Cross-cultural Eco-theology in an Indian Ocean Context

Cross-cultural Eco-theology in an Indian Ocean Context

Editors
Chilkuri Vasantha Rao
David Reichardt

2018

Cross-cultural Eco-theology in an Indian Ocean Context — published by the Rev. Dr. Ashish Amos of the Indian Society for Promoting Christian Knowledge (ISPCK), Post Box 1585, 1654, Madarsa Road, Kashmere Gate, Delhi-110006.

Online Order: http://ispck.org.in/book.php

Also available on amazon.in

ISBN: 978-81-8465-684-8

Cover credit: Internet sources

Laser typeset by

ISPCK, Post Box 1585, 1654, Madarsa Road, Kashmere Gate, Delhi-110006
• *Tel:* 23866323/22

e-mail: ashish@ispck.org.in • ella@ispck.org.in
website: www.ispck.org.in

Contents

Chapter - 2

Examining the ways in which the Christian faith has
both engaged and not engaged with the care of creation:
What are the obstacles before us?

Section Two
Using the Resources of Faith

Chapter - 3

Back to the Bible! How can the Bible be read
in the light of an environmental concern?

Chapter - 4

Christological Responses to the Groaning Creation

Section Three
Eco-theology and Eschatology

Acknowledgements

This Indian Ocean-spanning project is the brainchild of Rev. Dr. Ashish Amos, General Secretary and Director of the Indian Society for Promoting of Christian Knowledge (ISPCK). Dr. Amos' passion is to make available cutting edge theological literature in a high quality format at affordable prices to Indian pastors and interested laypeople.

This was made possible by each of the 14 authors not charging for their services. The authors' bios have been printed near the front of the book. Because this endeavour has been achieved through the sacrifice of time mention must be made of the authors' various places of work and family relationships who have lived in the tension of the "on the way" and the "not yet".

The project was also funded by Charles Sturt University's Public and Contextual Theology unit. Mr. Peter Walker was most helpful in this regard.

Associate Professor Clive Pearson liaised with Charles Sturt University, and gave the book much of its outline and shape, suggesting titles and content for each of its chapters and ancillary sections.

Mrs. Ella Sonawane, Asst. General Secretary, ISPCK and Rev. Dr. David Reichardt, Charles Sturt University have coordinated the project, finding suitable authors and encouraging them to write.

Rev. Prof. Dr. Chilkuri Vasantha Rao, Principal, United Theological College (UTC), Bangalore and Dr. Reichardt have done much of the initial editing.

UTC Bangalore provided Dr. Reichardt with hospitality and the College library provided him with a good working place for the editing process. Lady Willingdon Hospital, Manali has also provided him with a helpful working place.

Dr. Professor Mathew Koshy Punnackad and Dr. Samuel George have provided reflections at the end of each chapter.

Heartfelt thanks to each of these individuals and institutions.

To God be the glory.

David Reichardt

Foreword

The last decade has sent alarming reports and news which are both distressing and worrying for all God's creation.

Environmental crisis seems to have taken a front seat in terms of its seriousness and we as Christians especially need to address this.

In the Indian context, Mahatma Gandhi had rightly said, "Sanitation is more important than Independence". He was aware of the pathetic situation of Indian rural people at that time and he dreamt of a clean India where he emphasised on cleanliness and sanitation as an integral part of living. Unfortunately, after 71 years of independence, we have only about 30% of the rural households with access to toilets. President Pranab Mukherjee, in his address to Parliament in June 2014, said, "For ensuring hygiene, waste management and sanitation across the nation a "Swachh Bharat Mission" will be launched. This will be our tribute to Mahatma Gandhi on his 150th birth anniversary to be celebrated in the year 2019".

PM Narendra Modi has urged every one of us to pledge the following as a part of the Swachh Bharat Abhiyan:

"I will remain committed towards cleanliness and devote time for this. I will devote 100 hours per year, that is two hours per week, to voluntarily work for cleanliness. I will neither litter not let others litter. I will initiate the quest for cleanliness with myself, my family, my locality, my village and my work place".

Cross-cultural Eco-theology in an Indian Ocean is dedicated to all those who are stewards of God's creation and this book beautifully brings out the relationship of creation and theology. Eco theology is a theological view which stresses human responsibility for Creation both on the doctrinal and practical level (in the realm of Dogmatics as well as Ethics), because caring for Creation is one of the most fundamental assignments of human beings in the biblical book of Genesis.

We are God's creation and not just human kind is in danger but the entire creation. As stewards what is our responsibility to protect all life? As the Bible says we are all created in the image of God and as such we are to be responsible in looking after and nurturing creation.

In 2017 the UN Environment Assembly put ending pollution at the top of the global political agenda. If all the Assembly's commitments are met, more than a billion people will breathe cleaner air, many of the world's coastlines will be cleaner, and billions more will be mobilized for research into innovative programmes to combat pollution.

But as with all environment challenges, no government can go it alone. Citizens need to be informed and inspired to change their behavior. The coming together of people, governments and business has shown time and again that we can innovate our way out of any environmental challenge that comes our way.

Air pollution contributes to more than 6 million deaths every year, making it the single biggest environmental health risk of our time. The BreatheLife campaign, which UN Environment runs alongside the World Health Organization and the Climate and Clean Air Coalition, aims to partner with cities around the world to encourage them to act to clean up the air we breathe by 2030. With more than 8 million tons of plastic entering the oceans every year, our oceans could contain more plastic than fish by 2050.

Psalm 24:1 "A Psalm of David. The earth is the Lord's and the fullness thereof, the world and those who dwell therein." As we read in Revelation 11:18, those who abuse and destroy the earth will not go unpunished and knowing that the earth is not really ours, we should treat the earth with the respect of knowing it is God's own possession and not ours we are only caretakers and are answerable to him.

I congratulate the General Secretary ISPCK, Rev. Dr. Ashish Amos for identifying this grave global issue and encouraging the theological community to respond to this issue. I hope this book will bring not only our theologians but the church in fighting the cause of environment. I recommend all church leaders, pastors and lay to read this book as a tool to save the environment.

Let us challenge ourselves to move from commitment to action, from challenge to opportunity.

The Most Rev. Dr. P.C. Singh
Moderator, Church of North India

Preface

This volume is a textbook of eco-theology, designed to be read by Indian pastors and interested laypeople. It has been written by a group of 14 ecotheologians, of whom eight are Indians and six are Australians. Each chapter has been written by a different pair consisting of one Indian and one Australian. The degree of cooperation in writing has varied from simply setting what each had written alongside the other's contribution to treating the chapter as a conversation between the two authors.

Chapters are grouped into three sections. Section One, entitled "Beginning a Conversation", includes the first two chapters.

Professor Wati Longchar and Rev. Dr. David Reichardt have written Chapter One. It is entitled "Whose earth? Examining the state of the earth and the necessity for an ecotheology in an Indian context." The Christian faith is clear that "The earth is the Lord's", yet humans have disrespected, used and abused it as if it was ours. Because of India's great size, dynamism and increasing influence, and because this is simply a good thing to do, writing eco-theologies that arise from various Indian contexts are necessary and important. Chapter One includes an example of such an eco-theology.

Chapter Two, written by Dr. George Zachariah and Associate Professor Clive Pearson is entitled "Examining the ways in which the Christian faith has both engaged and not engaged with the care of creation. What are the obstacles before us?" This chapter examines the ways in which the Christian faith has both engaged and not engaged in the care of creation. Pearson has engaged with the topic by reflecting upon what our hymnals teach us about how we engage, and do not engage with creation. Zachariah has built upon Pearson's foundation, "interrogating" chants and doctrines as well as songs, all from the perspective of his passion for eco-justice.

Section Two, which is entitled "Using the Resources of Faith", examines what the Bible (Chapter Three), Christology (Chapter Four, Spirituality (Chapter Five) and Praxis (Activism) have to do with eco-theology.

Rev. Dr. Sunil Caleb and Dr. George Emeleus have cooperated to write Chapter Three, which is entitled "Back to the Bible!" This chapter examines the role that the Bible plays in eco-theology. Caleb and Emeleus address the question of how the Scriptures can be read in the light of ecological concern.

Associate Professor Pearson was in action again to write Chapter Four, collaborating with Dr. Eyingbeni Hümtsoe-Nienu to examine "Christological Responses to the Groaning Creation". The chapter studies how Christology, beliefs in and about Jesus Christ, should inform a Christian response to the care of creation.

Chapter Five, written by Rev. Drs. B. Silpa Rani and Jason John, is entitled "Eco-theological and Indian Tribal Spirituality: A Conversation". This chapter is in the form of a conversation between the authors, and the two rather different kinds of spirituality they represent. It examines the relationship between Christian spirituality and creation. It asks how, in light of the ecological problems before us, Christian Spirituality can provoke a change of heart, a new way of seeing things; what Pope John Paul II called "ecological conversion".

Chapter Six is called "Go, do likewise! Living out Eco-Theology in two contexts: India and Australia". This chapter addresses "ecological praxis". Given that the Christian faith is a way both of being and of doing, the authors, Rev. Subha Keerthana and Ms. Jessica Morthorpe, working closely together, describe how ecological communities of faith in their different contexts engage in ecological healing for Christ's sake.

Only two chapters, long, Section Three, "Eco-theology and Eschatology", turns the reader's attention to the future, then back to the present to prepare for whatever the future might bring.

Chapter Seven, written by Rev. Gracy Christina Mary R. and Rev. Dr. David Reichardt, is entitled "Beginnings...and Endings". It addresses the issue of secular and theological hope while recognizing that in a time of dangerous ecological degradation some things have already happened that may be beyond human capacity to set right. Nothing is impossible for God, but this may not be used as an excuse for inaction.

What humans do and do not do now affects the future. The final chapter has been written by Rev. Dr. Seferosa Carroll and Rev. Prof. Dr. Professor Chilkuri Vasantha Rao and is entitled "Living in the here and now". The employment of a handful of case studies from both islands in the Pacific Ocean and from India examines how a Christian environmental ethic both is and might be applied in particular situations. Issues of climate justice naturally come to the fore.

At the end of each chapter are several Questions for Discussion, a short "For further reading" list and a short reflection written by either Dr. Professor Mathew Koshy Punnackad or Dr. Samuel George.

The Bible version of preference is the NRSV (New Revised Standard Version).

Chilkuri Vasantha Rao & David Reichardt

Introduction
A Letter to the Indian Pastor

Namaste!

I bring you greetings in the Name of our Lord Jesus Christ from Australian sisters and brothers in the Faith. More than a year ago Rev. Dr. Ashish Amos, CEO of the publishing company ISPCK, requested me to write a textbook on eco-theology which would be a resource, especially for Indian pastors, but also for interested lay people. I am grateful for the trust that Dr Amos placed in me. I suppose he did this because I have lived several years in both the south and the north of India, and a few years ago ISPCK kindly published my PhD thesis in eco-theology in book form.

I asked Dr. Amos several questions. Why should an Australian write a book on eco-theology for Indians when there are already Indians doing this? Should not an Indian or Indians be involved in the writing? As a congregational pastor I find it difficult to write a sermon each week, let alone a whole book! Could there not be several authors writing a chapter each? Could a pair of one Indian and an Australian write each chapter? And should we not involve women in writing as well as men? Dr Amos agreed with my questions and suggestions. Coordinating a team of authors has certainly made the task of writing more complicated, but it has also enriched fellowship between Indian and Australian pastors and theologians.

Because the world-wide ecological crisis now affects each and every country on the globe it is important that Christians everywhere think about and act upon this important issue. And because of India's rapidly growing population and economy, and the enormous stress this rapid growth is placing on India's ecology, I suggest that it is particularly important that Indian Christians engage practically in caring for God's good creation. Even if your view of the end times (eschatology) causes you to think that we do not need to care about the fate of this earth, I hope that you will agree that already the damage being done to the environment is an issue of social justice. What does the Lord require of us? "To do justice, and to love kindness, and to walk humbly with your God?" (Micah 6:8) The need for the Church to respond as best we can with the small resources we have, trusting the God who through His Son Jesus stilled the storm, is becoming more urgent by the year. Indian pastors and church leaders have a vital part to play in efforts to meet the world's ecological crisis. Perhaps it does not seem like this if your congregation is in a small minority where you live, but churches are powerful formers of opinion. That is, God works powerfully through God's people to transform hearts and minds. The prophet Jeremiah wrote"[S]eek the welfare of the city where I have sent you...and pray to the Lord on its behalf, for in its welfare you will find your welfare." (29:7). My experience from both Australia and India is that when Christians cooperate with their community in practical environmental care people outside the Church are deeply impressed.

Many issues and people demand a pastor's time and energy. The daily grind of church life can steal our energy, motivation and joy in the Lord. It is difficult not to be consumed by "the tyranny of the urgent over the important". Yet the world's ecological crisis means that like the rest of society the Church will not be able to carry on with "business as usual". Recognizing this, in many places in India the Church is already doing good ecological work. As a volunteer eco-theological consultant several years ago to the Church of North India's Diocese of Amritsar I was present at several tree-planting ceremonies in the Punjab and Himachal Pradesh, and joined a large "Clean up Manali" campaign in Kullu-Manali. In Chapter Six my colleague Ms Jessica Morthorpe and her Indian writing partner, Rev. Shubha Keerthana, have described many practical steps in caring for creation that they have already been involved with.

It is both right and good for us and for God's creation that we care practically for it: "The Lord God took the man and put him in the garden of Eden to till it and keep it," wrote the author of Genesis. However, anyone can and should do that! Despite the importance of being practical the Church's vital contribution to any discussion is in theology, prayer and proclamation, and we pastors are the main theological thinkers and proclaimers our communities. This book has been written to provide you with an eco-theological resource that is both theological and practical.

We the authors invite you as a pastor (and of course you, dear reader, even if you are not a pastor!) to take the time to read this introduction to eco-theology and some of the other eco-theological works we have referred to, to think and pray. Studying and doing eco-theology have greatly enriched my understanding and love of the Gospel of Jesus Christ. I hope and pray that you will have a similar experience.

David Reichardt

Authors Profile

B. Silpa Rani is presently serving as the Assistant Professor in Bishop's College in the Department of Old Testament. She has completed her Master's of Theology degree in Old Testament from United Theological College, Bengaluru. She has been a part of Earth Bible Project initiated by the Church of South India and contributed Biblical sermons on ecology. She has also been resource person for seminars on Ecology and engages in re-reading of Biblical texts from ecological perspective. She belongs to Church of North India.

Chilkuri Vasantha Rao is an ordained Presbyter of the CSI Medak Diocese. He is Principal of the United Theological College, Bengaluru, India, and teaches in the department of Biblical Studies. His holds a Doctorate from Hamburg University, Germany. He was a visiting Professor at several international Universities including The Harvard University, Boston, USA. He has authored several books and published articles in Spanish, German, Protugese, Telugu and English, including in The Oxford Encyclopedia of South Asian Christianity. He is active in the CSI Synod department of ecological concerns.

Clive Pearson is a research fellow in the Centre for Public and Contextual Theology, Charles Sturt University. For the past 25 years he has been teaching and writing on environment, climate change and the Christian theology. In recent years he has taken a particular interest in the prospects of low-lying islands faced with rising sea levels. His most recent work has been on climate change and the doctrine of providence.

David Reichardt now works in Sydney as a minister following 2 years in north-western India as a volunteer ecotheological consultant to the Church of North India. During the 1980s he also volunteered as a scientific officer with The Leprosy Mission in Andhra Pradesh. An Al Gore-trained Climate Change Presenter with a PhD in eco-theology, David is deeply involved in ecotheological debate.

Eyingbeni Humtsoe-Nienu is a Senior Lecturer in Christian Theology at Clark Theological College, Mokokchung. She is the author of "God of the Tribes: Christian Perspective on the Naga Ancestral Idea of the Supreme Being" (CTC, 2014) and "Prayers and Litanies for All Occasions" (CWI, 2017). She also co-authored "Nagas: Essays for Responsible Change" (HPH, 2012) and "English-Lotha Dictionary of Christian Faith" (TDCC, 2015). She has also edited couple of books and written several essays for leading Indian theological journals and publications. She was also a guest editor for local daily "The Morung Express" and continues to contribute articles occasionally in local papers.

George Emeleus grew up in Northern Ireland, studied physics at Oxford and had a career teaching, mainly in universities in Tanzania, Papua New Guinea and Australia.   He then undertook biblical and theological studies.   He has a particular interest in how science and theology may work together to inform and guide Christians in response to the causes and consequences of climate change.

George Zachariah serves the United Theological College, Bengaluru in the department of theology and ethics.

Gracy Christina Mary R. is an ordained minister of Karnataka Northern Diocese, Church of South India. She was born and brought up in Bellary in a multi religious and multilingual context. She completed her Bachelor of Divinity from Karnataka Theological College, Mangaluru in the year 2014. She is currently pursuing her Master studies, Department of Old Testament at United Theological College, Bengaluru.

Jason John is an ecominister in the Uniting Church, previously in congregations and starting new outdoor faith communities, and presently at the Synod level with Jessica Morthorpe. His PhD combined his degree in zoology with his theological studies. He lives in a forest with his family, and maintains *ecofaith.org* plus the official church website, *unitingearth. org.au*

Jessica Morthorpe is a Uniting Earth Ministry Consultant and Founder of the Five Leaf Eco-Awards environmental program for churches. She is constantly delighted by all the amazing things churches are doing to care for the environment. She lives in Sydney with her husband, rabbit, two budgies and multiple stick insects; and loves preaching, bushwalking, planting trees and leading sustainability workshops.

Mathew Koshy Punnackad has been a pioneer in the field of ecology as a Green Church Campaigner since 1990. He has edited of three volumes of 'Earth Bible Sermons' and the 'Green Parables' published by CSI Synod. He is serving as the Hon. Director of CSI Synod Department of Ecological concerns.

Samuel George from Jammu is Professor of Christian Theology at Allahabad Bible Seminary (Serampore), Uttar Pradesh. Earlier, he served as the Principal of MCT (Serampore), Visakhapatnam. He is a Reference-Group member of EDAN-WCC. He has authored/edited 8 books apart from several articles in national and international journals. He is married to Dr. Atula Ao (an Old Testament scholar) from Nagaland.

Sef is a Fiji born Rotuman who spent her formative years growing up in Fiji. She migrated to Australia in 1987. Sef is an ordained minister of the Uniting Church in Australia. She currently works for UnitingWorld, the international partnership agency of the Uniting Church in Australia in the role of Manager, Church Partnerships, Pacific. Sef has a keen interest in the powerful role faith can play in changing people's lives, particularly in situations of violence against women and climate change.

Shubha Keerthana is an ordained presbyter in Karnataka Central Diocese, Church of South India,serving in two of the churches in Bangalore. She hails from Kolar Gold Fields in Karnataka,pursued her Bachelor's of Divinity at Tamilnadu Theological Seminary in Madurai. Presently , she is the Director of Ecological Concerns Department in her Diocese.

Sunil Caleb is an ordained presbyter of the Church of North India. He holds a Ph.D. in Christian Ethics from the University of Kent at Canterbury, U.K. Currently he is a Professor of Christian Theology and Christian Ethics at Bishop's College in Calcutta and also the Principal of the College.

Wati Longchar is Professor of Systematic Theology and Dean of the Center of Research and Extension Programmes of Indigenous Theology of Mission at Yu-Shan Theological College and Seminary, Hualian City, Taiwan. He earned his doctorate in theology in Serampore University, India. He has published widely, particularly in the areas of indigenous and Asian theology.

Section One

Beginning a Conversation

CHAPTER - 1

Whose Earth?

Examining the state of the earth and the necessity for an eco-theology in an Indian context

Wati Longchar & David Reichardt

Editor's Note

This book about eco-theology has been written primarily for Indian readers. However, eco-theology developed first in the West. So did the theology and worldview that gave rise to it, and so did the worldwide ecological crisis that stimulated its development. So, although this chapter examines the necessity for an eco-theology in an Indian context it is to the West we must go first for background to the story of eco-theology. For it is the West which industrialised first, increasing standards of living, but gaining great power with which to exploit nature.

India is now following a similar pathway. Given its huge population and swift development the environmental decisions India makes over the next few years will have great consequences for the whole world. Therefore it's not surprising that several Indian theologians have already written about eco-theology from an Indian perspective. You can find their names and the titles of their books in the For further reading list at the end of this chapter. That being so, how can a book on eco-theology, written by Indians together with Australians, and women together with men, add to what Indians have already been writing about? We the authors believe that writing cooperatively on the same project, though potentially complicated and messy, offers a greater variety and wealth of theological insights than doing it separately. Women see things that men miss, and vice versa. Australians look at things differently from Indians, and the outlook of southern Indians can differ from that of northern Indians. Following liberation theology and feminist theology, eco-theology is a form of theology in which "non-traditional" voices - from two thirds world contexts, from women, from the earth itself - are heard. It makes sense for these voices to be in conversation within the same book with more "traditionally heard" voices. All theology is a conversation; this book is the result of many discussions that by being published are being made public.

Introduction

In addressing the question "Whose Earth?" this introductory chapter examines the state of the earth and the necessity for an eco-theology in an Indian context. Western Christians need to continue to search within their own traditions for alternative answers to the question of whose earth they live in. The West has been all too ready to assume that the earth is theirs. Additionally, with India, like other countries, experiencing growing ecological problems it is all the more important that Indian Christians contribute their thinking to the discipline of eco-theology. In this chapter first Professor Wati Longchar, an Indian currently of Yu-Shan Theological College, Taiwan, then an Australian, Rev. Dr. David Reichardt, addresses these issues.

Wati Longchar

Towards an Indian Eco-theology: Let Us Redeem God's Creation

The Mother Earth, the 'Home' of humans and all forms of life, is being shaken by greenhouse gas emissions, global warming, rising sea levels, the alarming pollution of air, water and other essentials. Why is God's creation groaning? Who is responsible? Why do we have to talk about the redemption of God's creation? What went wrong to God's creation which sustains all lives? What are the humans' responsibilities in redeeming God's creation? These are some of the issues we need to address today. Redemption and preservation of God's creation is a justice issue. It is the foundation of all lives, and so also theology. The redemption of creation has to do with how human beings relate to Mother Earth. In this sense, eco-justice and social justice are so intertwined that one cannot be sought without the other.

Groaning of God's Creation

God's creation is groaning. The ideology that has contributed to the groaning of God's creation has four major streams of praxis. The confluence of these four streams has created a forceful current in the dominant Christian traditions that set aside the truth of the communion of human beings with God's creation. It is important to see how they have influenced the attitude of humans and contributed to the exploitation and abuse of Mother Earth.

a) *Mechanical view and secularization of creation*

This stream of thought is rooted in the Western Enlightenment tradition which makes a sharp contrast between nature and history. The advancement of the knowledge of science and secularization of nature is interconnected. The advancement of knowledge in the field of science and technology in the sixteenth and seventeenth centuries brought industrial capitalism, market economy, mass production, democracy and rationalism. The whole created order began to be viewed objectively. Using the tools of mathematical calculations and experimental data, humans began to claim that one could understand the specific nature of the physical matter constituting the Earth, and the changes within it. Thus, nature was seen purely from a utilitarian perspective; the mystery and sacredness of nature was taken away from the western worldview. People began to perceive that there is nothing amazing and sacred about the world; it is merely a sum-total of many material components and energies. Humans were capable of understanding, predicting, and controlling everything that relates to physical world; we are separated from, and masters of, the earth. Natural resources are given only in so far as they are useful for the development of science and technology. Hence, humans materialistic attitude today is greatly shaped by such ideologies. Many people visualize human civilization in terms of a highly mechanized and industrialized society. The booming of economic progress, high-tech mechanized life-style is perceived as attainment of higher quality of life. 'Growth' is seen as the only principle for liberation. The growth-driven and consumerist economic system and the one-sided development pursuits have led to colonization of others and laid ideological justification for the subjugation and exploitation of non-renewable earth's resources in a massive scale. The concepts of 'care for one another', 'just economy' and '(sabbath) rest for creation' are considered as non-productivity and the root of all human problems stem from poverty to sickness to political instability. Any attempt to slow down economic growth is labeled as immoral. Right to have dominion over God's creation is a biblical mandate and exploitation is seen as exercising humans creativity bestowed on them in the "Image of God' (Genesis 1:27,28). This Enlightenment paradigm of euro-centric modernity rooted in the conquest of nature is the major root cause of today's world crisis. Christian theologies have played its role in justifying exploitation of mother earth.

b) *Hierarchical structure of creation*

In the Hebrew thought, man is the helm of the hierarchy, ruling over the family, the women, the slaves, and all else. Several Christian theologians have explained God's creation within this hierarchical structure. According to Thomas Aquinas, God, the Creator, in the beginning, simultaneously created a hierarchy of creatures, ordered according to their degree of perfection. In this hierarchical order, angels are at the highest peak. Angels are created, but purely spiritual beings and they are above human beings. Humans are the highest among the created materials beings, having ultimate rights over the other creatures. This hierarchal order is by divine design because "the imperfect beings are for the use of perfect." Imperfect beings are created to serve the need of more noble beings, for instance, the plants draw their nutrients from the earth, animals feed on plants and these in turn serve humans use. Therefore, those lifeless beings exist for the sake of living beings, plants for animals and animals for humans. Having affirmed that, Aquinas went one step further and said that material creatures were created that they "might be assimilated to the divine goodness". For him, those creatures lower than the rational human creature in hierarchy simply assimilate to the divine goodness by fulfilling the needs of human creatures. The whole material nature exists for humans' needs because humanity alone possesses rationality. Human beings are above all creatures. In other words, the other non-human creatures are protected, preserved, and sustained by God to serve rational humans needs. This theology gives justification for manipulation and exploitation of other segments of God's creation.

c) Anthropocentric view of creation

The hierarchical and anthropocentric views of life are interrelated; they assume a similar theological position in regard to creation. This position views that humanity is the reference point of everything. Creation has meaning and values by serving the interests of humankind. In this view of life, Robert Borrong, an Indonesian theologian, underlines nine assumptions:

(1) Humans are separated from nature;

(2) The rights of human beings are prioritized over those of nature, but the responsibilities of human beings are not emphasized;

(3) The feelings of humans are prioritized as the centre of their apprehensiveness;

(4) There is a policy of management of natural resources in the interests of human beings;

(5) The solution to the ecological crisis is through population control, especially in the poor countries;

6) Adherence to the philosophy of economic growth;

7) The main norm is profit-loss;

8) Short-term planning is prioritized; and

9) One adjusts oneself to the prevailing political and economic system.

This view has become the basis for greedy exploitation and depletion of nature's resources in today's world.

Protestant theologies also gave theological justification to this view of life. Luther saw the whole creation of God as something which exists for the benefit of humans. He recognized nature simply as an existential springboard for grace. The ultimate purpose of creation is perceived as non-living, valueless; they are merely created so that human beings experience God's grace. Karl Barth advocated a similar theology. For him, God is the "wholly other", the transcendent Lord, who can be known only when He chooses to reveal himself, as He did pre-eminently in Jesus Christ. Barth said that the Word is not the foremost principle of creation which gives life to all created things; rather the Word is the first and foremost God's address to humanity in Jesus Christ. God is not known through His creation, but only through Christ. Barth is very explicit that salvation history begins from the incarnation of Jesus Christ, but not from the creation. Barth further argued that this great history of salvation cannot be actualized if there is no place or space for it to occur. It needs a "showplace" or a "theatre" outside of God and humans. This is the reason why God brought the created world into existence. It is very clear that Barth conceives creation simply as a show place/theatre for the saving works of God. Everything is created solely for the sake of the realization of God's covenant with humanity in Jesus Christ. However, nature is sustained, protected and upheld for the sake of election. Thus, creation is merely a stage. It has no history, and it is not redeemed, but merely used. Bultmann held a similar position. God is not to be perceived in the phenomena of nature but He is known and experienced in the 'cave of the heart', in the inner personal experience. Such theology places creation in a secondary position.

d) Dualistic view of creation

This stream of thought is of Greek origin with its dualism of body and soul. In Greek thought the soul was said to be the highest among all the created order. It finds its true destiny by escaping from nature, creation and the world. Marcion taught that the visible world is the creation of the God of Israel who is a lesser God than God, the Father of Jesus. Made out of matter, it is an evil work, destined for destruction. This view stressed that God is absolutely different and distinct from His created nature. A holy God cannot be related to the material world. Gnosticism held the view that the world is the creation of demonic power from the chaos of the darkness. The created world is purely material and fleshly, and a full expression of evil. Origen, the Early Father, held that God created the world because of a spiritual rebellion in heaven. Thus, the creation of the world was related to the Fall of man. The world is created for the fallen spirits and thereby it becomes a place of purification where fallen humankind could be educated through suffering to regain the pure state of the spiritual realm. Origen valued soul over the material world.

The influence of dualism is also evident among the Reformers. Nature and other material objects do not take part in the salvation and redemption of Christ. According to Luther, nature is not a witness to the glory of God. Nature is only a supplementary item for the salvation drama of human beings. This dualistic view of life influenced humans to believe that humankind is called upon to control nature and so the function of religion is simply to aid human beings in the execution of their task. This view contradicts the biblical testimony. God's creation is redeemed when human beings respect nature's rhythm and dynamic.

Most of the nineteenth century Evangelicals took this dualistic position. The Evangelicals recognized God's revelation only in Jesus Christ, but not in the total creation of God. One can know God only through Jesus Christ but not through creation. The teaching of heaven and hell further reinforced negligence towards and the undermining of God's creation. Evangelicals believed that the world is coming to an end, all that is material will be destroyed, but only the souls will be saved and live eternally in heaven; other materials will perish. This doctrine made people think that "This world is not our home. We are just passengers." Consequently, if this world is not our home, why should we take care of it?

The aim of this discussion is not to argue that theologians in the mainline Christian traditions have a negative attitude to creation. What we are trying to say is that because of their great interest in the uniqueness of God's action in history for human redemption, they were indifferent to God's other creation. It is understandable that serious attention was not given to creation theology as they did not face an ecological crisis as we do today. Moreover, one should not assume that Christianity does not have a theology of creation. Paul Santmire in his book, The Travail of Nature, has shown convincingly that it is not fair to blame Christianity and its traditions like Lynn White, to be 'ecologically bankrupt.' Santmire's book shows a long historical study in which he has demonstrated ecological promises in Christian theology. He has shown immense ecological insights in the theology of Irenaeus, Augustine and especially of Francis of Assisi. But the fact is that these voices have never become part of the dominant Christian traditions. Their voices are still unheard and have not been integrated as part of Christian praxis and ethos. It is a fact we need to acknowledge that the dominant Christian theologies have been too anthropocentric, hierarchical, mechanistic and dualistic in their approach and content.

The Judeo-Christian tradition bears to a certain degree of responsibility for today's ecological destruction. But there is no doubt that Christians have for too long neglected the theme of Creation in their theological reflection and teaching, and have accepted values and perspectives which are foreign to the biblical tradition. They have uncritically supported the modern domination of nature.

The dominant Judeo-Christian perceptions of life continue to promote the greedy exploitation and depletion of nature's resources. Today we realize that such theologies of creation are destructive to life. The mindless destruction of earth's resources, and marginalization and subjugation of the indigenous people through war, cultural genocide, alienation, denial and suppression are deeply rooted in such a view of life. It has contributed to reducing the indigenous people and nature to mere commodities. Such theologies are not adequate to respond to the present ecological crisis. We need a theology that promotes respect and a caring attitude towards all God's creation.

Re-vision God's creation

The biblical faith unfolds the fact that creation is God's first act of revelation: "In the beginning God created heaven and earth." Life begins from water. God cannot be perceived without water, wind, trees, vegetation, sky, light, darkness, animals, human creatures. In this first God's act of revelation, God revealed himself/herself as co-creator with the earth. The most striking aspect in this first act of God's revelation is that "God is present in creation." The presence of God makes this earth sacred. That is why God entered into a covenant relationship with all creatures. There are many stories, myths, parables, and even fairy tales of how the Sacred Power and the land sustain life together. This makes "the whole earth...full of God's glory" (Isaiah 6:1-3). To perceive God as detached from creation/earth or as a mere transcendental being, who controls life from above is not biblical faith. We believe in God because God as the Creator is present and continues to work with the land, river and sea to give life and hope. Everything emerged from God and was sanctified by His grace and love, and thus sacred. Human beings are no longer separate from nature, but form an integral part of it. This affirmation is the foundation of life.

The human body shares the power of nature in its composition of water, air and other elements of the Earth. Redemption of God's creation happens when humans maintain just communion and solidarity with all living and inanimate nature; it contributes to the maintenance of the whole Earth in its eco-systems, and all its equilibrium and balance.

Indigenous cosmology also gives inspiration to go beyond mere stewardship to affirming a spirituality of kinship with the Earth. This is signified by their totemic and taboo relationship with nature. Kinship expresses the reality of inter-dependence of humans and nature. A kinship relationship thus promotes a nurturing and a caring attitude and praxis towards all creatures.

The idea of sustainable development emerged from the realization that there has to be "limits to growth." This concept is also very much tied to an anthropocentric vision of reality. The dominant concern here seems to be the survival of humanity which is not possible when the environment is damaged, or the resources of nature are overexploited. Sustainable development does not focus on the present situation of poverty in a world where 20% of the population consumes 80% resources of nature. It seems to be concerned more about intergenerational equity by which is meant that the use of natural resources be such that we leave behind for future generations resources and means necessary to fulfill their needs. Hence the restraint on profit oriented massive scale development becomes imperative for human security. Such an orientation does not ensure justice to creation. It still looks at nature as an instrument/resources for present and future human well-being and progress, but not having value in itself. But Mother Earth is endowed with meaning and value in herself, not simply in terms of her utility for human beings. This vision of life needs to percolate through all relationships of human beings to nature, including economic activity. This would ultimately enhance the quality of human life. All forms of life, including human life, are dependent upon the Earth, its products, the biosphere and the eco-systems.

Therefore, we are called to redefine the following:

i)   Our understanding of church and mission. The Mission of God is not limited to conversion and planting of the church. Mission is inclusive. It involves calling persons to commitment to the kingdom of God, justice and peace, and ecological health of the land.

ii) Our understanding of Creation is not just that it supplies things to be exploited. Every living creature possesses an intrinsic value and rights. Therefore, preserving the integrity of the whole inhabited earth and promoting ecologically responsible development are matter of survival for the whole world.

iii) Our understanding of justice is not an abstract reality to be realized within human community alone, but it is how we live in the web of life in reciprocity with people, other creatures and the earth, recognizing that they are part of us and we are part of them.

iv) Our search for a new ethical principle. Human communities must bear a responsibility towards the earth and its wholeness. The earth, with its diverse life forms, is functioning as one coherent whole. The whole earth is God's creation and we need to respect its inherent values and rights. A lifestyle of high material consumption is unethical. Learning to live in a new way not based on exploitation and injustice would allow all to flourish in health and wholeness.

David Reichardt
The "Glocal" Ecological Crisis

Sometimes the Church is criticised for not becoming involved in the environmental movement earlier. That criticism may be a little unfair. To assess the charge properly we need to do some history of science. Although some of the first predictions regarding global warming and the "greenhouse effect" were made in the early nineteenth century, scientific concern about human-caused damage to the environment started to develop strongly only in the 1950s. To give two examples, in 1957 the American oceanographer[1] Roger Revelle helped to write a scientific paper that suggested that the Earth's oceans would absorb excess carbon dioxide being generated by humanity much more slowly than previously predicted by scientists. That suggested that emissions of gas caused by humans might create a "greenhouse effect" that would cause global warming over time.[2] About the same time concerns were developing about the effects that the insecticide DDT[3] was having on the strength of egg shells amongst birds that fed on insects on which it was sprayed. The American biologist Rachel Carson's book "Silent Spring,"[4] published in 1962, proved and gave voice to these concerns, and became a powerful stimulus for the environmental movement.

Yet another American, Lynn White, a Professor of medieval history, is usually credited with inspiring the modern eco-theological movement only shortly after his scientific colleagues. White's paper, "The historical roots of our ecologic crisis",[5] was published in Science Journal fifty years ago, in 1967. White argued, famously, that the western form of Christianity bears "a huge burden of guilt" for the ecological crisis which even then was becoming apparent in industrialised countries. This western form of Christianity, he said, was the most anthropocentric[6] religion the world has ever seen. By that he meant that western Christianity placed human interests above the concerns of the rest of the planet, including other forms of life.

Over a quarter of a century ago in 1991, still another American, the eco-feminist Sallie McFague, told her fellow theologians to pay attention to the ecological crisis:

> "The times are too perilous and it is too late in the day for [such] games. We need to work together, each in his or her own small way, to create a planetary situation that is more viable and less vulnerable."[7]

So at least some in the Church were aware of the world's looming environmental crisis, and were arguing quite early in the story of humankind's dealing with it that it must be addressed. Yet as late as 2007 the British economist Sir Nicholas Stern was still having to argue on the international stage that:

> "...scientific evidence is now overwhelming: climate change is a serious global threat, and it demands an urgent global response."[8]

Since then the situation has grown more urgent. To demonstrate this, and the importance of ecology even to theology we need to discuss both science and history.[9] As stated, knowledge about climate change has been developing for nearly 200 years.[10] The average temperature of earth's surface is kept within a narrow life-enhancing range around 15 degrees celsius by the so-called "greenhouse gases" - water vapour, carbon dioxide, methane and some other minor gases - in its atmosphere. Greenhouse gases are so called because the earth receives radiation from the sun which heats it, it radiates heat back into space, but the greenhouse gases trap some of that heat as a greenhouse traps heat within it. Without greenhouse gases the earth's average surface temperature would be about minus 6 degrees celsius, some 21 degrees colder than it is. The "greenhouse effect" was a feature of life on earth long before humans started to influence the climate. It is helpful for life. If the earth's temperature had not been this stable and warm it would have been much more difficult for human civilization to develop.

Over the past 250 years, however, a great deal of carbon has been released into the atmosphere in the form of carbon dioxide. This and growing emissions of other greenhouse gases are trapping too much heat and warming up the earth's atmosphere. While the world's "carbon cycle" was in balance the average concentration of carbon dioxide in the atmosphere was about 280 parts per million (ppm). The increase in the burning of fossil fuels brought about by the Industrial Revolution, starting some 250 years ago, upset that balance. It has been calculated that until 2009 over 600 thousand million tonnes (or gigatonnes, Gt) of carbon were emitted into the atmosphere from the burning of fossil fuels. That has increased the concentration of carbon dioxide in the atmosphere by about 43%, from 280 ppm in 1700 to over 400 ppm today.

Although almost all climate scientists[11] believe that increasing the concentration of greenhouse gases in the atmosphere is causing increased atmospheric temperature, this is still disputed. "The earth warms, the earth cools," commented a recent visitor, a layperson in terms of climate science. He was pointing to regular changes in the amount of sunlight falling on the earth's surface due to changes in the earth's orbit around the sun. These regular warming and cooling trends are called "Milankovitch cycles". Changes in the concentration of greenhouse gases associated with these Cycles have also contributed to changes in the earth's climate. Some also argue that changes in sunspot activity also result in cooling and warming cycles. However, it is important to note that the climatic effects of humans burning fossils are *additional* to these naturally-occurring phenomena. It is likely that the second half of the twentieth century was the warmest northern hemisphere period in the last 1300 years at the same time as both human burning of fossil fuels and the atmospheric concentration of greenhouse gases have been increasing dramatically.

The Effects of Climate Change

Of all the ecological degradation that humans are causing, the effects of climate change pose perhaps the most serious threat to life on earth. They are thought to be among the main causes of a mass extinction of species believed by many biologists to be going on. Perhaps the most obvious effects of climate change are extreme weather events. A decade ago the Oscar award-winning documentary on climate change called "An Inconvenient Truth" included a much-criticised graphic that depicted the flooding of the World Trade Centre site in New York as a real possibility. This did happen in 2012, and now similar flooding and coastal erosion are occurring around the world, notably in the Bay of Bengal. So are extreme flooding events upstream, such as the major floods along the Indus River catchment in Pakistan in 2010, and in Nepal, western Tibet and the Indian states of Uttarakhand, Himachal Pradesh and Uttar Pradesh in 2013. Although annual monsoons are a normal part of life and death on the Indian subcontinent, recent weather events such as these seem to be of a different type, or on a different scale. For example, in Uttarakhand the rain was so heavy that it melted the Chorabari glacier at the height of 3,800 metres, increasing vastly the size of the flood.

Floods are creating human floods of climate refugees. It is estimated that every metre in average sea level rise will create 100 million new climate refugees.[12] However, so strong are some recent extreme weather events that it is becoming more difficult to suppose that they are simply extremes in normal weather patterns. It seems more and more likely that the world is entering another, warmer kind of climate. Some scientists, convinced that the drastic effects of climate change have been caused by human activity, have invented a new word for what they see is the new geological epoch the world is entering: the "anthropocene".

There is good reason for this. Since when did a monsoon melt a glacier at an altitude of nearly 4,000 metres? Or the sea flood the subways of one of the world's greatest cities? The hottest temperatures since records began in 1859 produced the worst day[13] of fire conditions ever experienced in the Australian state of Victoria which led to the deaths of 173 people. Did these occurrences simply represent the extreme end of the normal climate regime? Was the likelihood that the drought which preceded Syria's civil war was the worst in 900 years an important cause of that war? Is the spread of the Zika virus into the United States due to an unfortunate set of circumstances, or has the United States warmed sufficiently to now accommodate the Zika virus's vector (carrier), the Aedes family of mosquitoes? A changing climate means changing temperature ranges on different parts of the planet, which causes both extinction and broadened range among different species.

As Al Gore has put it:

> "...the obvious and overwhelming evidence of the damage we are causing is now increasingly impossible for reasonable people to ignore. It is widely known by now that there is a nearly unanimous view among all scientists authoring peer-reviewed articles related to the climate crisis that it threatens our future, that human activities are largely if not entirely responsible, and that action is needed urgently to prevent the catastrophic harm it is already starting to bring. More importantly, Mother Nature is reminding us almost daily that the impacts of the climate crisis are growing steadily more severe, with more frequent and powerful climate-related extreme weather events. Every night, the TV news is like a nature hike through the Book of Revelation."[14]

Global in scope, climate change threatens to overwhelm both ecosystems and human societies, but it is only the most comprehensive of many forms of ecological degradation that are affecting local landscapes. The worldwide ecological crisis is "glocal,"[15] being both global and local in character. The challenge it presents is daunting.

Yet hope remains. Indeed, the transition away from the world economy based on fossil fuels to that based on renewable energy sources is being made far faster than had been predicted. There is a sense in which the issues have simplified and clarified. As Al Gore put it:

> "At this point in the fight to solve the climate crisis, there are only three questions remaining: Must we change? Can we change? Will we change? ...the overwhelming conclusion [is] that the answer to the first two of these three questions is a resounding "Yes." I am convinced that the answer to the third question—"Will we change?"—is also "Yes," but that conclusion, unlike the answer to the first two questions, is in the nature of a prediction."[16]

For Gore's prediction to come true the attitude and actions of India and the development of Indian eco-theologies will be of vital importance.

On Eco-theology as a Response to the Ecological Complaint

Christianity has traditionally paid attention to nature. This has often been expressed in the doctrine of creation and in natural theology. Chapter Three of this volume demonstrates the importance that the Bible places upon Creation. European theologians, from the medieval times from great Thomas Aquinas to the twentieth century's Paul Tillich, have long argued that the existence of a beautiful, ordered cosmos points to the existence of a good, powerful, benevolent Creator.

However, as we have seen, eco-theology approaches the relationship between ecology and theology differently. Lynn White's paper provoked much interest and criticism both within the Church, and in western and also non-western societies. His critique of western Christianity became known as "the ecological complaint" against Christianity. Opponents of the Christian faith were quick to use it as an argument that Christianity is actually hostile to this world.

Though Lynn White reached a controversial conclusion he did not argue that Christianity should be discarded in favour of some other belief system. Instead, he advocated finding resources from *within* the Christian traditions that would help humankind to address the problem of ecological degradation. He suggested studying and following more closely the life and thought of St Francis of Assisi, patron saint of ecology.

That stimulated Christian theologians and biblical scholars to search the Bible and Christian tradition and history, trying to defend the Faith against the ecological complaint. Some found other culprits to blame. The main one of these was **the Enlightenment,** the movement within **the West** in which human reason replaced faith in God as the primary source of knowledge and knowing. Others found that there were many examples within Christianity of love and care for Creation. And still others found much in the Bible itself that, re-read and re-interpreted, supports the idea that because a loving Creator has created a good Creation, God's special care-takers, humankind, are called to love and care for Creation too.

And there were those who admitted White's "huge burden of guilt", or at least took the charge seriously. Paul Santmire's "The Travail of Nature: The Ambiguous Ecological Promise of Christian Theology"[17] sought to explain how this could be by exploring contrasting "motifs" and "root metaphors" within Christianity. An eco-feminist, Sallie McFague spoke metaphorically of the earth being the "Body of God". Douglas John Hall argued that the biblical metaphor of "the Steward" best explains humankind's relationship with Creation and the Creator. Calvin de Witt has combined an evangelical respect for the Bible as the Word of God with a career as an environmental scientist. Similarly, Alister McGrath, a molecular biologist and historical theologian, has argued that the Enlightenment, western rationalism and scientific method have "disenchanted" nature, which needs to be "re-enchanted". Recently, scholars such as Celia Dean-Drummond have described eco-theology's growing maturity as a discipline within Theology as 'the turn to Ecology'.[18] That Indian authors such as Sarojini Henry, Solomon Victus and Mathew Koshy Punnakad are now writing eco-theologies from Indian contexts supports Dean-Drummond's view.

Whose Earth? On "Oikos" Theology and understanding Eco-theology

Another helpful way of approaching the subject of eco-theology is to think of the earth as a household, and then to ask to whom it belongs. There are three words with a common root that help us to do this: "economy", "ecology" and "ecumenism". Their "eco-" and "ecu-" syllables come from a Greek word "oikos", which means "house" or "home". "Eco-nomy" means "the law of the house". It's interesting to think of economics in this way! "Eco-logy" means "the study of the house". And "ecu-menism" means "the whole, inhabited house". In each case "house" means the earth itself. Huang Phoho has described Oikos theology and its potential for eco-theology from an Asian perspective.[19]

"Whose earth?" is a good question with which to begin a study of that fourth word that contains the "eco-" prefix: "eco-theology". It takes us to "theology", via the doctrine of creation. Following the meanings of the other three "eco-words", "eco-theology" could be said to mean "the theology of the house", where once again "the house" means the earth, itself. Another, simple description of eco-theology is "the greening of theology". There are other, more complicated definitions of eco-theology, but these will do for the moment. Similarly, there are many definitions and understandings of "theology", but Saint Anselm of Canterbury's famous statement, "Faith seeking understanding" is enough.

During the period of European history called "the Middle Ages"[20] the question of "Whose earth?" was easily answered:

"The earth and everything on it
belong to the Lord.
The world and its people
belong to him." (Psalm 24.1)

The ecological question of how all beings are related to each other was answered in detail by the concept of "the Great Chain of Being", a strict, religious, hierarchical structure, believed to have been decreed by God, that explained the place of all matter and life. The Chain started from God and progressed downward.[21] However, the Great Chain of Being was not originally a Christian concept. It came from the pre-Christian Greek philosophers Plato and Aristotle, and was promoted several centuries into the Christian era by their successors, principally the pagan philosopher Plotinus. Christian theologians such as Augustine of Hippo were much influenced, particularly by Plotinus, and again during the Middle Ages and in early modern Neoplatonism.

The movement of thought called the Enlightenment had its origins within the Christian West. However, by removing those above us in the Great Chain of Being – angels, demons, and ultimately, God - and placing human Reason at the head the Enlightenment removed restraint upon human selfishness. It provided the justification for human domination of Nature and removed philosophical, ideological and religious restraints; and the industrial revolution provided the means. Jesus' Parable of the Faithful Servant and the Evil Servant,[22] is an excellent illustration of what humans have actually done. With no constraints on our behaviour we tend to abuse our power. Indeed, the most popular image of who humans are in relation to God and creation - "the Steward" - is disliked by some because of our tendency to be bad, dishonest and exploitative stewards. "We need a model for being human that does not encourage us to harm nature," it is argued. Perhaps St Francis of Assisi's "Commonwealth of all Being" with its "Brother Sun" and "Sister Moon" would be helpful. Perhaps the Buddhist and Hindu ideas of non-violence, though Lynn White didn't think they would work either.

Who are we? On Eco-theological Christian Anthropology

How humans relate to creation is affected vitally by our sense of identity. The questions of "Whose earth?" and "Who (and whose) are we?" are closely linked. Alister McGrath has argued that one of the most important perspectives Christians bring to the study and care of nature concerns the place of humanity.[23] One approach to the question of human identity in relation to God and Creation is to list the main models that speak on the issue of human identity, seen from a Christian perspective in relation to ecology. It is worth taking them one by one.

We have already touched upon the question of who we are in God's "oikos", God's house.[24] Douglas John Hall has argued that the predominant biblical model is that of *the steward*.[25] This theme is probably the model by which most Christians would describe their relationship with creation. It finds much biblical support, particularly in a several of Jesus' parables. A major problem with it, however, is that, improperly interpreted, it leaves the biblical, medieval and Enlightenment hierarchy of human over nature unchallenged, allowing humans the potential to retain too much power and authority. Some theologians doubt humans' ability to withstand our own anthropocentrism and have developed other models. As mentioned, Lynn White was among the first to point to the need for another model, advocating that it be from within the Christian tradition.

St Francis of Assisi, widely regarded as the patron saint of the environment, lived out what might be described as a "*commonwealth of all being*".[26] Francis was convinced that humans are to regard themselves as being in a family, not a hierarchical, relationship with the rest of creation.[27] The American Catholic scholar Matthew Fox has sharpened this concept to the point where he has perhaps been in more trouble with his church authorities than even St Francis was! Neither has Fox's model gained wide respect among those Christians living in rural Australia.[28] The Swedish description of humankind as "***the crown of creation***" is not self-adulation but a fact of life for these people on the land.

The motif of humans' ***relationship with the land*** is particularly prominent in the Old Testament.[29] Ron Elsdon[30] has correlated the state of Israel's ecology with Israel's falling away from the Old Covenant: from a land "flowing with milk and honey"[31] to one in which

"Thorns will overrun her citadels, nettles and brambles her strongholds. She will become a haunt for jackals, a home for owls."[32]

The relationship of humans with non-human creation can thus helpfully be understood in terms of ***Covenant***, and the second great Commandment to love one's neighbour as oneself brings that perspective straight into the New Covenant.

"**Loving nature**"[33] can also be described as a model for relating to creation within the stewardship model. This model can be expressed in terms of the second great love commandment, to love one's neighbour as oneself, nature being the neighbour. For many people, particularly those who live closed to nature, being stewards of creation definitely meant loving creation.

The Australian Aboriginal model of humans as ***Custodians*** whose primary purpose in life is to "care for Country" emerges from a spirituality radically different from the Europeans' who took over Australia from them. Aboriginal spirituality emerges from the earth, European spirituality from the sky. For Aborigines, even Aboriginal Christians, the spirit world seems far more integrated with this world than for European Australians. Yet are these differences in worldview and spirituality as fundamental as many theologians believe? The children of Abraham are also called to "care for country". N.T. Wright has argued that the purpose of humans is not to be saved *from* earth but to work with God towards the restoration *of* earth. He argues that the *resurrection of the Son of God, as the first instance of the **new heavens and new earth***, is the motivation for Christians to work for earth's restoration, confident that whatever we do now will be used in God's restored, transformed creation.[34]

Thinking eschatologically, there is much to be gained from the biblical theme of '*the river of the water of life*'. Michael Wilcock calls this motif "'a tie-rod', running from end to end of the sixty-six books [of the Bible]", and argues that the third revelation of heaven in Revelation 21:9 – 22:19 is:

> "a summary of the biblical doctrine of creation…It concerns what Christ called 'the new world' (Mt. 19:28), literally 'the new genesis'. The first chapter of the Bible describes how God made the world; the last one shows how He will remake it. The creation as it was, and as it will be, is an immense organism alive with the life of God, for the stream flows 'from the throne of God and of the Lamb', and thence 'through the middle of the street of the city'."[35]

Orthodox theology, represented by Paulos Gregorios, speaks in terms of the human as a *microcosm of all creation*. Another Orthodox priest, Metropolitan John Zizioulas, has suggested that humans are *priests in and of creation*, offering creation back to God. At the Eucharist we do this by bearing bread and wine, representing the fruit of creation, forward to the altar. This model also allows humans a central, but not anthropocentric place in creation.[36] This, Zizioulas wrote, is:

> "…an idea more or less corresponding to that of *love* in its deepest sense. In all this the underlying assumption is that there exists an interdependence between man and nature, and that the human being is not fulfilled until it becomes the *anakephalaiosis*, the summing up of nature. Thus man and nature do not stand in opposition to each other, in antagonism, but in positive relatedness. This cannot be achieved in any other way except through liturgical action…"[37]

Conclusion

In the light of the worldwide environmental crisis this first chapter of this textbook of eco-theology has begun a conversation about Creator, Creation and humans, and our relationship with each other. It has examined the question "Whose earth is this?" It has entered the domain of science and examined the "state of the earth". And it has both introduced the theological discipline called "eco-theology", presented an example of an Indian eco-theology and argued that the world needs more Indian eco-theologies.

Questions for Consideration

1. Think about the four areas mentioned at the end of Wati Longchar's contribution. How would you re-define them?

2. Which of the models for understanding how you as a human being relate to the Creator and the Creation speaks most powerfully to you? Why?

3. How do you relate your Christian faith and the environment in which you live? Do you need eco-theology?

For Further Reading

Pope Francis. *Laudato Si': An encyclical letter on Ecology and Climate* Città del Vaticano, Libreria Editrice Vaticana, 2015.

Sarojini Henry. *We're One Earth Community*. Delhi: ISPCK, 2013.

John Houghton. *Global Warming: The Complete Briefing*. Cambridge: Cambridge University Press, 4th Ed. 2009.

Huang Phoho. *"Embracing the Household of God: A Paradigm shift from Anthropocentric Tradition to Creation responsibility"* in Doing Theology, PTCA Study Series No.7, Kolkata 2014.

Mathew Koshy Punnakadu. *http://www.drmathewkoshy.com* See "Published articles"

Solomon Victus. *Eco-Theology and the Scriptures: A Revisit of Christian Responses*. Delhi: Christian World Imprints, 2014.

Lynn White Jr., *"The historical roots of our ecologic crisis"* Science, New Series, Vol. 155, No. 3767 (Mar. 10, 1967), pp. 1203-1207.

Published by: American Association for the Advancement of Science Stable URL: http://www.jstor.org/stable/1720120.

Endnotes

[1] An oceanographer is a scientist who studies oceans.

[2] Revelle, R., and H. Suess, "Carbon dioxide exchange between atmosphere and ocean and the question of an increase of atmospheric CO_2 during the past decades." *Tellus* 9, 1957, pp. 18-27.

[3] Dichloro diphenyl trichloroethane.

[4] Rachel Carson, *Silent Spring* Harmondsworth: Penguin Books Ltd, 1962. Silent Spring has been re-published by other companies since.

[5] Lynn White Jr. *"The historical roots of our ecologic crisis"* Science, New Series, Vol. 155, No. 3767 (Mar. 10, 1967), pp. 1203-1207. Published by: American Association for the Advancement of Science Stable URL: http://www.jstor.org/stable/1720120.

[6] Means "human-centred", selfish.

[7] Sallie McFague, "An Earthly Theological Agenda," *The Christian Century* 108, no. 1. 1991.

[8] "Stern Review: The Economics of Climate Change" (Cambridge: Cambridge University Press, 2007).

[9] The information in this section comes from John Houghton *Global Warming: The Complete Briefing.* 4th Ed. (Cambridge: Cambridge University Press, 2009), 21-23.

[10] The French scientist Jean-Baptiste Fourier first recognized this warming effect as early as 1827. The Englishman John Tyndall measured the absorption of infra-red radiation (the sort that travelled back out towards space) by carbon dioxide and water vapour. In 1896 a Swedish chemist, Svante Arrhenius estimated that doubling the concentration of carbon dioxide would increase the global average temperature by 5 to 6 degrees Celsius, which is quite close to what climate scientists think today. Around 1940 G.S. Challender was the first to calculate the warming due to the increasing carbon dioxide produced from the burning of "fossil fuels" – coal, petrol, diesel and the like.

[11] 97% according to a study conducted several years ago.

[12] From "An Inconvenient Truth" slide show.

[13] 7 February, 2009.

[14] Al Gore, An Inconvenient Sequel: Truth to Power: Your Action Handbook to Learn the Science, Find Your Voice, and Help Solve the Climate Crisis. New York, Rodale, 2017,13.

[15] To use Roland Robertson's composite term, introduced to theology by the Catholic missiologist Robert Schreiter.

[16] Al Gore, An Inconvenient Sequel: Truth to Power: Your Action Handbook to Learn the Science, Find Your Voice, and Help Solve the Climate Crisis (New York: Rodale, 2017), 10.

[17] Paul Santmire's *The Travail of Nature: The Ambiguous Ecological Promise of Christian Theology* 1 ed. 1 vols. (Philadelphia: Fortress Press, 1985).

[18] Celia Deane-Drummond, *Eco-Theology*, (London: Darton, Longman & Todd, 2008), p.viii.

[19] Huang Phoho: *Embracing the Household of God: A Paradigm shift from Anthropocentric Tradition to Creation responsibility in Doing Theology* (PTCA Study Series No.7, Kolkata 2014).

[20] From the 5th to the 15th centuries CE (Common Era, previously known as AD.)

[21] to angels, demons (which were thought to be rebel angels), stars, the moon, kings, princes, nobles, common people, wild animals, domesticated animals, trees, other plants, precious stones, precious metals, and other minerals.

[22] Luke 12:35-48.

[23] McGrath, *The Re-Enchantment of Nature*. 15.

[24] The South African theologian Ernst Conradie has written extensively on this.

[25] Hall, *The Steward: A Biblical Symbol Come of Age*, Elsdon, *Greenhouse Theology: Biblical Perspectives on Caring for Creation*.

[26] The current Pope has taken his name from St francis. See his encyclical Pope Francis *Laudato Si': An encyclical letter on Ecology and Climate* Città del Vaticano, Libreria Editrice Vaticana, 2015.

[27] St Francis' famous Canticle to the Sun expresses this well.

[28] The author conducted a study on such Christians on how they related their Christian faith to the environment in which they lived.

[29] Walter Brueggemann's *The Land* is perhaps the best-known treatment in recent years. Geoffrey Lilburne has written in similar vein of the Australian context. William Dumbrell has contributed with *Covenant and Creation: A Theology of the Old Testament Covenants*.

[30] Elsdon, *Greenhouse Theology: Biblical Perspectives on Caring for Creation*.

[31] Exodus 3:8 is the first of many references.

[32] Isaiah 34:12-4.

[33] James Nash *Loving Nature: Ecological Integrity and Christian Responsibility*. 1 ed. Nashville: Abingdon Press in cooperation with The Churches' Center for Theology and Public Policy, 1991.

[34] This summarizes the argument of Wright, *Surprised by Hope*, N. T. Wright, *The Resurrection of the Son of God*, 1 ed., Christian Origins and the Question of God (London: SPCK, 2003).

[35] Michael Wilcock, *The Message of Revelation*, ed. John Stott, The Bible Speaks Today. Leicester: Inter-Varsity Press, p. 216. 1975.

[36] I used this model as the basis of a prayer I was asked to give by The Hon. Al Gore in September, 2007 at the beginning of a day in which he trained some 160 people to deliver his Climate Change slide show that formed the basis of the Oscar award-winning film "An Inconvenient Truth". The sense of being representative, both of creation and of the diverse communities from which trainees had come from across Australia and abroad was much appreciated.

[37] John Zizioulas, "Preserving God's Creation (Part 1)," *Theology in Green*, no. 5. p. 18. 1993.

Reflection

The article of Wati Longchar is an excellent exposition of dominant Christian theologies and justifies the reason for not having an eco-theological perspective in Christian faith. Most of the Christians In India are following the prevailing dominant western theological thinking. It is a fact we need to acknowledge that the dominant Christian theologies have been too anthropocentric, hierarchical, mechanistic and dualistic in their approach and content. Several Christian theologians have explained God's creation within this hierarchical structure. Human beings are the highest among the created materials beings, having ultimate rights over the other creatures. Luther, Barth and Bultmann held somewhat similar positions. Evangelicals believe that the world is coming to an end, all that is material will be destroyed, but only the souls will be saved and live eternally in heaven; other materials will perish. This doctrine made people think that "This world is not our home. We are just passengers." Consequently, if this world is not our home, why should we take care of it? Serious attention was not given to the creation theology as they did not face an ecological crisis as we do today. Christianity does have a theology of creation, but most of the Christians are not ready to accept this point. The presence of God makes this earth sacred. That is why God entered into a covenant relationship with all creatures. We believe in God because God as the Creator is present and continues to work with the land, river and sea to give life and hope.

David Reichardt, in his article explains the present ecological crisis in a systematic way. Western Christianity placed human interests above the concerns of the rest of the planet, including other forms of life. That has increased the concentration of carbon dioxide in the atmosphere by about 43%, from 280 ppm in 1700 to over 400 ppm today. The effects of climate change pose perhaps the most serious threat to life on earth. David explains that eco-theology came as a response to the Ecological crisis. He states that another helpful way of approaching the subject of eco-theology is to think of the earth as a household, and then to ask to whom it belongs. The questions of "Whose earth?" and "Who (and whose) are we?" are closely linked.

This chapter is a good introduction to the book and it gives good insight to all those who are interested to know more about eco-theology.

Mathew Koshy Punnackad

Examining the ways in which the Christian faith has both engaged and not engaged with the care of creation:

What are the obstacles before us?

Clive Pearson & George Zachariah

Editor's Note

Chapter two continues with the task of setting eco-theology in its theological and ecclesiological context. Clive Pearson's choice of the hymnal as a means of doing this is perhaps surprising...until one thinks of one's own formative Christian experience. I learned my Bible by singing "Scripture in Song" choruses and much of my basic theology from Wesleyan hymns. George Zachariah has built on Clive's foundation. The "hermeneutical tools" he employs - "suspicion and retrieval" - sound much less inviting than a good sing along until one realises that this is about listening for the human side of every biblical text.

Clive Pearson

Part A: Sing a New Song

It has often been said that Christians receive their understanding of faith through what they sing. That may seem like a surprise given the importance we attach to the Bible. It is our primary witness to God's ways with the people of Israel, firstly, and then through Jesus Christ and the work of the Holy Spirit in the early days of the church. And yet what we sing in our services of worship can shape us as much, if not more, than what we read in the Scriptures.

On reflection that should not come as too much of a surprise. There is a lot of singing in the Bible anyway. In the New Testament the gospel of Luke is full of songs that mark the announcement and birth of Jesus. If we turn to the Hebrew Bible (or the Old Testament), then the book of Psalms is the most obvious collection of songs. The Greek word used to translate the Hebrew title is psalmoi. That words means "instrumental music" – by extension it comes to mean "the words accompanying the music". There are many themes and images covered in this collection of songs.

Of particular interest for us in caring for creation are those psalms that call us to "sing a new song" and the ones where the created order is praising God. Examples of such are Psalms 19, 93 , 96 and 98. Here the "all the trees of the forest sing for joy", "the sea roars", "the floods clap their hands" and the "hills sing together for joy". Comparisons here can be made with the prophetic literature where "the mountains and the hills before you shall burst into song, and all the trees of the field shall claps their hands" (Isaiah 55:12).

One of the dilemmas that face leaders of worship is that the great majority of hymns- and song-books were published before climate change and the care of creation became so important. So many of the older hymns are of a more personal nature. They make much more use of 'I' statements and how the self relates to God. Sometimes the personal pronoun is changed to a 'we' and carries with it an understanding of the church:

what it is called to be and what does it see as its part in the mission of God? There is a tendency in these hymns to privilege heaven more than life lived on earth. What belongs to the moment in time of our personal existence is seen in terms of a journey into the nearer presence of God or to our true home where there is no more hardship, weariness, war or rumours of war, or tears. "We blossom and flourish like leaves on the tree, then wither and perish".

It is also not uncommon for hymns to evoke a landscape other than the one which we inhabit. Sometimes the hymn situates us inside the geography of the biblical lands – Bethlehem and Jerusalem, the river Jordan and Bethel, for example. What is happening here is that the biblical references may bind us into the experience of Jesus or the people of Israel; alternatively, or at the same time, the biblical geography becomes a metaphor for the stage of our own life's journey of faith.

For those of who live in Australia there can be another sense of dislocation. So often the hymns carry the ecology and environment of another country. The seasons, the landscapes, the descriptive language has more the feel of England where so many of our traditional hymns have been composed. It is not the environment of an Australia that possesses a different range and timing of seasons, a different geography and geology; nor is its bird life, insects, reptiles and mammals those of a faraway land captured in the lyrics (which is more often than not England). No doubt the same is true for Christians in India.

Now and then the words of what is sung capture the wonder and beauty of creation. Hymns like "All things bright and beautiful" and "For the beauty of the earth" remind us of how we share our lives with the rest of creaturely existence. There are a number of others that are designed to lead us into the praise of God as "the king of creation", who, "has made all things well". These are hymns that are often used at the beginning of a service as hymns of adoration and a recognition of how we are now self-consciously coming into the presence of God who is reckoned to be creator, sustainer and redeemer: "I sing the mighty power of God / That made the mountains rise / ... Thou, God, art present here". These hymns of praise can be placed alongside more seasonal hymns of harvest where there is a mood of thanksgiving. They are inclined to express gratitude for the providential care of God. "We plough the fields and scatter / the good seed on the land / But it is fed and watered / by God's almighty hand".

These received hymns hand onto us a rather mixed message. There is praise of God the creator and a recognition of its wonder and its God-given nature. There is also a strong message to be more concerned with a life beyond our existence in this passing day. It has been argued that the dominant tradition of the Christian faith is to look upon this world more like a staging post for personal salvation; it is ultimately not as important as the next life. One Australian scholar of the Hebrew Bible (the Christian Old Testament), Norman Habel, reckons that this tradition and so much of our popular understanding of the Christian faith is inclined to too much 'heavenism'. It regards this world as 'disposable'.

Sometimes this way of thinking can be expressed in a very extreme form. Sometimes the claim is made that we do not care for this Earth, for this created order, because the book of Revelation speaks of a new heaven and new earth. There is the expectation of the second coming of Christ which raises the question as to why should we bother with the caring of creation. That particular expectation is often associated with biblical images that speak of the sun being darkened, the moon not giving its light, and the stars falling from heaven. It can even be argued that failure to care for the environment might even hasten the day of the Lord and the winding up of human history.

It is important for us to be mindful of how there are biblical traditions that can play down the need for us to show concern for the well-being of God's creation. The problem is not to be found just with these end-times texts. One of the most troublesome texts has been Genesis 1:28-30. In this account of creation human beings are created on the sixth day. It is said that both male and female are made in the image of God. Humankind are then told to be fruitful and multiply; they are told that they have dominion and authority over everything 'that has the breath of life'. The plant life – all that yields seeds – is for their use.

The language of dominion can lend itself to a sense of responsible stewardship of the created order. That would at face value seem to be an advance on being indifferent to the care of creation. In more recent times, however, that reading of the text has become more of a problem. The model of stewardship still leaves humanity in control: it does so in a way in which the management of the earth's resources can also be an invitation to exploitation of the earth's resources and disregard of other creatures.

It should perhaps come as no surprise then that Lynn White Jr. argued that the Judaeo-Christian tradition should bear a 'huge burden of guilt' for the ecological crisis of our day. For much of our history there has been a dominant tradition that has desacralized nature and emphasized the otherness of God. That text – Genesis 1:28-30 – becomes a symbol of what is called humanity's instrumental use of creation. What is meant by this turn of phrase is that a tree, for example, only possesses value insofar as we convert it into a door, a table, a house. It gets its value by how we put it to use. The alternative is to value a tree for simply being a tree. Here it has what is called intrinsic value.

Lynn White Jr. was one of the first to make the case against the ecological record of the Christian faith. Now he was not writing as someone without a faith who wanted to humiliate the church through time. White also referred to what has been called a minority tradition within the Christian tradition. For him that lesser tradition it was associated with St. Francis of Assisi whom he called 'the patron saint of ecology'. It was within this tradition that Pope Francis dedicated his encyclical, Laudato Si': On Care of Our Common Home. This minority tradition is evident in St Francis' Canticle of the Sun where the relationship between humanity and the rest of creation is expressed through the language of kinship - for example, brother and sister.

That there is this minority tradition is something to celebrate. Those who have a concern for the environment and the rest of creaturely existence speak of the need to 'sift the traditions' that have been handed down to us. That call is not to ignore those texts that are indifferent or potentially damaging to the environment – although those texts may be susceptible to a different interpretation. One example of that is the way in which the combination of the dominion understanding of Genesis 1:28-30 and the end times texts are used. The Princeton theologian, Daniel Migliore, described how the practice of willing the hastening end of this creation is a form of 'apocalyptic terrorism'. It fails to recognize how the Genesis story also speaks of each of the six days of creation being described by God as 'good'.

This sifting of the traditions can lead us to consider how we might read the Bible through 'ecological eyes'. It has sometimes been said that far too often we read the Bible as if we have 'word blindness'. We do not pay attention evenly to what is actually in the text. We are likely to privilege the words to do with God, Christ, the Spirit and the human subject and not notice what is happening with regards the rest of creation.

It is one thing to read the Bible with ecological eyes; it is another thing to sing a 'new song'. The latter becomes important if our claim that most people form their understanding of faith through what they sing is true. The dilemma is that the majority of our hymns from the past do not address the themes to be found in the Pope's encyclical. There he refers to climate as a 'common good'; the Earth is our 'common home, our only home'. He refers to the 'throwaway culture' of the west and notes that it is the poor and most vulnerable who are most likely to feel the deepening effects of climate change.

We now know that the Earth system is changing. The Earth system refers to all those sciences which deal with how our planet functions in terms of its air, water, soils, rocks. It includes volcanism and glaciation. There are now so many signals of how humankind has influenced the Earth's system – so much so that it is said that we are passing into a new period in the Earth's deep history. We are crossing over into the Anthropocene – the age of humans – and leaving behind the Holocene which was a time of relative stability in the Earth's climate which allowed for cultures, civilisations and faiths to flourish.

It is critical for us to find a new song to sing. It is well known that music – like dance – has the capacity to inspire us and inform us in a way that is deeper than words. It is not uncommon for some Christian scholars to say that humankind now stands in need of an ecological conversion. In the language of the parable of the prodigal son it is time to "come to our senses" (Luke 15:17). The other side of this coin is to become aware of how denial is expressed.

Kari-Marie Norgaard is a sociologist of everyday emotions. She had made a study of a number of towns in Norway in order to explore what do they know about the threat of climate change and how they then handle that knowledge. Sometimes the problems can seem so large and we suffer from what is called 'psychic numbing': we know there is a problem but we are so small; what can we do?; so we do nothing. One of Norgaard's findings was that the news media regularly made folk aware of ecological problems. Some people in these towns pursued livelihoods that were very sensitive to weather change. The common response was one of denial.

Norgaard drew upon the work of an English sociologist, Stanley Cohen, then in order to describe different forms of denial at work. There is outright denial: what you say is not happening. Then there is the kind of denial where you acknowledge what is happening but then pursue inappropriate responses. Here in Australia that might mean recognizing that fossil fuels release adverse levels of carbon emissions into the air, but we decide to build another coal station when other options for renewable energy are available. The third and final form of denial Cohen identified was to mask the effects of what is happening. During recent wars the language of 'collateral damage' of bombing was used to avoid speaking about the incidence of innocent civilian deaths.

The singing of a new song can weave together the words we use with the emotions of our hearts and minds and the physicality of our bodies. The words we sing can help form our Christian understanding and inspire us to do what is possible for the sake of our neighbour and our life together. For a Christian concern for the environment - for ecology and climate change; for life in the Anthropocene – these new songs must be able to establish a link between what is now happening in our world with the language of the faith we profess. There are two stories to hold together. The first has to do with the vulnerability of God's good creation; the second has to do with how we are bound to God the Creator, the Holy Spirit as the source and giver of life, and the Word who became flesh, the cosmic Christ through whom, in whom and for whom all things were made.

Let us finish with a couple of hymns that stand at the dawning of this new age. The two I have selected are often found in hymn books around the world today, but that does not exhaust the list of possibilities. There has been a proliferation of hymns seeking to address ongoing concern for God's good creation. The first of my selected hymns was composed by Shirley Murray from Aotearoa-New Zealand. It was first published in the early 1990s and at that time was one of the very few hymns to address the realities of ecological threat. It differs markedly from those hymns of praise and adorations we began with and could be sung in tandem with them.

> Touch the earth lightly, / Use the earth gently, / Nourish the life of the world in our care:
> Gifts of great wonder, / Ours to surrender, / Trust for the children tomorrow will bear.

> We who endanger / Who create hunger / Agents of death for all creatures that live,
> We who would foster / Clouds of disaster /God of our planet, forestall and forgive!

> Let there be greening, / Birth from beginning, / Water that blesses and air that is sweet,
> Health in God's garden, /. Hope in God's children, / Regeneration that peace will complete.

> God of all living / God of all loving / God of the seedling, the snow and the sun,
> Teach us, deflect us, / Christ re-connect us, / Using us gently and making us one.

The second hymn is "Beauty for brokenness" by Graham Kendrick. It demonstrates an holistic concern for a kingdom of justice joy and peace. It is framed in the nature of an appeal to "God of the poor, friend of the weak". It does so against a background of the fragility of life. The third verse situates a world of strife and bitterness alongside the pain of Christ's cross. The fourth verse names ecological damage and does so in the context if a longing for our darkness to be lightened, for justice to burn brightly and the nations learn the ways of salvation and praise God:

> Rest for the ravaged earth, / oceans and streams /
> plundered and poisoned, / our future, our dreams, /
> Lord, end our madness, / carelessness, greed; /
> Make us content with / the things that we need.

George Zachariah
Part B: Interrogating Our Songs, Chants, and Doctrines

Ecological crisis is a reality and we are all affected by this crisis. But how far the sources of Christian faith enable us to actively engage in eco-justice ministries is a question that calls for serious attention. Is Christian faith sensitive to the groaning of creation? Does Christian faith discern the ecological crisis as a wakeup call for conversion and transformation? Or is Christian faith responsible for the destruction of the earth? Does Christian scripture legitimize violence against God's creation? These are self-reflexive questions which we ought to wrestle with in our times. At the same time, we also need to retrieve life-affirming traditions from our sources so that it may inspire the faith communities to be sensitive to the groaning of creation and to be a healing presence in our context. This chapter is an attempt to explore the ecological significance of the sources of Christian faith using the hermeneutical tools of suspicion and retrieval to enable us to become credible witnesses in the context of the distress of mother earth.

What is the place of God's creation in our spirituality? Do we think that our hymns, liturgies, sacraments, and lectionaries inspire us to engage in ministries of creation care? These interrogations lead us to a critical examination of our spiritual resources that facilitate our faith formation. A cursory look at the hymnals—English and vernacular—that we use in our churches exposes the ecological bankruptcy of our hymns and lyrics. None of these hymns talk about God's creation or the place of the rest of the creation in the redemptive purpose of God. The subject index in our hymnals include; The life to come, The second coming of Christ,

Heaven anticipated, The redeemed in heaven, and Death and resurrection. As these titles indicate, these hymns articulate an earth-denying faith, anticipating the glorious union of the saved individual with the Lord in the world to come. Our earthly life is just a preparation for our life after death. Earth is a waiting room for the saved who are eagerly waiting for the trumpet sound.

The theology of mission propagated through our hymns and lyrics also require our critical evaluation. Most of the hymns proclaim the conquering love of God manifested on the cross of Christ and invite us to conquer the people living in darkness with the light of the gospel. The mission motif that we find in these hymns is again a theology of preparation—preparing people to escape from the eternal fire of judgment and to be with the Lord in the world to come. In other words, it is a theology of mission which excludes God's creation from God's grace and salvation. Metaphors like pilgrims and sojourners further admonish the faithful from engaging in ministries to protect and nurture God's creation. Earth is simply a transit point in our journey from birth to death, and our mission is not to get settled down in or beautify the transit point.

Along with the hymns, our liturgies and sacraments play a significant role in our theological formation. As the Orthodox tradition believes, liturgy is the kerygma (proclamation) of the Church. Liturgical prayers and rituals affirm the faith of the Church. From an ecological point of view, the two dominical sacraments are so rich with their nature symbolism. The sacrament of baptism is celebrated around water, whereas in Eucharist we celebrate the bounty of creation and human labor in the bread and wine. But unfortunately, these two sacraments neither theologically tell us about God's plan and purpose for the community of creation nor inspire us to engage in the mission of redeeming God's creation. Instead, we are being presented as a called out and separated community by the blood of Christ, not to be contaminated by our engagement in the world.

The Eucharistic liturgy celebrates the passion of Christ as a new covenant for the forgiveness of sin. But this experience of salvation is limited to human beings, and hence, the rest of the creation falls outside the sphere of the saving grace of Christ. The prayers of confession that we use in our liturgies do not help us to discern our ecological sins. As a result, our worship does not lead us to the experiences of genuine introspection and repentance.

The ecumenical creeds are the concise articulations of the faith of the Church, and they occupy a prominent space in our faith formation and Christian life. A critical reading of these creeds from the perspective of the earth reveals the disturbing fact that the communion of creation created and found good by God does not find any room in the creeds of the Church except in the affirmation of God as Creator. The critical analysis that we have done so far categorically exposes the ecological bankruptcy of our spiritual practices, liturgies, hymns, creeds, and the sacraments. This ecological bankruptcy not only obscures the significance of earth in Christian faith and mission, but also legitimizes our ecological sins.

In spite of the ecological bankruptcy of our traditional faith formation and spirituality, there have been attempts to reclaim the ecological vision of Bible and to engage in ministries of creation care. Inspired by Christian faith, communities are involved in the mission of responding to the groaning of the creation all over the world. However, realizing the potential threat of this public protest against the prevailing order of economic exploitation and ecological pillage, Bible and Christian theology have been extensively used to sabotage the eco-justice ministries. We may not take these theological and biblical arguments seriously. But the very fact that these arguments are posed by heavily funded and learned Christian leaders and theologians with large number of followers indicate that several of our Christian brothers and sisters are yet to recognize care of creation as a mission imperative. As a result, the ecological crisis does not generate any response of guilt or moral indignation or conversion in us. As long as we legitimize theologically and scripturally the present state of the earth and the corporate plunder, our faith communities will not approach ecological crisis as a moral issue demanding faith response.

The theological arguments of legitimization are primarily committed to protect and perpetuate the prevailing order. Anything that disturbs or questions the existing social relations or power equations is considered as a threat against God. For those who consider carbon civilization as

God's blessing, a call to reduce our carbon footprints is a negation of God. The climate change discourses emerging from the margins exposing the historical emissions of the developed nations, and their reluctance to be part of the global initiative to reduce carbon emissions are perceived as attempts to destroy the imperial powers of our times. For people who earnestly believe that it is the God of the Bible that leads their countries in their neo-colonial economic and ecological assault of other nations and the nature, it is blasphemous to accept carbon civilization as sin.

Yes, as Christians, it is our responsibility to discern the crisis of our times, and to enable the faith communities to respond to the ecological crisis. However, before we venture into that mission, we need to do an introspection to expose the ways in which our biblical interpretations continue to legitimize and perpetuate the distress of the earth. That means, the crisis that we face today is primarily a theological problem; a problem that emerges from our perceptions of God, ourselves, and the rest of the creation that sanctions our abusive relationship with nature.

In his controversial article "The historical roots of our ecological crisis," the American historian Lynn White Jr. argued that the Judeo-Christian theology is fundamentally exploitative of the earth because (1) The Bible asserts human dominion over nature and establishes a trend of anthropocentrism, and (2) Christianity makes a distinction between human beings as created in the image of God and the rest of the creation, which has no "soul" or "reason" and is thus inferior. Our current ecological crisis is caused by the commodification of nature by the profit mongering corporations and nation states in the name of progress, growth and development. Is Christianity responsible for our current ecological crisis, as White accuses? To answer this question, we need to explore what Christianity tells people about their relationship with the environment. The biblical creation narratives present us with a vision about who we are in relation to the rest of the creation. This is the theological anthropology that guides us in our social and ecological engagements. The first creation narrative in the book of Genesis portrays human beings as the crown of creation. We are distinct from other created beings because we are created in the image of God. Further, the theological understanding that we are endowed with the right to have dominion over the created order and to subdue the earth lies at the very heart of the ethos of imperialism, capitalism, globalization, and our growth-oriented development paradigm. Human beings have got intrinsic worth; the rest of the creation has only instrumental value. God created the natural world as a super market for human beings to plunder and exploit in order to quench their unjustifiable thirst for more. Creation has no worth other than being useful to human needs and greed. In other words, an anthropocentric theological anthropology emerging from the Judeo-Christian tradition reduces non-human beings into commodities without intrinsic worth. Such a theological anthropology legitimizes human exploitation and pillage of nature.

It is also important here to remember that Christianity with its missionary zeal, supported by exclusive claims, continues to reject and desecrate indigenous religious traditions and their practices of earth care. Pantheistic religions and their ecological practices are condemned as nature worship. Panentheistic ethos of Christian faith has been sidelined fearing idolatry. The whole concept of sacred grove is alien to Christianity, and Christian missionaries have chopped down several sacred groves in India to destroy idolatry. Once the intrinsic worth of the nature is theologically destroyed, then it is easy for the human beings to construct the destiny of the nature. Yes, Christianity bears a huge burden of guilt for the exploitation and colonization of nature.

In the face of the ecological crisis, a good number of devout Christians genuinely believe that God is punishing us. God has been considered as the agent causing floods, storms, droughts, and other "natural" catastrophes. God is punishing us or abandoning us is the standard Christian response to the ecological crisis. This theological position stems from a fearful sense of apocalyptic doom that only waits for God's inevitable judgment on planet earth and the sinful creatures. Why is God punishing us? Where is God in this crisis? These are the questions reverberate from the ground zeros of ecological destruction.

Climate change and other ecological disasters are explained as the consequence of God's wrath and curse. The God whom we see in this theological and biblical project is a God who is angry with the sinfulness of human beings, and hence is cursing the earth. According to this theological and biblical interpretation, ecological crisis is just an indication that the world is fast approaching its end. These are all signs of the end time. Our task then is to prepare ourselves to meet the Lord. Differently said, rather than inspiring us to engage in bearing public witness in the context of the distress of earth, our theological and biblical reflections tend to indoctrinate us to focus our attention on our personal salvation leaving behind the sinful world to its inevitable doom and destruction. In spite of the fact that all of us experience the impact of global warming in diverse forms, the theological and biblical reflections of the Christian community all over the world in general are geared up toward an otherworldly spirituality refusing our call to redeem the earth.

If at all we are encouraged to engage in eco-justice ministries of creation care in the context of the ecological crisis, it is not theologically articulated as an expression of our faith. Ecological engagement is considered as "social" involvement because we lack the theological imagination to understand our eco-justice ministries as part of the redemptive work of God initiated in Jesus. In our understanding, salvation and redemption are limited to human beings. Nature is soul-less, and hence it falls outside the redemptive work of Christ. As a result, nature cannot be redeemed. That means, our ecological struggles to protect our planet from ecological destruction is not a "Christian" mission. This distorted understanding of salvation and redemption does not stir us to seriously engage in the struggles for ecological justice.

Questions for discussion

Think about your favourite hymns: how do they refer to the rest of creation?

How important do you think it is for us to "sing a new song" that expresses care for God's good creation?

Reflect upon the two hymns by Shirley Murray and Graham Kendrick: what do you think we should "do" as a consequence of singing such hymns?

For Further Reading

Clive Ayre, Earth, *Faith and Mission: The Theology and Practice of Earth care.*,.
     Eugene: Wipf and Stock, 2015.

Celia Deane-Drummond. *Eco-Theology*. London: Darton, Longman and Todd,
     2008.

Celia Deane-Drummond. *A Primer in Ecotheology: Theology for a Fragile Earth*.
     Eugene: Cascade, 2017.

Elizabeth Johnson, *Creation and the Cross: The Mercy of God for a Planet in Peril*.
     Maryknoll: Orbis, 2018.

Pope Francis. Laudato Si': On Care of Our Common Home. Vatican City:
     Libreiria Editrice Vaticana, 2015.

Reflection

The chapter has been an eye opener for many of us who think the 'inherited' Christian faith has adequately dealt/engaged with the issue of ecological crisis and care of creation. The writers have pointed quite succinctly that it has not been the case. Creation has not found adequate place in our Christian faith, which we have received in the form of doctrines, hymns etc. These 'acquired' hymns are mostly based on the ecology of the mother church/country and most of these hymns are out rightly heavenistic (therefore, other-worldly) in nature. Therefore, care of the creation is given very less importance. Another notable problem with these faith affirmations was its language of dominion. Human beings are the masters of the whole created order. Creation is to be used (misused) for the needs and greed of humanity.

Renowned Indian ethicist, K. C. Abraham has rightly pointed out that unless we consider the ecological crisis as a spiritual problem, we continue to spoil the creation of God. He said,

> The ecological crisis is a spiritual problem. God created humans to be in partnership with nature. Humans are given special responsibility to take care of the creation. The role assigned to them is that of stewards and gardeners. Tenderness and care are the spiritual mode of this relationship. But humans became conquerors and exploiters of God's creation. This distorted relationship is the root of ecological crisis.[1]

The spiritual problem that Abraham speaks of is the creation of a 'distorted' and individualistic spirituality and theology we have inherited. Christian faith is intrinsically connected to Creation. In the Bible, God created the creation and put the human into the beautiful, ordered, complete and sufficient creation. The Bible is quite forthright in its message about caring the creation – "The Lord God took the man and put him in the garden of Eden to **till it** and **keep it**" (Genesis 2:15, NRSV). The command is to "work it/cultivate it" and "maintain it/preserve it." Cultivating the earth in the spirit of preservation is the command of the creator. The need of humanity for sustenance is not denied (cultivate it) but not at the expense of destroying it (therefore, preserve it).

As noted earlier, it is a spiritual problem. Therefore, it has to be addressed in a spiritual manner too. Spiritual methodologies need to be found to address it. How to go about it? Few suggestions are made here:

What should we do?

- Help congregations to hold "Creation Sunday."

- Start Bible Studies on what the Bible says about the environment. Consider holding 'outdoor' services.

- Hold a public prayer event with emphasis on care of creation, and stewardship.

- We need new hymns/songs that sings of care of creation.

- Emphasis on ecological conversion. Then only the ecological bankruptcy in our lyrics, hymns, doctrines, preachings, and liturgies will be overcome. This can be done by re-reading the Bible from an ecological perspective, thereby reclaiming the eco-vision of the Bible.

- Start a "Creation Club" for kids and youths of the church.

- As a faith community we need to invest, cooperate and indulge in eco-justice ministries.

- Plant trees around the church to provide natural shade to the building instead of putting up energy-guzzling air conditioners.

- Seriously consider to conduct an energy audit of your church and implement improvements.

Endnote

[1] Cf. K. C. Abraham, "Ecology: Some Theological Challenges," *Asian Christian Review* 3, no. 1 (Spring 2009): 39 (39-49).

Samuel George

Section Two

Using the Resources of Faith

Back to the Bible! How can the Bible be read in the light of an environmental concern?

Sunil Caleb & George Emeleus

Introduction: Why read the Bible for Guidance on Environmental Concerns?

The primary benefit of using the Bible in connection with an environmental concern is that we are able, as Christians, to discover the way in which God relates to the environment and to the whole non-human creation. We then can see what is God's plan for the human relation to the non-human creation. Though the severity and breadth of environmental problems were perhaps not present in the times when the words of the Bible were written, yet it is amazing how the Bible reveals clearly God's will regarding the use and care of God's created environment.

As Christians, the Bible is at the centre of our traditions and beliefs. At every time and place in Christian history, people have read the Bible for guidance on how to live rightly in relationship with God and with each other. Jesus summed up living rightly by quoting the two great commandments. The first and greatest commandment is: "You shall love the LORD your God with all your heart, with all your soul and with all your mind" and in the second one which Jesus described as like it: "You shall love your neighbour as yourself." (Matthew 22:37-39. Also Deuteronomy 6:5, Leviticus 19:18, Luke 10:27). In these commandments, the obvious emphasis is on relationships between people and God, and people with each other. However, when we look more deeply into what the Bible teaches us about right relationships with God and each other, we soon find these relationships also depend on how we relate to non-human creatures, and how we relate to the environment in which we live.

If we love God, and desire to live so that we reflect the image of God, then that means seeing as good all that God has created (Genesis 1). It also means acting with God-like, loving creativity. We are called to care for the parts of our environment which we influence, so that the God-given ability of all creatures to re-create themselves and to thrive is sustained. In doing so, we find Jesus present, as Christ who is with God and in God in the creation and sustaining of all things. (John 1:1-3, Colossians 1:15-17).

If we love our human neighbours as ourselves, then we will be concerned that they have a healthy environment in which to live, just as we want this for ourselves and our children. When Jesus answered the man who asked him "Who is my neighbour?" he told the parable of the Good Samaritan. The message is clear. We are true neighbours to those in need when we act in practical ways to care for them. Our neighbours could even be traditional enemies (Luke 10:29-37). Love for other people is to be shown in practical ways and not limited by social and political barriers and prejudices.

Today, the world-wide population is far greater than in biblical times, and we are interconnected in ways unimagined at that time. The whole world is our neighbourhood, in the sense that the way people live in one place may affect other people and their environment anywhere in the world. Our interdependence with other people, other creatures and our environment is so strong that we even could think of all creatures with which we share Earth as our neighbours.

Although we live in a world which is in many ways very different from how it was in Bible times, many things have not changed. The Bible describes famines, when the environment is stressed and unable to support essential agriculture, so that crops fail and animals die. When we read the descriptions of what happened, we may see exactly the same thing happening today (e.g. locust plagues: Joel 1:4, drought: I Kings 17) or may make an informed guess (e.g. toxic algae: Exodus 7:20). Sometimes the famines are linked to God's judgment, and sometimes no theological interpretation is given (e.g. Acts 11:28). Destructive human activity today may be very similar to the sort of activities which led to famines described in the Bible, and which are interpreted as a result of God's judgment. War still causes famines. Rich people still drive traditional farmers into poverty and debt. They still seize their land and use it to generate riches for themselves.

Today, environmental stress, its causes, and the threats it brings, cause great concern at every level from villages to national governments and to international organizations such as the United Nations and its agencies. Farmers, politicians, economists, scientists and many others are making great efforts to find ways to manage threats due to environmental stress, and to reduce its causes. For Christians, the Bible brings treasures of wisdom to the most difficult questions of all. These questions are about with how we live in relation to God, to each other, and how we live in the world and care for it and all its creatures.

In this chapter we explore how some of these biblical treasures of wisdom and insight may be applied to our environmental concerns today. There are three sections. In the first, we look at biblical themes of God as Creator, and humankind as creatures among, and sharing with, all of creation. In the second we explore use of analogy, where Biblical stories of human misuse of God's gracious gifts led to disaster, followed by redemption and hope. In these stories the patterns of human behaviour then are similar to the patterns of human behaviour causing environmental problems today. In the third we explore how Jesus' teaching about the kingdom of God may guide our responses to environmental concerns.

1.   **God the Creator: Humans created with a duty of care towards all creation**

Creation and the Hebrew Bible (Old Testament)

Overall the primary fact that the Bible reveals to us about God's relation with creation is that God is the Creator and God says that the Creation is Very Good. (Genesis 1:31). Writings on the presence of ecological themes on the Hebrew Bible often concentrate upon the accounts in Genesis 1, where God gives the human race 'dominion' over non-human life (Genesis 1.26) and Genesis 2 where Man is put in the Garden of Eden and told to 'till and keep it' (Genesis 2.15). From these verses it is deduced that since the word 'dominion' means responsible lordship, and since the Man was told to tend the garden, there is certainly evidence that the Hebrew Bible is strongly in favour of 'responsible stewardship' of the natural resources of the earth.

Many modern authors have found this biblical vision too anthropocentric, and have blamed it for the current environment crisis.[1] According to them, the trend of treating nature as something separate from God was begun by the Judeo-Christian tradition. However, in response to this criticism, a rediscovering of ecological concerns in the Bible has taken place. Ecological theologies also have been developed. These seek to explain the care of God for creation, either through the work of the Spirit of God or in ways of relating nature to God through relationships such as that of the human-body relationship or family relationships.[2]

In fact, in the Hebrew Bible, commitment to the health of the natural world is not just a matter of giving human beings advice about responsible use of the natural world (which could be interpreted as an anthropocentric activity), but is fundamental to the whole purpose of God in creation. Thus, there is seen particularly in the Hebrew Bible, a fundamental link between injustice, greed and sin in society, and ecological destruction. This link, for the writers, took the form of a 'cosmic covenant' that connected 'all orders of creation and linked them with rituals, ethics and society of humans'[3] and was recorded in Genesis 9. Hence, within the Hebrew Bible, there are clear signs of the view that injustice in the social order, particularly in the conduct of kings and the elite, leads to disharmony in the ecological order. Thus, for instance, Jeremiah links ecological devastation and the abandonment of the worship of God, and the obeying of the commandments of God, when he says in chapter 18:14-16a,

> "Does the snow of Lebanon leave the crags of Sirion? Do the mountain waters run dry, the cold flowing streams? But my people have forgotten me, they burn offerings to a delusion; they have stumbled in their ways, in the ancient roads, and have gone into bypaths, not the highway, making their land a horror, a thing to be hissed at forever."

The call for all creation to praise God in Psalm 150 shows us that God depicted in the Hebrew Bible has not just provided for human beings, but has provided the things necessary to live for all creation, and therefore expects a response of gratitude from even the trees and the birds. This concern for the needs of the land and the animals is seen in the requirement that even they be given a Sabbath rest. Thus Exodus 23:10-12 speaks of the need for the land to be left fallow in the seventh year and for domesticated animals to be allowed to rest in the seventh day of the week. As Robert Murray puts it,

> When the Bible's teaching on God's creation and our place in it is duly digested, I believe that it cries out to us 'you are brothers and sisters of every other human, and fellow creatures of everything else in the cosmos; you have no right to exploit or destroy, but you have duties to all, under God to whom you are responsible.[4]

Thus, the view of the writers of the Hebrew Bible is not only concerned with people. It also takes the needs of the land and the animals into account. However, since it is the human race that is responsible for the imbalances that appear, it is the responsibility of human beings to fulfil their duty to look after God's creation. It is therefore clear then, that only ecologically sustainable economic development has the support of the writers of the Hebrew Bible.

Creation in the New Testament

According to the New Testament, the resurrection of Jesus Christ is the transforming event in human history, the vindication of all that Jesus stood for. It is also the event, when 'the original goodness and moral significance of the created order, and of humanity's significant place in

that order, are reaffirmed and restored.'[5] The death and resurrection of
Christ brings nearer the transformation of the created order, for 'through
him God was pleased to reconcile to himself all things, whether on earth
or in heaven, by making peace through the blood of his cross' (Colossians
1.20). Until that process is complete, Paul views the whole of creation as
groaning like a woman in labour, waiting for the new, restored creation
to emerge (Romans 8.18-23).

Thus salvation in the New Testament is not only the restoration
of the relationship between God and human beings, but includes the
reconciliation of nature and human beings and the reconciliation of
human beings to one another. Hence it is true that Christ atones for our
debts to the creation, as well as to one another and to God.[6]

It is therefore clear, that the health of the environment is very much
part of the concern of God the Holy Spirit, as He seeks to draw human
history towards its 'final fulfilment in the eternal plan of God which is
revealed in Jesus Christ.'[7] In order that this plan may be fulfilled, we
are called upon to cooperate with God the Holy Spirit as He seeks to
encourage humankind, to use the natural resources of the world in a
sensitive and sustainable manner.

2.   Relationships and Patterns: Using Analogy

Some of the particular concerns that we have today may be unlike anything
described in the Bible. When that is so, we have to look deeper to find
how God speaks to us through the Bible about these concerns. Our
circumstances may be very different from those of the Bible writers, but
at a deeper level the cause of things going wrong for them, and for us,
is the same. We have to look deeper into the great themes of the Bible,
such as the revelation of God's love for the world, God's holiness, and
how our Lord Jesus Christ makes it possible for people to be reconciled
to God and be led on the path of right relationship with God. Damaged
relationships with each other, non-human creatures and our environment
are symptoms of a deeper failure. That deeper failure is brokenness in our
relationships with God, from which all brokenness and sin follows (Psalm

51:4). As we read the Bible with environmental concerns, God speaks to us about all our relationships, and how they may be healed.

When we read the Bible and learn what happens when people ignore God, we see events in Bible times unfolding in ways similar to the way in which events unfold today. The biblical narratives may then be used as an analogy for what is happening today. The similarities which make up the analogy then allow us to use the Bible as a guide to God's judgment and mercy at work in issues of concern to us today, including environmental concerns.

An example of analogy: The unfolding disaster of global warming and climate change, and the decline and fall of the kingdoms of Israel and Judah

Today, global warming and the climate change which it is causing are of great concern. This concern is felt at every level from those who live off the land and from the sea to the highest levels of governments and international organizations like the United Nations. Scientific research on climate change explores its causes, and what is likely to happen in the future. This research is perhaps the largest world-wide scientific co-operative effort ever undertaken. It shows that global warming mainly is the result of the way in which industrialization has taken place, and continues to do so. The underlying cause is emission of gases coming from burning coal, oil and gas, including when these are used to generate electricity, from land-clearing, and from making steel from iron ore and cement from limestone. Carbon dioxide is the most significant of these gases. Carbon dioxide in the atmosphere occurs naturally, and is one of the gases which traps heat so that the Earth remains warm enough for life to thrive. This is known as the "greenhouse effect". However, since the start of the industrial revolution, human activities are resulting in steady increase of atmospheric carbon dioxide, causing extra global warming. The extra heat trapped in the atmosphere already is changing weather patterns, melting polar and glacial ice, and warming the oceans. Extra carbon dioxide dissolved in the oceans makes them more acidic, disrupting the life-cycles of the micro-organisms on which ocean food-chains depend.

Large-scale industrialization, enormous global population increase, global warming, climate change and the scientific understanding of how these are linked, are modern issues. The Bible has nothing direct to say about them, but it has much to say about human behaviour when God gives people opportunities to live well on Earth. The modern story of industrialization, climate change, and scientific research is a story about humans using the Earth's resources to seek a better and more prosperous future. At the same time, this modern story exposes greed, injustice, and terrifying destruction in recent times, now, and into the future. It is the story of how humans have accessed fossil fuels (coal, oil, gas) from the Earth, and used the energy from them to transform how humankind lives on Earth. We may think of fossil fuels as a gift from God, with promise of blessing if it is used wisely. However, where this gift is used unwisely, it causes suffering and injustice. The result is curse – curse on people, on land, and now on the Earth as a whole, through global warming and climate change.

In the Hebrew Bible, the story of the Israelites entry to the Promised Land, how they lived there, and how they were crushed by the Babylonians and exiled, is also a story of gift, promise, blessing and curse. We may use this story as an analogy for our present woes due to climate change. As the Israelites ended their forty years wandering in the wilderness, they neared the land promised to them by God. It was God's to be gift to them, so that they could experience blessing from God. When the Israelites were about to enter the Promised Land God, through Moses, gave them covenantal promises of blessing if they lived righteously, in right relationship with God and each other. However, God also solemnly warned them that if they neglected God and God's ways, the blessing would turn to a curse. These themes of gift and promise, blessing and curse come together in Deuteronomy 26.

Once they were settled in the Promised Land, the Israelites began to neglect and ignore God the Giver. People exploited each other so the rich became richer and the poor poorer. From Judges to II Chronicles, we have the story of blessing and of curse as the judges, and then the kings, led the nation through good times and bad. In that period, whenever idolatry and unrighteousness and injustice increased, the prophets spoke out, and were contradicted and persecuted. The downward path of broken relationships and of ignoring calls to repentance led to disaster first for the kingdom of Israel, and then finally for Judah.

In the Hebrew Scriptures, the deepest cause of these disasters is the broken covenant in which God, through Moses, promised blessing for obedience, and curse if the people forgot God. The final depths of disaster occur when the Babylonians besieged Jerusalem from about 589-586 BCE. When the city walls were broken down, the Babylonians burned the city, destroyed and burned the Temple, and took captive the people who survived, exiling many to Babylon. These terrifying events are described in II Kings 25. They are remembered in many other places in the Hebrew Scriptures and the New Testament. Jewish people have continued to remember them, every year for over two and a half thousand years. Some examples of these memories are Psalms 74,79 and 80 and the book of Lamentations, and in these scriptures there are expressions of intense grief and of repentance, and also of hope.

The prophets continued to speak out as the remnant struggled to survive in exile in Babylon, offering words of hope. That hope was possible only because it was hope in the LORD, the Creator of all that is, whose glory would finally be honoured (e.g. Psalms 74:22 and 79:9).

In the last three centuries, industrial use of fossil carbon (coal, oil and gas) has transformed how humankind lives. It has provided most of the energy on which today's industries, communications and cities depend. It has driven research and technology, including in medicine, promoting human survival and the great increase in human population. We may think of that as fulfilling God's command to increase and fill the Earth (Genesis 1:28). These changes have made life better and longer for a great many people. For those who have benefited from use of fossil carbon, it is like a gift from God, a sort of "Promised Land", with the promise and experience of blessing. We see here that the biblical themes of gift, promise and blessing are being repeated. However, these "blessings" for some of humankind have been developed in ways which have been a terrible curse for many other people. The rich have become richer at the expense of others, some of whom are driven into deeper poverty. The industrial developments dependent on this "gift" have been used to industrialize war, causing great suffering and destruction. Now, the industrialized parts of the global economy are causing changes to the atmosphere and oceans, through greenhouse gases and the changes to climate which they cause. This threat is so serious that it is hard to imagine its impact in the future.

When we compare humankind's experiences of living in today's world, under the threat of climate change, and how the Israelites experienced the promised land, we can see common themes. In each case God has given a precious gift, so that people may be blessed (the Promised Land/Fossil fuels to give energy to make life better). The gift comes with a promise of blessing, conditional on keeping right relationship with God, amongst people, and with our God-given environment. Certainly, the Promised Land did bring blessing for some for a time, and so too has fossil carbon today. However, then and now, the gift has been misused, allowing some people to exploit many others. Then, and now, the Giver has been ignored and idols worshipped instead. Prophets warned of coming judgment, called their people to repent, and warned of coming disaster, and they were often ignored and persecuted. Today, on environmental and social issues, people still speak prophetically, warning, calling people to change their ways. They too are too often ignored, and even sometimes persecuted. Then, when disaster struck Jerusalem and a remnant were taken to exile, prophets spoke words of hope.

Today, we too face possible exile from a world of uncertain peace and reasonably predictable weather to a much more terrifying one. The time is likely to come when very many people will be displaced from their homes due to climate change, as sea levels rise and agricultural land turns to desert. There will be migration and conflict, and a widespread sense of hopelessness. In Hebrews 12:1-3, the writer brings together the faith and hope of the Israelite ancestors, and the hope which Christians have through Christ. Faith keeps going, even in terrifying situations which cause despair (Hebrews 12:1-2). As the writer reminds us, God created "the worlds" through the Son, who "sustains all things by his powerful word" (Hebrews 1:1-3). God's delight in all creation, and love for the "world" (John 3:16) are so great that we can only begin to imagine them. Are our concerns a reflection of God's concerns?

3.   Environmental Responsibility and the Kingdom of God

In the time of Jesus' earthly life, the Jewish people longed for the coming of God's chosen one, the Messiah. They expected him to be heralded by a prophet like Elijah (Matt 11:14), and that he would be greater than David (Matthew 22:43-45). He would "redeem Israel" (Luke 24:20) and his kingdom would have no end (Isaiah 9:7). People wanted to force Jesus to become their King, expecting him to lead a revolution (John 6:15), but Jesus already had rejected taking on the powers of evil on their own violent terms (Luke 4:1-13). In John's gospel, the contrast between the kingdom of God which Jesus was bringing in, and the violent force of earthly kingdoms, is summed up when Pilate questions Jesus:

> "Are you the king of the Jews?" Jesus answered, "Do you ask this on your own, or did others tell you about me?" Pilate replied, "I am not a Jew, am I? Your own nation and the chief priests have handed you over to me. What have you done?" Jesus answered, "My kingdom is not of this world. If my kingdom were from this world, my followers would be fighting to keep me from being handed over to the Jews. But as it is, my kingdom is not from here." Pilate asked him, "So you are a king?" Jesus answered, "You say that I am. For this I was born, and for this I came into the world, to testify to the truth. . ." (John 18:33-37).

Jesus' incarnation as Emmanuel, "God with us" (Matthew 1:23) makes his whole life and teaching about the incoming reign, or kingdom, of God. There are many scriptures in which Jesus specifically refers to the kingdom of God or, in Matthew, the kingdom of Heaven. He taught about the attitudes of heart and mind that make it possible for people to be part of the kingdom, and to be children of God (e.g. Matthew 5:3-11, 7:21, 19:14). He taught many parables which provoked thought about what the kingdom is like. He also looked beyond living as part of the kingdom in the here and now, to when the "Son of Man" would return in glory (e.g. Matthew 24:29-34). In the New Testament letters, and the Book of Revelation, there is a great deal more teaching about the kingdom of God. Some of it contains apocalyptic ("revealed") visions of the end of the "world" as we know it, the Lord's return, and the fulfilment of all things. There are scriptures which refer to redemption and fulfillment for all creation (e.g. Romans 8:18-25), and there are others which dramatically describe the destruction of the earth (e.g. II Peter 3:10), to be replaced by a "New Heaven and the New Earth" (Revelation 21).

The kingdom of God is sometimes described as "already" but "not yet". It is eternal, transcending and transforming every-day life, because that is what Jesus did before his death, and it is what he continues to do as the risen Lord, in the power of the Holy Spirit.

We need particular care and wisdom in how we interpret the biblical visions of the fate of the earth as we know it, and of the "New Heaven and the New Earth", and in how these influence the way we live now. Some Christians use end-time scriptures such as II Peter 3:10 and parts of Revelation to say that caring for the environment is not important, because it will be destroyed in the day of judgment. Some people even say that the growing environmental crisis today is a sign of the end, and that destroying the environment will speed up Christ's return. However, that is doing what Paul condemns in Romans 6:1 where he asks "should we continue to sin in order that grace may abound?" When interpreting particular scriptures, it is necessary to interpret them in view of the overall teachings of the scriptures. The first Christians expected Jesus to return in glory in their lifetimes, but they had to be reminded that when Jesus returns is known only to the Father (Matthew 24:36). The important thing is to live in a way that is formed by love of Jesus, and the faith that we shall, in his time and way, "see face to face" and "know fully, even as (we) have been fully known" (I Corinthians 13:12). We are answerable to him, now and eternally, for how we live all the time. That includes how we live with environmental responsibility.

We may speak of loving Jesus, but who do we say he is? (Mark 8:29) Who, indeed, is the King whose kingdom Christians are called to be part of? In John 1:1-5, he is the Word: "He was in the beginning with God, and without him not one thing came into being". In John 3:16, God "so loved the world that he gave his only Son, so that everyone that believes in him might not perish but may have eternal life." The Greek word translated "world" is *kosmos*, and its meaning includes the idea of how things are ordered. It could be translated "world order", or "cosmic order". The focus of John 3:16 is on people being transformed by God through faith. However, transformation of people occurs within the wider "world order" or *kosmos*, which God so loves. There is profound disorder in the world, in human affairs, and in the influence of humans on other creatures and the environment. God, the Creator, loves all creation, and people who are alive to Christ will find Christ's presence where all life, and the environment, are cherished and cared for.

As we wrote in section 1, the death and resurrection of Christ bring nearer the transformation of the created order, for 'through him God was pleased to reconcile to himself all things, whether on earth or in heaven, by making peace through the blood of his cross' (Colossians 1.20). Until that process is complete, Paul views the whole of creation as groaning like a woman in labour, waiting for the new, restored creation to emerge (Romans 8.18-23). Thus salvation in the New Testament is not only the restoration of the relationship between God and human beings, but includes the reconciliation of nature and human beings and the reconciliation of human beings to one another. Hence it is true that Christ atones for our debts to the creation, as well as to one another and to God.

As people "in Christ", Christians have a particular responsibility for the process of reconciliation. Paul puts it this way: "So if anyone is in Christ, there is a new creation: everything old has passed away; see everything has become new! All this is from God, who has reconciled us to himself through Christ, and has given us the ministry of reconciliation . . ." (II Corinthians 5:17,18). Paul's focus in this scripture is on reconciliation between people and God. That takes place as part of the reconciliation of all things to God. The process of reconciliation of all things includes seeking God's will, guidance and empowerment to respond to environmental concerns.

Conclusion

The Bible does have many texts which speak directly about the environment, but reading the Bible with environmental concern goes much further than these texts. For guidance on environmental concerns, we need to consider them in light of the great themes of the Bible, such as creation, judgment and redemption, and the coming of Jesus as the Messiah who brings in the reign, or kingdom of God.

Creation, and the renewal of creation, are the first of these themes. The environment in which humankind lives is part of all creation, which God has made and which God declares good. For Christians, Jesus Christ is God with us, and he is with God and in God in the creation and sustaining of all things. This makes the whole of creation sacred, a sign of and a witness to the grace and glory which the Son shares with the Father. All creation does not simply exist for human benefit. It has great beauty and sacredness quite apart from humans. Looking at the stars and the heavens, and all that God has made, makes known God's majesty and glory and the extraordinary love of God for humankind (Psalm 8). Although we are small creatures in a very much greater God-glorifying creation, we are beloved by God and have been created with special responsibilities within the creation.

Of course, people always live in particular times and places, and depend most of all on their immediate environments. The environments in the Bible usually are described to give context and background to the human story. What is happening in the environment (e.g. rain, floods, lightning, droughts, wild animals, plagues of locusts) is sometimes interpreted theologically, and sometimes it is described without such interpretation. We depend on human relations, and relationship with our environments in order to live. Everything we depend upon is a gift from God, who promises blessing if the gifts are used wisely, but warns of potential disaster when God is forgotten and idols take God's place.

In the New Testament, Jesus brings in the kingdom, or reign, of God which is already becoming present in our everyday world. Christians are called to live in, but not of, the world, even as Jesus was in, but not of it. That means not conforming to the world-order, particularly when human actions are destructive. Instead, Christians are called to the ministry of reconciliation and healing of relationships. That is an essential part of how God's kingdom is expressed on earth. We are taught to pray: "Your will be done on earth as it is in heaven." As God's will includes the reconciliation of all things to himself, we may confidently and in faith respond to environmental concerns as part of our Christian calling.

Questions for Discussion

Name something which is an environmental concern to your community. How do you, and others in your community, respond to this concern? What themes and particular scriptures help you to make your responses a definite part of your Christian discipleship?

Can you think of ways in which the Exodus drama could be used as an analogy for our generation and future ones living with climate change? *(There is some good thinking on these lines by the Jewish scholar Jonathan Sacks. This may be found with an on-line search (Jonathan Sacks Exodus Climate Change)).*

What sort of actions in response to environmental problems could be thought of as signs of the Kingdom of God? What Biblical teaching about the Kingdom of God supports seeing these actions in this way?

For Further Reading

Conradie, Ernst. *An Ecological Anthropology: At home on Earth?* Aldershot: Ashgate, 2005.

Deane-Drummond, Celia. *Eco-Theology.* London: Darton, Longman and Todd, 2008.

Edwards, Denis. *Ecology at the Heart of Faith. The Change of Heart that leads to a New Way of Living on Earth.* New York: Maryknoll, 2006.

Moltmann, Jurgen. *God in Creation: An ecological doctrine of Creation.* London: SCM, 1985.

Moltmann, Jurgen. *Sun of Righteousness Arise! God's Future for Humanity and the Earth.* Minneapolis: Fortress Press, 2010.

Northcott, Michael S. *The Environment and Christian Ethics.* Cambridge: Cambridge University Press, 1996.

Jantzen, Grace. *God's World, God's Body,* London: DLT, 1984.

Nalunnakkal, George Mathew. *Green Liberation: Towards an Integral Ecotheology,* Delhi: ISPCK, 1999.

Zachariah, George. *Alternatives Unincorporated: Earth Ethics from the Grassroots.* London: Equinox, 2010.

Wielenga, Bastiaan. *Towards an Eco-Just Theology.* Bangalore: Centre for Social
      Action, 1999.

Endnotes

[1] The most famous example is Lynn White's essay, 'The Historical Roots of
our Ecological Crisis', *Science,*155. 1967, 203-7.

[2] Examples are Jurgen Moltmann, *God in Creation: An ecological doctrine
of Creation* (London: SCM, 1985), Grace Jantzen, *God's World, God's Body*
(London: DLT, 1984) and Sallie McFague, *Models of God: Theology for an
Ecological, Nuclear Age.* (Philadelphia: Fortress. 1987).

[3] Michael S. Northcott, *The Environment and Christian Ethics* (Cambridge:
Cambridge University Press,1996),168.

[4] Robert Murray, *The Cosmic Covenant: The Biblical Themes of Justice, Peace
and the Integrity of Creation* (London: Sheed & Ward.,1992),174.

[5] Michael S. Northcott, *The Environment and Christian Ethics,* (Cambridge,
U.K.: Cambridge University Press, 1996),200.

[6] Stephen R.L Clark, *How to think about the Earth: Philosophical and Theological
models for the Earth,* (London: Mowbray,1993), 140-141, 1993.

[7] Michael S. Northcott, *The Environment and Christian Ethics,* p.202.

Reflection

The authors have excellently emphasized the need to read the Bible from an ecological perspective. At every time and place in Christian history, people have read the Bible for guidance on how to live rightly in relationship with God and with each other. Ecological issues were not a serious issue during the time of Jesus. Hence if we want to understand the Bible we have to retell biblical narratives addressing the present crisis. The salvation in the New Testament is not only the restoration of the relationship between God and human beings, but includes the reconciliation of nature and human beings and the reconciliation of human beings to one another. The Bible does have many texts which speak directly about the environment, but reading the Bible with environmental concern goes much further than these texts. The environment in which humankind lives is part of all creation, which God has made and which God declares good. For Christians, Jesus Christ is God with us, and he is with God and in God in the creation and sustaining of all things. This makes the whole of creation sacred, a sign of and a witness to the grace and glory which the Son shares with the Father. All creation does not simply exist for human benefit. Our understanding of Christian mission develops in response to issues and questions that arise in living out our faith. Theology is not formed in a vacuum but emerges in response to concrete situations or crises that stimulate study and reflection. The issues shaping our approach to mission today are different from those our ancestors struggled with and, in all likelihood, will not be cutting-edge concerns sixty years from now. As each new crisis is addressed, however, our perspective on the nature of the Christian mission is enriched and enlarged. One of the great contemporary matters requiring an informed missional response is the environmental crisis.

Mathew Koshy Punnackad

Chapter - 4

Christological Responses
to the Groaning Creation

Clive Pearson & Eyingbeni Hümtsoe-Nienu

Editor's note

Dr Hümtsoe-Nienu wove her work within Associate Professor Pearson's effort.

By what authority?

The distinguishing mark of being a Christian is, of course, belief in and about Jesus of Nazareth. So much about how we organise our lives as the church, the body of Christ, depends upon how we understand his ministry and the purpose of his crucifixion and resurrection. At face value that seems rather removed from his ministry of healing, his teaching in parables, and the controversies he attracted. The latter was concerned with the law, the observance and purpose of the Sabbath, and what one eats and with whom.

The importance of focusing on Christology for the sake of an eco-theology is well appreciated by Celia Deane-Drummond. Writing in her *eco-theology* she declared that the person and work of Christ lies at the heart of the Christian faith; Christology is a 'crucial' and 'core element' of Christian belief. If Christ can somehow be woven into an ecology, then this way of Christian believing offers an alternative to 'vaguer references to a world-view affirming God as Creator that could [albeit mistakingly] be pushed to the margins of discussion'. Writing in the anthology, *Christian Faith and the Earth* (2014), Deane-Drummond noted that the 'distinguishing mark of Christian faith is ... belief in Jesus Christ'.

It is only relatively recently that talk about the person and work of Jesus Christ has been put to use in the discussions over the environment and climate change. That should come as no surprise. The received tradition has been to think of Jesus (and the risen and ascended Christ) being more concerned with the forgiveness of sins and the salvation of those who will follow.

The Jesus who lived in first century Palestine was not an ecological activist ahead of his time. Nor was the care of God's good creation a feature of the world in which he lived – while the grim prospects of climate change that now confront us were unthinkable. Jesus did not preach on climate change and global warming.

Jesus of Nazareth belonged to another time and place. It is, at first glance, hard to imagine why we should speak of him in terms of this deepening current crisis to do with the ecological well-being and future of God's good creation. It is not self-evident that we should place his life and teaching, his death and resurrection, alongside the work of climate scientists, the Intergovernmental Panel on Climate Change (IPCC), Al Gore and his concern for 'an inconvenient truth' and any one of a number of Indian thinkers and NGOs committed to ecological justice.

And yet, for a Christian, the right to preach, teach and act on such matters must – in some way – flow from our confession of faith in Jesus of Nazareth who becomes the risen Christ. That may seem like an obvious claim but is it? Writing in his *Jesus and the Earth* James Jones noted that so often the biblical references for works on the environment and sustainability feature texts from the Old Testament rather than the gospels.[1] Have we any authority, then, that looks back to Jesus for a twenty-first century concern for the earth?

The Wisdom of God

In the biblical tradition, wisdom is always closely associated with God's work of creation and its right and just ordering. Wisdom has the capacity to weave together the care of creation, justice, compassion and hospitality. It is a rich theme to be found in the books of Job and Proverbs especially. It is no surprise that wisdom has become a spiritual theme identified with the well-being of creation.

In the of book Proverbs wisdom comes to be expressed in the person of a woman - *Sophia*. In Luke and in Matthew the case can be made for Jesus being both a prophet and a personification of wisdom. On several occasions Jesus will explicitly refer to the practice of wisdom; at other times his parables and teaching represent a way of wise teaching. In our time of climate change this theme of wisdom can lead us to consider what the wise thing to do for Christ's sake is. The way in which we might then respond in Christ's name will assume our capacity to discern what is good and what makes for life. It would assume a concern for justice as well as compassion for the most vulnerable. It would assume a mindfulness of how this Earth, its system and its resources, are God's good creation and gift.

Jesus – *Sophia* – the wisdom made flesh, as Elizabeth Johnson[2] puts it, encourages believers in Christ to consider the relationship between flourishing of the earth and Jesus' fleshly act of liberation (Romans 8:19-22) and thereby be responsible for every human action that may do harm or good to our planet. The Indian wisdom narrative drawn from the image of *shakti* – the feminine energy or power who destroys evil and upholds righteousness – is an apt category to think about how humanity can draw wisdom from Jesus in order to ensure the fertility and prosperity of the earth while at the same letting go of humans folly that perpetuates 'ecocide'.

The Coming of Christ into Our World

There is a close link between this emphasis on wisdom and the way in which the prologue to John's gospel makes use of the Word: "In the beginning was the Word, and the Word was with God, and the Word was God. He was with God in the beginning. Through him all things were made; without him nothing was made that has been made."

In both instances wisdom and the Word are pre-existent. This means that they 'exist' before creation itself. They are with God. If Jesus of Nazareth is to be the wisdom and Word of God then there is this presence with God before creation itself. The birth of Jesus represents the wisdom and Word of God coming into the world in human form. It is an incarnation.

At this point we might like to take a step back from the way in which we usually understand this claim. In John's gospel the text refers to the Word being made "flesh" (John 1:14). That word flesh does not simply refer to our human bodies. In Paul's epistles flesh and spirit are in contrast with one another. That which is flesh is that which is created; it is matter and it encompasses the rest of creaturely existence. In other words the incarnation is not just about the Word and wisdom of God becoming human; it is also very deeply concerned with how the Word and wisdom of God enter into this material world of all those are in existence – and, that includes our environment.

Ramanuja's interpretation of the *Isvara* – the revealed Brahman – the Absolute Being – provides an Indian framework for understanding the idea of divine em'body'ment in Christian belief. Being the *Saguna* Brahman, *Isvara* appears to the world in all his divinity, indwelling the universe as the *antaryamin* (inner controller) and actually functioning as its body.[3] In tribal thoughts similar correlations are identified between Jesus and the incarnate divine. In the Ao[4] belief – *Lijaba* – is the one who "enters the earth"[5] to empathize with the poor and oppressed by providing bountiful field harvest and more. Traditionally, the Lothas[6] believed in the physical and visible personification of the divine in the characters of *Ngazo* and *Ronsü* who were seen to be in charge of agricultural produce and *Jüpvüo* who was considered to have mastery over aquatic life.[7] In all the above instances divinity is seen as permeating the material world, not as an "outsider" but ontologically. The coming of Christ into our world happens to be in the same level. This calls for a serious consideration of Christian attitude towards all of creation. The relevant theological question would be to ask, "If God indwells all things in Jesus, is there any part of creation that must be excluded from the ambit of Christian life and concern"? The answer clearly is, "none".

The Gaze of Jesus

In his *Laudato Si': On Care for Our Common Home* Pope Francis concludes the chapter on 'The Gospel of Creation' with a section entitled 'The Gaze of Jesus.'[8] The purpose here is to draw attention to the way in which Jesus "invited others to be attentive to the beauty that is in the world because he was himself was in constant touch with nature, lending it an attention full of fondness and wonder."[9] For the sake of the kingdom of God he proclaimed Jesus made use of the natural world to teach his disciples as well as illustrate his parables he addressed to the crowds. One of the first such references the encyclical isolates is John 4:35. Jesus is speaking to his disciples: "Lift up your eyes, and see how the fields are already white for harvest". In a like manner Jesus draws attention to the sparrows (Luke 12:6) and "birds of the air" (Matthew 6:26).

Pope Francis confesses that "Jesus lived in full harmony with creation". Jesus himself was not an ascetic; he did not withdraw from the world. The Pope emphasizes how Jesus "was far removed from philosophies which despised the body, matter and the things of the world". The way in which Jesus lived out his life was not like the spiritual guru who shuns this world.

Pope Francis concludes by calling upon us "to direct our gaze to the end of time". That will be "when the Son will deliver all things, to the Father, so that God may be everything to every one' (I Corinthians 15:28)". Here the Pope is situating the Jesus who lived in this world inside "the mystery of Christ" that lies beyond our current experience. There is an otherness to Jesus Christ that is bound to God and to the "destiny of all creation". The Pope reminds us that the "New Testament does not only tell us of the earthly Jesus and his tangible and loving relationship with the world. It also shows him risen and glorious, present throughout creation by his universal Lordship".[10]

Let's unpack this vision a little more.

Embedding Jesus in Nature

One of the most common practices is to situate the textual Jesus in the natural world. The fact that the incarnation occurs through being Christ's being human can lend itself to us looking at the "life of Christ" purely through human spectacles. Our attention is concentrated more upon what he says and does in and with people, albeit in the sight of God. The point is well made by Ian Bradley: "we miss an important dimension of his life and work if we concentrate simply on Jesus' interaction with other human beings".

Jesus was "not just the man who healed lepers and made the blind to see. He was also the man who stilled the storm and walked on the water, whom the wild beasts do not harm; who chose to enter Jerusalem seated on a colt; who often communed with nature, going up to the hills to pray or walking by the side of the lake." The healing miracles can also incorporate the anointing of eyes with clay and washing in the sacred pool of Siloam. In terms of his teaching Jesus chose to put across his message in the form of parables filled with images from the natural world - from mustard seeds and grains of sand to vineyards and fields of wheat. The natural world is also employed to illustrate the care of God for human beings, most notably demonstrated at Matthew 6:26-30 - the comparison is made with the birds of the air and the lilies of the field.

For Edward Echlin the intention is to develop an understanding of Jesus "embedded in nature".[11] This is significant in the context of India that shows 70% of its 1.23b population as agriculturists. The sight of fields full of mustard, sugarcane, rice, millet, pulses, onions, tomatoes, potatoes and many other vegetation and food items, ought to interest Christians in seeing Jesus being embedded in the soil and all its produce. Doing so develops an ecologically sensitive perspective of Christ that sees his hand in and eyes upon every creature – plants, animals or human - instilling in Christians and churches the sense of godly attribute in earthcare.

"The Son of Man"

Jesus and his contemporaries belonged to a world that knew about floods, storms, and droughts. The gospels themselves include accounts of storms that take the disciples by fright; the capacity of Jesus to still a storm provokes awe. It leads to a fascinating confession that would, on the surface, have relevance for us today.

The world in which Jesus lived was nevertheless aware of potential endings. In the Hebrew past the day of the Lord was most usually associated with judgement and a visitation of the wrath of a loving God. This understanding of the day of the Lord is sometimes associated with Jesus' teaching in his office of being the Son of Man. That is how Jesus often refers to himself in the gospels, especially in Mark. It is a Hebrew concept rather than a Greek one. The son of man is a translation of the Hebrew *ben adam*. That word/name *adam* is of particular interest because of its connection to *adamah* which means 'ground' or 'earth'. In the genealogy to be found in Luke Jesus is referred to as 'the son of man' in a line of descent that goes back to the first Adam.

Whether Jesus himself was aware of it potential ecological role is doubtful. The phrase 'son of man' has its roots in the Hebrew Bible, in the books of Daniel and Ezekiel in particular. It can be a roundabout way of expressing the personal pronoun 'I'. It is certainly evident that Paul was willing to define Jesus over and against Adam (Romans 5; I Corinthians 15).

From an ecological perspective we may draw out a handful of implications while mindful that Jesus was not addressing these contemporary concerns. The first has to do with his 'authority on earth to forgive sins' (Matthew 9:2-8). The immediate context is the healing of a paralytic man: our context is one in which we are becoming progressively more aware of the first sin of Adam which led to the earth being cursed. In the light of this text, we might ask: does Jesus then have the authority to forgive our sins against the earth?

Signs of the Times

That sense of the kingdom of God drawing near and being in the midst of life is captured in Jesus' only 'weather report'. It can be found at Luke 12:54-55. The setting is one of Jesus' teaching the crowds on the risk of hypocrisy. Towards the end of this teaching Jesus said to the crowds, "When you see a cloud rising in the west, you immediately say, 'It is going to rain'; and so it happens. And when you see the south wind blowing, you say, 'There will be scorching heat'; and it happens. You hypocrites!

You know how to interpret the appearance of earth and sky, but why do you not know how to interpret the present time?"

The word for that 'present time' is *Kairos*. It is not the same as *chronos* time which refers to our watches, calendars, the way we date a year. *Kairos* time is the right time, the opportune time – and, in matters of faith, the God-given moment in time. Sometimes the language of interpretation carries with it the capacity to 'discern the signs of the times'.

It is not unusual now for Christian thinkers to say that climate change is one of the signs of our times. We are being invited to interpret the weather patterns of our day and consider what insight they can give us into the drawing near of the kingdom of God.

Owing to the socio-economic reality, India relies much on weather predictability. Among the tribals, seasons determine all of life activities – farming and festivities included. Climate change implies that survival itself is a threat. Availability of basic needs such as food and entertainment such as traditional festivals will turn into a luxury. Jesus' warning of the "signs of the times", which today includes the issue of global warming is not to be taken lightly by Indian churches. His wisdom that foresees the future state of those in this century must educate modern churches to pay heed to the severity of the problem and instil in its members the urgency to turn the tide against climate change.

"Your will be done"

The changes to our climate form one part of the context in which we now hear Jesus' teaching. We might say that we are a little bit like the prodigal son who features in one of Jesus' parables in the gospel of Luke (Luke 15.11-32). He has led the kind of life where he has enjoyed himself and what wealth he has. Now he finds himself in a pigsty – we might say a world that has been messed up: it is time to "come to his senses".

What we can see here is the possibility of hearing a familiar biblical story in a new way. It is not uncommon for those who care deeply about the welfare of God's good creation to talk about 'coming to our senses' or 'having a change of heart', or 'seeing with new eyes'

Being aware of the signs of the times can also inform our understanding of the Lord's Prayer. We often say this prayer very quickly – so quickly we may miss the significance of what we are actually saying. Why not slow down? Why not take one line at a time? On occasions why not let the line lead to a reflection on what might it mean for us in a time of rising sea levels, droughts, storms, climate change? The prayer speaks of God's will being done on earth as it is in heaven. In other words, the earth matters. It recognizes our sin and our request for forgiveness. We might reflect on the ways in which we have misused the earth and other creatures. Give us this day our daily bread. How does our pattern of living affect others if we take more than we need – and, if we exploit the earth in doing so? Lead us not into temptation. What happens if we are tempted to make use of the environment around us for purposes which are not good for its well-being in the long run? How do we match our needs to make use of the creation with our needs to preserve and protect?

The moment we begin to think about the Lord's Prayer in this light it can lead to other parts of Jesus' teaching about the kingdom of God. It is not surprising that the parable of the Good Samaritan now comes into view. This particular parable is an invitation to discern who is our neighbour. Pope Francis has rightly described climate as a 'common good'. It is a planetary phenomenon which can lift our concern for the neighbour beyond those who are close at hand, those we know, those who are like us. The parable, of course, relies on the actions of the Samaritan who provides care across cultural suspicion stereotype and enmity. In a world of climate change our neighbour may be close at hand or far away in another part of the world. They may belong to another faith or no faith – but they are in need of care.

The Birth Pangs of a New Creation

Now and then activities within the natural world emphasize something more deeply symbolic, however. The Son of Man language is bound to apocalyptic events that signify the day of the Lord and the drawing near of the Kingdom of God. Both the crucifixion and the resurrection of Jesus are accompanied by earthquakes (Matthew 27:51, 28:2). These two earthquakes should be seen alongside two others to be found in Matthew

(24:3, 8). Here the earthquakes are included within a list of catastrophic events that Jesus declares to be the 'beginnings of the birthpangs'. The other quake to be found in Matthew is obscured by the way in which the Greek word *seismos* is translated as storm rather than an earthquake. Jesus is in a boat, crossing the Sea of Galilee, when a *seismos* occurs and the boat is threatened with being swamped by a great wave.

Analogically speaking, Sallie McFague's argument for an ecologically conscious model of Christology that views the world as divine body, because of his embodiment,[12] is significant beyond the feminine experience of birthing pains. It points to the extent to which Jesus' work of salvation is manifested in and through the natural elements. Hence, in the economic scheme of things it may surprise us to realize that a phenomenon like an earthquake is not necessarily a disaster as we are wont to think. In Christological narratives, it appears like a bursting forth of his inner self to convey his renewing work in creation. If the world is likened to the body of divinity, it then should not be surprising that Christ not only engages but also permeates nature to fulfill his salvific plan – historically and eternally.

The Cross

Christian faith is not just about the life and ministry of Jesus. It is also about his death, resurrection and ascension. The Easter events can turn our attention to suffering, woundedness, shame, humiliation and desolation. The cross speaks into the presence of God, Christ and the Spirit in the dark places of life and this earth. From the perspective of climate change the cross possesses a capacity to envisage how Christ suffers with the creation as a whole: this earth, this good creation, has been violated. One Christian poet and hymn writer speaks about the crosses we seldom see and note: those crosses are those suffered by creatures other than those of our own species.

The cross as a symbol of the suffering of Christ can find relation in Indian indigenous folklores that tell of their "saviour" who had to suffer bodily in order change circumstances for the oppressed subjects. The Ao Nagas speak of Lijaba who disguises himself as a sore infested, poor and dirty visitor who blesses two orphaned and socially discriminated sisters because they took him in when none of the village people did.

His rejection and humiliation as a cause for great suffering has led tribal theologian to identify Jesus as co-sufferer, liberator and defender of the poor.[13] The Ho-Adivasis tell of a similar story in which God took the form of a psoriasic servant boy – Toro Kora – and sacrificed himself to ensure that the people did not run short of iron, since they were iron smelters.[14]

Whatever the imagery, the suffering of Christ is as real as the wholeness he brings as a result of it. Churches thus ought to engage in restoring the suffering beings – nature – into their state of wellness (John 10.10). The cross/suffering has accomplished it and the church remains to actualize the "ecological significance of Christ's suffering and death, a death that unites him not only with all living creatures but with earth itself."[15]

The Cosmic Christ

The resurrection is a sign of how the cross is not God's last word. It turns our gaze to that mystery of Christ that Pope Francis referred to in *Laudato Si'*. One of the effects of the threats to our created world has been the recovery of one aspect of that mystery. The early Christians were deeply aware of what has become known as the cosmic Christ. Of particular references for us today are the appropriate references to be found in Ephesians 1 and Colossians 1.15-23. Here we have a 'gospel of creation' wherein all things were made in, through and for Christ.

The Colossians text is like a text for our time. It lifts our Christian faith out of a concern for just our own personal selves – and for humankind apart from the rest of creation. Paul declares himself to be the servant of the gospel that has been proclaimed to every creature under heaven.

Furthermore, the cosmic Christ as the *pantokrator* – holder of all things[16] – in his embodiment is rightly asserted by Moltmann as the end of "God's works in creation", "God's work of reconciliation" and "the redemption of the world."[17] In other words, "these works of creation, reconciliation and redemption also surround and mould the living character of created reconciled and redeemed men and women...as being part of this history of God with the world."[18] This inclusive idea of the cosmic Christ enlarges the scope of the church's mission and message of God's work to embrace all lives.

Conclusion

An ecologically sensitive Christology will become meaningful only when the whole of the Christ-event is brought into focus within the concerns surrounding our eco-sphere. The doctrine of Christ's coming as flesh, to all flesh, and all flesh eventually returning to him is at the centre of eco-Christology. To perpetuate the notion that Christ redeems only people and their souls is to miss out the universal redemptive purpose of God. The church's teaching, preaching, liturgy, prayers and service would be incomplete without necessarily including the natural world, the realm in which God's beauty, grandeur and grace is explicitly manifested. Today, we see more of the suffering of Christ in nature that has been left devastated by human greed, selfishness and indifference. Can the church, particularly in India, continue the *Missio Dei* embodied in Jesus, the Christ?

Questions for Discussion

1. How important do you think it is for a Christian ecological concern to be bound to our understanding of Jesus?

2. Which of the themes – e.g. wisdom, gaze, Jesus being embedded in nature, the cosmic Christ etc – speaks most to you in your particular context? Why?

3. How would you interpret the parable of the prodigal son in order for it to release a concern for the care of creation

For Further Reading

Ernst Conradie, Sigurd Bergmann, Celia Deane Drummond, eds. *Christian Faith and the Earth: Current Paths and Emerging Horizons in Ecotheology.* London and New York: Bloomsbury T & T Clark, 2015.

Celia Deane-Drummond. *Eco-Theology.* London: Darton, Longman and Todd, 2008.

James Jones. *Jesus and the Earth.* London, SPCK, 2003.

Michael S. Northcott and Peter M. Scott, *Systematic Theology and Climate Change: Ecumenical Perspectives.* Abingdon and New York: Routledge, 2014.

Endnotes

1 James Jones, *Jesus and the Earth* (London: SPCK, 2003), 5.

2 Elizabeth A. Johnson, *She Who Is: The Mystery of God in Theological Discourse* (NY: Crossroad, 1992), 54 (?)

3 Cf., Mathew Vekathanam, *Indian Christology: Perspectives and Challenges* (Bangalore: Asian Trading Corporation, 2004), 69ff.

4 A Naga tribe.

5 A. Wati Longchar, "Lijaba – The Earth Entering Supreme Being: The Ao-Naga Concept of God and Ecology" in *The Tribal Worldview and Ecology*, Ed., A. Wati Longchar and Yangkahao Vashum (Jorhat : Tribal Study Centre, 1998), 29.

6 A Naga tribe.

7 Eyingbeni Humtsoe-Nienu, *God the Tribes: Christian Persepctive on the Naga Ancestral Idea of the Supreme Being* (Mokokchung, CTC: 2014), 94.

8 Pope Francis, *Laudato Si': On Care For Our Common Home*, 81-84.

9 Ibid., 82.

10 Ibid., 84.

11 Edward Echlin, 'Jesus and the Earth Community', *Ecotheology*, January 1997 (2): 31-47.

12 Cf., Sallie McFague, *The Body of God: An Ecological Theology* (London: SCM, 1993).

13 Takatemjen, *Studies in Theology and Naga Culture* (New Delhi: ISPCK, 1998), 61-63.

14 Cf., Joshy Xavier, "Liberative Motif: Towards an Adivasi-Christian Dialogue" in *New Life Theological Journal*, Vol 5/2 (July-December 2015): 115-16.

15 Larry Rasmussen by Duncan Reid, "Enfleshing the Human: An Earth-Revealing, Earth Healing Christology," *Earth Revealing, Earth Healing: Ecology and Christian Theology*, Ed., Denis Edwards (Minnesota: The Liturgical Press, 2001), 82.

16 Jürgen Moltmann, *The Way of Jesus Christ: Christology in Messianic Dimensions* (London: SCM, 1990), 279.

17 Jürgen Moltmann, *God in Creation: A New Theology of Creation and the Spirit of God* (NY: Harper Collins, 1991), 245-6.

18 Ibid., 246.

ଉ ଥ

Reflection

The author of the article is trying for an ecologically sensitive Christology. He says that it will become meaningful only when the whole of the Christ-event is brought into focus within the concerns surrounding our eco-sphere. Jesus who lived in first century Palestine was not ecological. Jesus did not preach on climate change and global warming. Ecologically sensitive perspective of Christ that sees his hand in and eyes upon every creature – plants, animals or human - instilling in Christians and churches the sense of godly attribute in earth care.

Whether Jesus himself was aware of its potential ecological role is doubtful. From an ecological perspective we may draw out a handful of implications while mindful that Jesus was not addressing these contemporary concerns. Sometimes the language of interpretation carries with it the capacity to 'discern the signs of the times'. Jesus' warning of the "signs of the times", which today includes the issue of global warming is not to be taken lightly by Indian churches. His wisdom that foresees the future state of those in this century must educate modern churches to pay heed to the severity of the problem and instil in its members the urgency to turn the tide against climate change.

The parable of the Good Samaritan is an invitation to discern who is our neighbour. The words in the Bible 'love another' 'neighbour' have a wider meaning including all the creations. The Bible is not good news for human beings alone, but for the whole Creation. 'Go into all the world and proclaim the good news to the whole creation (Mark 16:15). "A new command I give you: Love one another. As I have loved you, so you must love one another. By this all men will know that you are my disciples, if you love one another" (John 13:34-35). We can see the rhythm of God only through the rhythm of nature. When the rhythm of human beings harmonizes with the rhythm of Nature, then harmony and peace will follow. As the plant kingdom has no vested interests, it is moving as per God's will in the rhythm of God. The creation is a symphony where we find a variety of creatures each singing and worshipping the Maker in tune with the rhythm of God. Nature is the best example to study the rhythm of God. If we follow Nature's rhythm we can bring peace and harmony. Jesus through his life and ministry shows us how to be a disciple by following the rhythm of God. We read in the Bible, Jesus spent forty days and forty nights in the wilderness, an area essentially undisturbed by human activity together with its naturally developed life community to study the rhythm of nature. In order to disturb God's rhythm, the tempter came to him and said, "If you are the Son of God, tell these stones to become bread.". Jesus observed the rhythm of Nature through his life in the wilderness. Bread is made of grains which will be produced by the growth of seed from the earth. Converting stones to bread is an unnatural process which is against the rhythm of nature. The second temptation was "If you are the Son of God, throw yourself down". The tempter again tempting Jesus against the rhythm of Nature. Jesus overcomes the second temptation which is against the natural rhythm. The third temptation is in favour of worshipping Nature. Jesus overcomes the third temptation. Nature is not for worshipping it but for understanding God's revelations through its rhythm. Through forty days training Jesus understood the rhythm of nature which is the reflection of God's rhythm. That is why during his ministry, Jesus said " Look at the birds of the air; they neither sow nor reap nor gather into barns, and yet your heavenly Father feeds them...... Consider the lilies of the field, how they grow; they neither toil nor spin, ... But if God so clothes the grass of the field, which is alive today and tomorrow is thrown into the oven, will he not much more clothe you—you of little faith?" Therefore do not worry, follow the rhythm of God, then your heavenly Father knows that you need all these things. A disciple of Christ should follow the rhythm of God which we can learn from Nature. Then harmony and peace will prevail.

Mathew Koshy Punnackad

Chapter - 5

Eco-theological and Indian Tribal Spirituality: A Conversation

In light of the Ecological Problems before us how can Christian Spirituality Provoke a Change of Heart, a New Way of Seeing Things?

B. Silpa Rani & Jason John

Editor's note

Silpa's and Jason's approaches to spirituality are enrichingly different, and reflective of their respective contexts. The material they have provided has been edited lightly into an imaginary conversation in order to highlight this.

Silpa's Introduction

"To introduce this chapter I would like to start by defining "spirituality" in the midst of ecological issues around the globe. Most of the time it is defined or commonly understood as self-pietism, where "spirituality" is only confined to it and it is beyond one's imagination to even think of "spirituality" in relation to ecology. Spirituality "is nothing but a process of a deep sense of being. Hence, eco-spirituality becomes a process of connection between the divinity, the creation and the created beings."

"This connectedness also reminds us that we should learn to share because everyone and everything is in the web of connectedness. Eco-spirituality is about "All my relations." "It's all alive, it's all connected it's all intelligent and it's all relatives." [1] However, the anthropocentric ideology dominates relationship between creation and the divine, and always glorifies the relationship between human being and God. The comprehension of a deep sense of self pietism of human being, a formal individualistic relationship one has with God, has supported in the disintegration of the earth in light of the relationship between God, human and nature has been injured, deserting a miserable and vulnerable circumstance for the earth. The present ecological crisis is the consequence of lost spirituality that breaks the web of connection between divine, creation and human beings."

Jason's Introduction

"We could also introduce the topic of spirituality by going straight to Jesus. We know the stories. Jesus spent days, even weeks wandering with his disciples from town to town; retreated to isolated places to pray; considered the birds of the air and the lilies of the field; spent his last night of freedom in a garden; and indeed his first days of ministry preparing himself in the wilderness. The same Spirit who brooded over creation at its beginning compelled Jesus out into the wilderness at his ministry's beginning. We worship the God in whom all things live and move and have their being."

"So, Jesus' spirituality was nurtured and formed outdoors, as well as by Temple and Scripture. His call to reject wealth, to be content with having enough and ensuring that others did too, was a call to live sustainably before that word existed."

"It was after his forty days in the wilderness that his cry first rang out, "Repent!" For the kingdom of God has come near." It was on the mountains and plains that he called people to follow him, to see things in a new way. He warned against all forms of greed, and against storing up wealth for ourselves. He told the parable of the prodigal son, who repented from his selfish, wasteful living, and humbly returned home."

"Since Christians follow Jesus, we could reasonably expect that Christians would also have a spirituality which provokes a sustainable way of life. Looking at Jesus, and then at the ecological crises around us, how could a Christian spirituality *not* provoke an 'ecological conversion?'"

"Yet the evidence of 2000 years since Jesus walked the earth, especially in western industrial countries, forces us to admit that Christian spirituality, at least in the west, has not automatically led to sustainable living, or ecological conversion. Often quite the opposite."

"We will return to Jesus' tale of the prodigal, reimagined in the light of the ecological crisis, at the end of this chapter, as we consider which of the brothers we are: the wasteful one or the one who always lived well with the family. But first, let's briefly consider whether a Christian spirituality, *can* help us live more sustainably, and whether it *should*. Then we will look at the two paths laid before us by the Genesis creation stories, before concluding with a third path suggested by the prodigal son, in which the elder brother cannot afford to simply wait for the prodigal to come to his sense but must act to make him."

Silpa: Eco-spirituality as Just Spirituality

"That sounds complicated. I still think spirituality is nothing but a process of a deep sense of being. Ecology is a matter of faith and creed. Ecology speaks of the ways in which living things interact with each other. In the web of life eco-justice is a celebration of relationship- being fair to all forms of life. In an eco-vision of the earth community 'giving what is due to each component of the whole', is a divine mandate to establish just relationship that leads peace. This is well stated in Genesis 2:7 where we read that Adam is created out of *Adama* (the ground/soil). The relation between man and the ground is deep and intense. Once Adam is alienated from *Adama,* the land lies fallow. Community becomes morally stagnant and unjust. "Dust you are and to dust you will return" (Genesis 3:19) is a classic Bible text for the just relationship.[2] In the Torah the Lord warned, "When you enter the land I am going to give you, the land itself must observe a Sabbath to the Lord," But if you will not listen to me and carry out these commands... I will lay waste the land... All the time that it lies desolate, the land will have the rest it did not have during the Sabbaths you lived in it". The deep wisdom of the Old Testament includes reverence for the land.[3] A harmonious existence of the symbols of life could be called prevalence of just peace in God's creation. Any kind of imbalance/disorientation is a state of alienation. The petition in the Lord's prayer "your kingdom come on earth as it is in heaven" (Matthew 6:10) urges us to make a meaningful relationship in God's order of creation anything that disrupts or disregards the bond of uniting tie in Creation is to be considered as injustice to its core.[4] This beautiful relationship between Divine-Human-Creation can be well understood by the psalmist, 'the Earth is of the Lord's and all that is in it, the world and those who dwell therein' (Psalms 24:1)."

Silpa: Eco-centric Indigenous Spirituality in India

"Space, creation and land together serve as the foundation of indigenous people's concept of life, relationship and interdependence. Indigenous worldview is creation-centred and is characterized by understanding the interdependence and the inter-relatedness of all creation, including human beings.[5] Given this reality, indigenous theologians have argued convincingly that an indigenous theology must begin with space and creation and not with humans. Space-creation centred theology calls for critical re-evaluation of our ways of life, our Christian spirituality, and our attitude towards all God's creation. The ecological crisis with which we are confronted today is primarily a spiritual crisis. Looking from the indigenous people's holistic view of life, there is no separation between what is physical and spiritual, matter and spirit and everything including human, spirits and the rest of creation are interrelated and interconnected. For the indigenous people, spirituality is, therefore, a way of life; our living style, habit and the way we conduct and relate with other fellow human beings and creation are all integral part of their spirituality.[6] This worldview of spatiality essentially accentuates and locates the all-important life qualities of relationships among and between human beings and the whole creation. This understanding extends and embraces the way indigenous peoples view the world and relate themselves to the spirits and God. For the indigenous thinkers, the western intellectual tradition, is quite alien to the indigenous people and is in fact destructive to their livelihood. From the indigenous people's point of view, therefore, a space-creation centred theology provides a corrective to the human-centred theology of the dominant Christian tradition. Indigenous theology affirms that the world is our home; it is the home where God, spirit, human and the whole creation live together as a universal family."[7]

Silpa: Tribal cosmology: God-Human-Creation Relationship

"The fact that indigenous people see themselves as interrelated in all their life totality to the whole creation, can be seen from the creation myth, and other practices and beliefs. For example, in *Tangkhul Naga* creation myth, which tells the story of the great assembly of all creatures was convened by *Kasa Akhava* (God) to determine of day and night.[8] *Kasa Akhava* is in the profoundest way asserted as the creator and sustainer of the universe. The whole creation is depicted as a family with *Kasa Akhava* as its head. In the tribal society one most prominent practice is that, important decisions are taken by the family sitting around the hearth-fire. This is indicative of the universal family, which requires the participation and co-operation of all family members in decision making and carrying out the given responsibilities. The whole creation is depicted as co-workers responsible partners- in caring for *Kasa Akhava*'s created world. The second story comes from the *Khasis* of Meghalaya. The *Khasis* believed that their ancestors descended from heaven/sky world. The story unravels how from the very beginning God and human family are connected to each other. The third story is about the log-drum of the *Wanchos* of *Tirap* district of Arunachal Pradesh. Log-drum constitutes as one of the finest symbols of the *Wancho* people's culture. It is a drum curved out of a huge tree. In the past, log-drum is used for a number of purposes and occasions ranging from organizing defense mechanism, announcing natural calamities to heralding the beginning of community festivities and celebrations. A number of different beats symbolized meanings to the villagers."[9]

"Indigenous spirituality has given due recognition to the place of flora and fauna in expressing the inter-relatedness of the whole cosmos. The Creator God is to be worshipped and adored where God manifests God's majesty at the best. Indian festivals like Onam, Pongal and Deepawali could speak to the devotees in the language of ecology. The use of mango and neem leaves, which are traditionally used in the cultural festivals our tribal context of India, would also find a place in Christian worship. There are several universal eco-symbols, like dove, water, air and fragrance, which could be used as images for conveying spiritual truths. In, India nature symbols like sandal wood paste, lotus flower, and coconut, milk and palm leaves are to be widely used in worship service. The offering of flowers/leaves in a tray or bowl in worship services could be introduced as a mark of respect for the created order. The open-air worship services under the shade of a tree or the sea shore/river banks could make worship eco-friendly and lively. The offering of nature's gifts in worship service has a long tradition in the life of the Church. But the offering of money gradually replaced all other offerings without giving adequate place for the offering of the other product of the earth.[10] This brings out how human and nature maintain their interdependent living relationship, especially humans towards the nature.

Silpa: Spirituality and Eco-centric Ecclessia

"Most of the churches today are not ecological. The Sunday sermon is not about flourishing of God's whole creation rather it is aimed at the care and comfort of human individuals. The gospel and the good news is usually addressed to human needs and failings. The well-being of the whole of God`s creation is not seen as part and parcel of gospel message. It is usually an add-on. Christian theology has been anthropocentric concerned mainly with the well-being of human beings. But can human beings thrive apart from nature? If salvation is understood as eternal life for some humans, then perhaps the answer is yes. But if salvation means the flourishing of all God`s creature here and now on this earth, then the answer is no. the world cannot be left out. The Church must become ecological, and it is by cultivating ecological virtues of material simplicity, sharing of power, and the reverence for life that a just world can be built up. The need of the hour is nothing less than a world ethic of sustainability that enables people to cooperate with one another and to live in harmony with nature. The needed changes for this are as radical as they are essential, so much so that we need deep convictions to awaken our moral sense.[11] An attempt must be made to restore the spiritual relationship of Divine-Creation-Human and to heal the wounds inflicted on the earth, which calls us to realise that ecological justice is necessarily tied up with social justice. There can be no saving of the planet earth, without tackling the basic issues of justice. When justice is perverted, misinterpreted as a justice for a few, resulting in accumulation of wealth, greedy spending of natural resources, love of consumerism, the whole earth suffers along with humanity."[12]

Jason: *Can* a Christian Spirituality help us? The three paths

"Silpa, it's great you are so keen about the ecological credentials of Indian tribal spirituality. But my question is still, *Can* a Christian Spirituality help us? As Paul Santmire has demonstrated, the relationship between Christian theology and a healthy attitude to the rest of life on earth is ambiguous,[13] but not without promise.[14] Though Lynn White criticises especially *Western* Christianity as the most anthropocentric religion the world has ever seen,[15] culpable in large part for the ecological crisis, he also holds out Francis of Assisi as a beacon of hope, proposing him as the patron saint of ecologists."[16]

"Some theologians responded defensively to White's critique, for example Alister McGrath,[17] but his defence largely proves White's point: that Christian theology, especially in the West, showed little to no interest in ecological issues until after Santmire's paper was published. Santmire offers a sustained defence of White against McGrath."[18]

"The ambiguity around whether Christianity *can* help us live in better relationship with the rest of Earth, is based on an historical ambiguity about whether it *should*. Why should Christians care whether the planet is degraded? Here we briefly survey several reasons put forward to argue that Christian's *should* be concerned about Earth, before addressing whether our spirituality can help us do something about Earth's degradation."

Jason: Should a Christian Spirituality help us?

"In the industrialised West, where the separation between humans and the rest of Creation is well advanced for many, concerns have been raised about the psychological effects of human beings on living in increasingly bland city and even mono-cultural farm landscapes. Raised in the 1980s by E. O. Wilson, and especially in a book he edited in the 1990s,[19] there has recently been a flurry of research into "nature deficit disorder" in children[20] and adults.[21] This has been anticipated, to some extent, by Christian theologians concerned about the effect of a degraded ecology on our spirit and soul."

"Catholic theologians tend to be at the forefront here. Thomas Berry claims that our souls are diminished in proportion to the diminishment of Creation's diversity,[22] a sentiment forcefully echoes by Paul Collins.[23] Rosemary Radford Ruether argues that the degradation of the environment leads to a loss of "aesthetic imagination" which robs us of the moral urge to value life.[24] It is not surprising to find such sentiment in those from the ecologically engaged part of the Roman Catholic tradition, which has a long standing theology of creation as sacrament. This assumes that we can, through contemplating life around us, connect with the Creator of Life. Denis Edwards, for example, believes that, "… *Earth* reveals. It is the place of encounter with the Holy Spirit (emphasis mine)."[25] In this encounter we engage God the uncontrollable Other, the Spirit who blows where it will."[26]

"Another call to action is a reaction not to our damaged souls, nor psyches, but our bodies. The Evangelical churches in particular emphasise the link between degraded ecosystems and worsening conditions for the poor. Climate Change is addressed primarily as a threat to our 'Poor Neighbour.' TEAR Australia[27] was a leader in this movement in a time when it was still controversial amongst many Evangelicals to become "distracted" by environmental issues."[28]

"All of the above reasons focus on human benefit- psychological, spiritual and practical. What about the benefits to all the other creatures we share this planet with?"[29]

"Early on, other protestant churches tended to emphasise the needs of the rest of creation in calling people to work for a healthier ecology, often called eco-justice. The World Alliance of Reformed Churches emphasized not only the rights of future generations, but also the rights of Nature itself.[30] The Uniting Church in Australia, echoing the repeated refrain in Genesis 1, declares that the natural world is good "in and of itself.[31]""

"Several decades on from Lynn White's criticism, in an era when there is much more communication between denominations than ever before, theologians, preachers, and teachers in the different traditions now tend to include all of the above reasons for caring about Creation, addressing both 'what's in it for us?' and 'what's in it for the rest of Creation?'"

"These two questions, and the ambiguity about whether Christian spirituality actually can lead to a change of heart, go all the way back to the creation stories in the Hebrew Scriptures, which suggest to us two quite different spiritual paths. Genesis 1 focuses on the rest of Creation being for humanity, Genesis 2 imagines that humanity exists for Creation. We will now explore these two paths, before suggesting a third which arises out of the interaction of Christian faith and the new elements of our Creation story being discovered by the sciences."

Jason: Path 1 (Genesis 1). Earth is Created for humanity

"The Lutheran Scholar Norman Habel, one of the founders of the Earth Bible project, repeatedly encourages us to stop attempting to harmonise the two creation accounts in Genesis, and instead to read them on their own terms, as largely irreconcilable stories of the relationship between God, humanity and the rest of Creation[32]."

"Whether you agree that Genesis 1 and 2 are fundamentally different stories, it is well worth examining their differences."

"In Genesis One humanity is presented as being fundamentally separate from the rest of Creation, and much more like God. As the final, ultimate act of Creation, humans alone are created in the image and likeness of God (Genesis 1:26-27). We are then told by divine decree to fill and *subdue* the earth. We are given *dominion*, over all things. Although this is quickly constrained by the imposition of a vegetarian lifestyle, this is eventually overturned in Genesis 9:1-3, which is effectively the end of the story, when *all things* are delivered into the hand of Noah and his sons[33], which then live in fear and dread of us,

'The fear and dread of you shall rest on every animal of the earth, and on every bird of the air, on everything that creeps on the ground, and on all the fish of the sea; into your hand they are delivered. Every moving thing that lives shall be food for you; and just as I gave you the green plants, I give you everything.'" (Genesis 9:2-3, NRSV)

"Despite attempts to make this story sound less hostile to other creatures, there is no escaping the violent nature of the word subdue (*kabash*) which throughout scripture refers to the defeat of, and enslavement of enemies[34]. It is combined with the phrase, "delivered into your hand," which always refers to conquest and victory, so there is no way that subdue could mean anything benign."

"Genesis 1 is the Creation story favoured by Western Christianity, with its emphasis on the unique, dominating place of humanity, with the God given mandate to tread down the rest of creation, which belongs to us as God's gift. Long after Christianity faded as a force in the west, this attitude to the rest of Creation is evident everywhere."

"There may be a redeeming side to Genesis 1. Mark Brett[35] argues that Genesis 1 is not addressing ecological questions, or the relationship between humanity and Earth. It was written whilst the Jewish people were in exile in Babylon, and it reshapes the creation story of their captors to make one vital claim: that it is not the king of Babylon, but *all people* who are created in the image of God. All are equal. Contrary to the claims of the Babylonian religion, that their king was the image of the gods, given the right to rule over and subdue all the earth, the Jewish story claims that *all people* are meant to have access to the riches of Earth."

Genesis 1 is, if Brett is right, primarily a story about ancient equality, even democracy. When humans are not treating each other as equally valued by God, as equally entitled to the Earth's abundance, then Genesis 1 is being violated. In our world, where less than 1% of the population controls more than 50% of its wealth,[36] is a world completely at odds with Genesis 1.

A Genesis 1 spirituality is an asset in our relationship with each other, but a stumbling block to our relationship with Earth.

Jason: Path 2 (Genesis 2). Humanity is Created for God's Garden

White argues that Genesis 1 is the story of the Western Christianity. If so, Genesis 2 is the story of Francis of Assisi.

Genesis 2 is a much older story, probably dating back to Hebrew oral traditions. In Australia, it is best read around a campfire, like a Hebrew Dreaming story. Like Aboriginal spirituality, it emphasises the close connection between humans and the rest of Earth.

The *Adam* is created from the *Adamah* (Genesis 2:7). The Earthling created from the Earth. Why is the earthling created? Not to rule over the Earth or subdue it, but to *'abad* and *shamar* it. *'Abad* is usually translated "till" in modern translations, perhaps reflecting our agricultural bias, or maybe even that of the people who finally compiled the bible. But far more often *'abad* is translated "serve" in the scriptures.

Shamar is translated "keep," not meaning "own," but "protect."

So in a Genesis Two spirituality, Earthlings are created out of the Earth, to serve and protect God's garden. Not our Garden, God's.

Earthlings are still special, it is only into the *Adam* that God specifically breathes the breath of life.[37] And of course we are given a special role: being servant and protector implies both humility and ability. It resonates much better with Jesus' call to a leadership of service, not domination (Mark 10.42-45).

This story of serving and protecting God's garden doesn't end well. In Genesis 3, humans don't accept the implied limitation of their power. As a creation myth, this raises important questions of humility, wisdom, and the existence of so much pain and difficulty in a world which the scriptures claim was created by a good God, who loves us.

As a myth read in the 21st century, however, it raises significant problems.

Most obviously, within the story itself, the punishment for human rebellion falls disproportionately on Eve, and through her all women,

> "To the woman he said, "I will greatly multiply your pain in childbearing; in pain you shall bring forth children, yet your desire shall be for your husband, and he shall rule over you."" (Genesis 3.16, NRSV)

Men may have to weed and sweat as they plough, but Women are ever after subjected to excruciating pain, which too often leads to death, every time they give birth. Not only that, it appears that God's punishment is visited especially on poor women, when we look at the mortality rates for mothers around the world.[38] As if that wasn't punishment enough, God institutes patriarchy: from now on men will no longer listen to their wives, but instead will rule over them: exercise dominion over them.

Genesis 2, which started with such ecological promise, ends with nothing but bad news for women, and any men who value their comradeship.

Fortunately, reading the stories as we now do in the light of all we have learned from the sciences over the last centuries, and especially the science of evolution, we can read the Genesis 2-3 creation story in a way which emphasises its intuitions about our close relationship with the rest of life, without being bound by its explanations for the realities of painful childbirth and the patriarchal structure of Judaism and subsequent societies. A third path has opened before us:

Path 3 (The Prodigal). The humble return home.

A Christian spirituality must learn from the creation stories in the scriptures, as well as the creation stories now being revealed in conversation with cosmologists, geologists, geneticists and evolutionists. Many of the pioneers in these disciplines were Christian, and even pastors and priests.[39]

Through science, we have come to see that Earth is a tiny planet in the whole universe, and that humans are a tiny chapter in the billions of years long story of life on Earth. Genetics has shown that we are all related through common descent from one ancestor: the first living thing. We are part of one giant family of life on Earth. Ecology has stressed our interconnectedness: what happens to one ecosystem affects others, and humans are dependent on the web of life like every other species. Climatologists have emphasized that connection through the growing realisation that humans, mostly in rich nations, are affecting the climate in which every creature lives and moves and has its being. Those nations who are contributing least to the problem are suffering the most consequences, or more specifically, the poor in most nations are the lowest producers of greenhouse gasses, but suffer the consequences of increased climate variability the most.[40] Before climate change was an issue, the poor suffered because the rich used their technology to enable them to exploit resources from far away, and dump their waste far away, so those who benefitted the most from technological advances suffered the least consequences.

India, one of the poorest nations *per capita*, is predicted to suffer increasingly from Climate Change,[41] and was one of the hardest hit by Climate Change effects in 2016.[42]

So we see, crucially, that when we talk about Climate Change's causes and impacts, we are not talking about what "we" are doing, or suffering, as if humanity was a single unified mass. There really is an "us" and "them," more specifically a "poor" and "rich." And here we enter into territory frequently addressed by Jesus.[43]

It may be that the rich will never listen, and that we are going to live out the story of the rich man and Lazarus at a global level. But there is still a little hope that we might instead find ourselves living the spiritualities of the Prodigal son, and older brother.

Jason: Prodigals and elder brothers in Australia

The Prodigal: Western Christian Colonisation

A comprehensive review of the ways in which the first white people in Australia acted like the prodigal son, wasting resources with no thought of tomorrow, is beyond the scope of this chapter, so a single example will have to suffice: a report of the wasteful approach of the first cedar cutters,

> "The devastating axe of the timber-getter has made dire havoc among the cedar brushes, and where a few years ago immense quantities of the wood were to be found, there is not now a single tree worth the

cutting. The sawyers are a most wasteful set of men. They spoil more timber than they use. They cut and square only the very best parts of a tree, leaving great masses of cedar… to rot unheeded in the brushes[44]"

Of course, not all white people had a "Prodigal Son" attitude to the bush. However most either did, or were indifferent enough to accept the luxuries that came from a spirituality of separation from the land, and thus rapid exploitation of it. The multiple evidences of Australia being turned into a "pig pen" reveal a Prodigal attitude at work.

The Elder Brother: Aboriginal resistance and return

In contrast stands the Elder brother in our story: the oldest inhabitants, the Aboriginal people of hundreds of tribes or nations. Whilst their impact on the ecology of Australia was far reaching, and much greater than appreciated until recently,[45] those groups that survived until white invasion were the descendants of those who, like the Older Brother, had lived within the family's means, as *part of* the family.

Many Aboriginal Christians retain this spirituality of connection, of belonging to Mother Earth as part of the family,[46] and the Uniting Church in Australia, at least, has committed to having its spirituality shaped by the First People, or Elder Brother and their unique insights into God's ways in Australia.[47]

Silpa, would you repeat the Prodigal story, but in an Indian context?

Silpa: An Indian Reading of the Parable of Prodigal Son (Luke 15. 11-32)[48]

"The first part of the Prodigal Son dynamic also played out in India…"

"Then Jesus said, 'There was a Jamindaar (Land Lord) in a village who had two sons and 100 Acres of ancestral property. 80% of the land was used for cultivation and 20% of the land for growing cattle feed. His family depended upon the land for their livelihood. His elder son was working in the field along with his father to get a good crop and his younger son was studying in a town. He took his graduation in Civil Engineering and wanted to become a big millionaire by establishing his own business. So the younger son forced his father to divide the property. The Jamindaar tried to explain to him about the natural production from the agricultural land which would be more than enough for them to survive. But his younger son did not listen and persisted on receiving his share from the property. So his father divided the property between them. The younger son sold his immoveable properties, took the money, went to the city and started a business along with his partners; a real-estate business and 1000 houses were planned for construction. They made a residential venture on cultivable land with a good capital amount. In the very first year they sold almost all the houses and received a huge amount of profit so he enjoyed lavishly and spent his money on all sorts of pleasure.

Gradually his business failed and the other partners and workers left him and soon he became bankrupt. As he lost his business he was left with no money to survive. He tried for ways to work to satisfy his hunger. He found a job in a nearby hotel but was not satisfied with a day's meal. So he started eating the food everyday which was already prepared for the customers. One day the owner found that he was eating the food in the kitchen without telling the owner. Immediately he was dismissed. At this juncture he came to his senses and remembered his father's house where plenty of food was available for the entire household including servants and the cattle. He knew that he was no longer able to provide food for himself and would starve to death. So he decided to return to his father and to beg for forgiveness, saying, "Father, I have sinned against God and you. I am no longer fit to be called your son. Please give me a place among your servants so that I would help you to see that you produce a good crop with the help of natural chemicals and pesticides." As he was nearing home, his father saw him from a distance and with tear filled eyes he ran towards him hugged him, kissed him, and took him home. The young man fell at his father's feet and asked forgiveness for what he had done. His father had compassion on him and ordered his servants to give him good clothes and a place to live and presented a gold ring. The Jamindaar ordered them to make arrangements so that they would celebrate his son's return. His elder son came back from the field tired from the day's work but to his surprise there was a celebration going on in the house. He was shocked for a while and asked his servants about this celebration. One of his servants replied and said that this celebration was for his brother's return. The elder son became furious and refused to go inside. His father pleaded with him to join the feast. But he complained about his brother and said that your younger son has taken all your property and spent it lavishly and now you are celebrating a feast for him. And he also said that I have never disobeyed you but never gave me anything to celebrate with my friends. His father said to him my dear son you are always with me and all that is mine is yours so don't worry, go and enjoy the feast. Hence forth both the brothers started working in the field to get a good crop through organic farming.'"

Jason and Silpa: Prodigals and elder sons in India

Jason asks: "Silpa, what about the relationships between prodigals and elders sons in the Indian context?"

Silpa replies:

"For instance, in the Indian context it can be noted to interpret the parable of the 'prodigal son' with allegorical symbolism. The elder brother in such a scenario could be the Dravidians, Adivasis, and the tribal people of India whose existence dates bated to the Pre-Aryan era. During the Pre-Aryan era the country, then borderless, was a composition of people whose spirituality's heart was dignity, respect and interconnectedness with one another along other earth communities. Worship of trees, animals, forests, rivers, and the sun, and considering the earth itself as Mother Goddess was embedded in Indian culture. Thus, Indians articulated the need to sustain and promote the ecological balances of nature through sacred incarnations and systematized rituals for the sustenance of life on the earth. Eco-cultural socialization was the core value that Indian spirituality then practised. At this point on the Indian spiritual timeline humans and nature dwelt hand in hand."[49]

Silpa: The Prodigal Son: Western Christian Colonisation

"On the other hand," Silpa continued, "the prodigal son can be symbolise a common human who lives with a colonial mind, a western intellectual soul that only wishes to 'subdue' and have 'dominion.' Though many assume Christianity came into India through colonisation, the reality that Christianity existed in India even before it reached the colonies, is no fairy tale. However, it was during colonisation that Christianity began to penetrate in and through the heart of culture with the added flavour of European imposition. This only broke the unique relationship that existed between God and Humans, Humans and Creation. In such a context Indian Christian theology sprouted like a western theology yet recovered to replenish itself with the Indian fragrance. However, the interconnectedness that existed then, are now traces that are hard to find."

Jason: A Christian Spirituality for the Elder Brother, and his allies

"The ecological version of the Prodigal Son story has some key differences from Jesus' tale, of course. These are played out in Australia but also on the world stage.

The Ecological Prodigal did not simply leave the family, taking his share of resources. Through technologies, as he ran out of assets he continued to take more and more from the family, and from the Elder Brother. No matter how frugally and wisely the Ecological Elders live, their homes continue to be plundered. It is not possible, then, for God and the Elders to wait for the Prodigals to come to their senses, or all will be lost. Whatever spirituality sustains them must empower them, and those Prodigals who have returned to join them, to turn over the tables of exploitative commerce which stand in the way of people and their communion with God and each other.

As the chapter heading implies, we cannot simply wait for a change of heart, our Spirituality must provoke it. As long as the Ecological Prodigals can maintain their lifestyle by creating new pig pens on the Elder's lands, they will do so, and there will be no hope for a true change of heart and a humble return to the family, the occasional permaculture community notwithstanding.

If a Christian spirituality is going to help, it will have to be a spirituality of the Elder Brother, one which moves beyond patient (or even resentful) waiting for the rich to come to their senses.

But none of this is news to the Indian reader, after the decades long campaigns to end British colonial exploitation. The Prodigal did not simply come to their senses, they were confronted, and cajoled. The tables were turned, and the money poured out. Finally, as external factors pressed in on them, namely the shattering their economy received in World War II, they relented.

In this new situation, the external factor is Climate Change, as it begins to affect not only the poor, but also the Ecological Prodigals. If the Elder Brother refuses to continue to be exploited, then finally the Ecological Prodigal might just return home, humbled, whilst there is still a home to return to.

What does, what might, that Elder Brother Spirituality look like in the Indian context, given what worked in the past?

Silpa, the last word goes to you."

Silpa - Conclusion

"The human race's rat-race of becoming 'numero-uno' in the corporate circle has made the world a harsher place to expect such interconnectedness between humans and creation. In Odisha, especially in the Western part of Odisha, people experience heat waves, high temperature, and scarcity of water and so on. The reason is the establishment of industries destroying the forest resources and contaminating the water resources. This passage is a reminder for our vocation as Christians to take care of the earth and resources of the earth. Earth should not to be objectified but the creation is also a partner of God in the salvific acts of God, as are human beings. We need to follow the simple life without greed and we should understand the difference between greed and need as K.C. Abraham put it, "Greed is identified as the source of the problem of ecology. By adopting a simple life-style they showed a way to suppress greed."[50]

Living in harmony with nature and keeping the needs to a minimum follows the monastic community which proclaims that the earth is the Lord's and that it should not be indiscriminately used to satisfy human avarice and greed. It is also a powerful protest against a wasteful lifestyle that is devoid of any responsibility for the world of nature. The problem lies not in how interconnected God, humans and creation are, but rather in how humans too are part of creation itself in a cycle God created. It is in such realisation that one can understand that the soul of creation in relation with God is a spiritual expression. Thus, human spirituality must move from an anthropocentric spirituality to a spirituality that includes humans as a part of creation, and relate to God. Therefore, Indian spirituality can be revived by establishing interconnected relationship between God and creation (in which humans too are a part). The role of the Indian Church in such a context is to facilitate the congregation to encounter God in this realisation. In this manner we would not only return to our "father" but also unite with the elder brother as in the parable of the 'prodigal son'."

Questions for Discussion

1. "Jesus' spirituality was nurtured and formed outdoors." Do you agree? If so, how is, and could, your spirituality and your congregations be nurtured outdoors too?

2. The chapter does not mention the story of Zacchaeus, but his very practical spirituality is very relevant: giving up half his wealth, and refunding everyone he has defrauded four times over (Luke 19:1-10). What might this mean in the Indian context?

3. Do you identify more with Genesis 1 (dominion for all people, over creation) or Genesis 2 (the earth creature created to serve and protect the garden)?

For Further Reading

Habel, Normal C. "Bible Study Session 2- Humanity Sunday." http:// seasonofcreation.com/worship-resources/bible-studies-for-the-season-of-creation/bible-studies-humanity-sunday/.

"India: Climate Change Impacts." The World Bank, http://www.worldbank.org/en/news/feature/2013/06/19/india-climate-change-impacts.

More on worship outdoors: "A Walk in the Park" Jason John 2008, self published, http://ecofaith.org/books/a%20walk%20in%20the%20park.pdf

A video version of some ideas in the chapter: https://www.youtube.com/watch?v=ETniiHdtSr4&t=20s

Anything by H. Paul Santmire

Endnotes

[1] L. C. Jain, *Eco-Spirituality for Communal Harmony or Philosophy of Being* (Bangalore: Ecumenical Christian Centre, 2003), 6.

[2] Hubert M. Watson, ed., *Eco-Justice: Implication For Faith and Theology* (Bangalore: Indian Theological Alumni of the University at Regensburg and BTESSC, 2011), 184.

[3] R.L. Sarkar, *The Bible, Ecology and Environment* (Delhi: ISPCK, 2000), 234.

[4] Hubert M. Watson, ed., *Eco-Justice: Implication For Faith and Theology*, 184.

[5] Yangkahao Vashum, "Eco-Theology from Tribal/Indigenous People's Perspectives of the North-East India" in *Tribal Ecology* edited by Razouselie lasetso, Marlene Ch. Marak and Yangkahao Vashum (Jorhat: ETC Programme Co-ordination, 2012), 40.

[6] Yangkahao Vashum, 43.

[7] Yangkahao Vashum, 42-43.

[8] Yangkahao Vashum, 43.

[9] Yangkahao Vashum, 33-34.

[10] M.J. Joseph, *The Eco-Vision of the Earth Community* (Bangalore: BTESSC/SATHRI, 2008) 86.

[11] Viji Varghese Eapen, George Zachariah and P. Mohan Larbeer Ed. *The Word and the Worlds: Biblical Reflections on Climate Change* (Bangalore: BTESSC & CSI, 2013), pp.27-28.

[12] Andreas Nehring, op.cit., 303.

[13] H. Paul Santmire, *The Travail of Nature : The Ambiguous Ecological Promise of Christian Theology*, Repr ed. (Minneapolis: Augsburg Fortress, 1992). He also published a shorter summary of Western preoccupation with the story of God and humanity, at the expense of the story of God and Creation in "Healing the Protestant Mind: Beyond the Theology of Human Dominion," in *After Nature's Revolt: Eco-Justice and Theology*, ed. Dieter T. Hessel (Minneapolis: Fortress Press, 1992).

[14] *Nature Reborn : The Ecological and Cosmic Promise of Christian Theology*, Theology and the Sciences (Minneapolis, MN: Fortress Press, 2000).

[15] Lynn White, Jr., "The Historical Roots of Our Ecological Crisis," *Science* 155 (1967): p. 1205.

[16] Ibid., pp. 1206ff.

[17] Alister McGrath, "Respect for Nature: Christianity and Ecological Concern," in *The Re-Enchantment of Nature* (London: Hodder & Stoughton, 2003).

[18] H. Paul Santmire, "The Re-enchantment of Nature: The Denial of Religion and the Ecological Crisis," *Christian Century* 120, no. 2 (2003).

19 Edward O Wilson, "Biophilia and the Conservation Ethic," in *The Biophilia Hypothesis*, ed. Stephen R Kellert and Edward O Wilson (Washington, D.C.: Island Press, 1993).

[20] Richard Louv, *Last Child in the Woods* (London: Atlantic Books, 2005).

[21] The Nature Principal: Reconnecting with Life in a Virtual Age, (Chapel Hill: Algonquin Books, 2012).

[22] Thomas Berry, "Christianity's Role in the Earth Project," in *Christianity and Ecology : Seeking the Well-Being of Earth and Humans*, ed. Dieter T. Hessel and Rosemary Radford Ruether (Cambridge, Mass: Harvard University Press, 2000),127-28.

[23] Paul Collins, *God's Earth: Religion as If Matter Really Mattered* (North Blackburn, Vic.: Dove, 1995), 3-4.

[24] Rosemary Radford Ruether, *Gaia & God : An Ecofeminist Theology of Earth Healing* (San Francisco: Harper, 1992), 102.

[25] Denis Edwards, "For Your Immortal Spirit Is in All Things," in *Earth Revealing, Earth Healing: Ecology and Christian Theology*, ed. Denis Edwards (Collegeville, Minnesota: Liturgical Press, 2001), 65-66.

[26] Ibid., 65.

[27] https://www.tear.org.au/resources/climate-of-change/

[28] Chapter eight explores this approach in more detail.

[29] There is also the question of the benefit to God of a diverse and abundant ecosystem, explored further in Jason John, "Biocentric Theology: Christianity Celebrating Humans as an Ephemeral Part of Life, Not the Centre of It" (Flinders University, 2005), 305ff, 288ff.

[30] Lukas Vischer, "Rights of Future Generations, Rights of Nature, Proposal for Enlarging the Universal Declaration of Human Rights," in *Studies from the World Alliance of Reformed Churches* (World Alliance of Reformed Churches, 1990).

[31] "Statement to the Nation: Australian Bicentennial Year," news release, 1988.

[32] A brief, web based example is Normal C Habel, "Bible Study Session 2- Humanity Sunday." See a longer more detailed argument in Theodore Hiebert, "The Human Vocation: Origins and Transformations in Christian Traditions.," in *Christianity and Ecology: Seeking the Well-Being of Earth and Humans*, ed. Dieter T. Hessel and Rosemary Radford Ruether (Cambridge, Mass: Harvard University Press, 2000), 136ff.

[33] But not his wives or daughters.

[34] For a quick concordance search: http://www.blueletterbible.org/lang/lexicon/lexicon.cfm?Strongs=H3533&t=KJV

[35] Mark Brett, "Earthing the Human in Genesis 1-3," in *The Earth Story in Genesis*, ed. Norman C. Habel and Shirley Wurst, The Earth Bible (Sheffield: Sheffield Academic Press, 2000).

[36] Anonymous, "Global Wealth Report 2017: Where Are We Ten Years after the Crisis?," Credit Suisse Research Institute.

[37] Although see Gen. 7.15 where the animals are also given the breath of life.

[38] For every 100,000 births, the number of mothers who die is 174 in India, 6 in Australia, and the worst rate is 1360 in Sierra Leone, according to https://www.indexmundi.com/g/r.aspx?v=2223

[39] For a substantial list see various, "List of Christians in Science and Technology," Wikipedia.

[40] David Eckstein, Vera Künzel, and Laura Schäfer, "Global Climate Risk Index 2018: Who Suffers Most from Extreme Weather Events?," (Germanwatch, 2018), 2,10.

[41] Anonymous, "India: Climate Change Impacts," The World Bank.

[42] Eckstein, Künzel, and Schäfer, 5.

[43] For example Matthew 19, Mark 10, Luke 1, 6, 12, 16, 18, 21.

[44] Robertson, "Visit to the Tweed River," *The Sydney Morning Herald*, 26 August 1869.

[45] See for example Bill Gammage, *The Biggest Estate on Earth: How Aborigines Made Australia* (Crows Nest, NSW: Allen and Unwin, 2011) and Bruce Pascoe, *Dark Emu Black Seeds: Agriculture or Accident?* (Broome: Magabala Books Aboriginal Corporation, 2014).

[46] For example Galarrwuy Ynunpinga, "Concepts of Land and Spirituality," in *Aboriginal Spirituality: Past, Present, Future*, ed. Anne Pattel Gray (Blackburn, Vic: Harper Collins, 1996); Rainbow Spirit Elders, *Rainbow Spirit Theology: Towards an Australian Aboriginal Theology* (Melbourne: HarperCollins, 1997).; and John, 28, 40ff.

[47] Uniting Church in Australia, "The Revised Preamble to the Constitution," (2010).

[48] B. Jawaher Paul, *Green Parables*, (Chennai: SCI Ecological Department Publication).

[49] http://shodhganga.inflibnet.ac.in/bitstream/10603/73994/11/11_chapter%204.pdf

[50] K.C. Abraham.

৶৶

Reflection

The chapter was an attempt to understand eco-theological world view and vision of Indian Tribal Spirituality.

We know that Ecology, was earlier a minor topic in biology. Now it a universal political discourse and a significant theology category that can mobilize many people. It is the ecological crisis that made it possible. Today, it finds place in almost every discussion.

Christian Theology is the discourse on the inter-relationship between God-human-creation. It is what the renowned Indian Catholic theologian, Raimundo Panikkar calls – *Cosmotheandrism*. Theology, therefore, is as Anselm said, "faith seeking understanding." Faith that is ecologically grounded. Unfortunately, this ecological aspect of Christian faith was seldom emphasised. That left a deep wound in Christian approach to ecological crisis. People like Lynn White squarely put the blame on us Christians for the ecological crisis in the world. Should we then not be concerned?

Our theology has affected our spirituality too. In our spiritual endeavour we have become too other-worldly that we have hardly any concern for the environment and the ecological crisis we face. What we need is an 'eco-conversion.' An eco-spirituality is the need of the hour. Eco-spirituality is a "process of realization of a deep sense of being, where an interconnectedness is sought between the divine, the creation and the created being." What better way to understand this spirituality from the tribal/indigenous cultures. Spirituality for them is the fabric that forms the complex web of linkage to the cosmos. Their spirituality is intrinsically interconnected with the bio-diversity of, which they are but one part. Foremost in the tribal/indigenous spirituality is a deep-rooted respect for all forms of life. The divine pervades everywhere, in everything. Creation is sacred for them. Therefore, sacrilege cannot be committed.

Another important lesson to be learned from the tribal/indigenous spirituality is its emphasis on holist approach to spirituality not the anthropocentric ideology, which dominates the worlds spiritualities today. Human is one part of the created order not the whole. The present ecological crisis is due to this emphasis on human as the master of the universe.

Ecological crisis is a spiritual crisis. For the indigenous people, spirituality is, therefore, a way of life; our living style, habit and the way we conduct and relate with other fellow human beings and creation are all integral part of their spirituality.[1] Such a spirituality is a just spirituality. Can we today talk about an Eco-centric ecclesia? What about Christian spirituality? Can it be eco-spiritual? As noted in the second chapter, the command of God to humanity is a spiritual command – Till and Keep. *Till* in terms of serving and *keep* in terms of protection. Service and protection of the creation therefore, is a spiritual command.

Today, we need an ecological theology. A theology of ecological liberation hears the cry of the poor and the cry of that great poor figure, the earth itself. Both must be liberated.[2] It is a Christological imperative too. The Incarnation of Jesus means taking on matter and becoming part of the cosmic process. It is eschatological too. Caring for the earth and its vast riches means caring for ourselves and assuring our common future.[3]

What should we do?

- Read and learn from tribal/indigenous spirituality.

- Invite tribal/indigenous scholars and practitioners to church services, listen and learn from them the ancient spiritual truths regarding caring the creation.

- Making eco-tours to tribal/indigenous communities as a church.

- Developing viable eco-spirituality and theologies based on tribal/indigenous world-views.

- Re-reading the Bible from an eco-spiritual perspective. Recovering and reclaiming the eco-vision of the Bible.

Endnotes

[1] Yangkahao Vashum, "Eco-Theology from Tribal/Indigenous People's Perspectives of the North-East India" in *Tribal Ecology* ed. Razouselie Iasetso, Marlene Ch. Marak and Yangkahao Vashum (Jorhat: ETC Programme Co-ordination, 2012), 43.

[2] Leonardo Boff, "Ecology," in *Dictionary of Third World Theologies*, eds. Virginia Fabella and R. S. Sugirtharajah (Maryknoll, New York: Orbis Books, 2000), 81.

[3] Ibid., 82.

Samuel George

CHAPTER - 6

Go, do likewise!

Living out Eco-Theology in two contexts, India and Australia

Shubha Keerthana & Jessica Morthorpe

Editor's note

Shubha and Jessica, representing their two contexts, India and Australia, have shared in detail the eco-friendly practices their respective Churches are developing. This chapter takes the form of a conversation between them.

Introduction

Christian faith is a way of both being and doing. James 2.14-17 tells us:

> "What does it profit, my brethren, if someone says he has faith but does not have works? Can faith save him? If a brother or sister is naked and destitute of daily food, and one of you says to them, "Depart in peace, be warmed and filled," but you do not give them the things which are needed for the body, what does it profit? Thus also faith by itself, if it does not have works, is dead."

Our faith tells us to care for and protect God's creation, to participate in ecological healing for Christ's sake, so how can we live this out in the lives of our churches and members?

All around the world, we are seeing exciting growth in this area, often springing from grassroots passion and faith, and bearing much creative fruit. This chapter outlines some of the actions Shubha and Jessica have seen in India and Australia, to offer you inspiration for action in your own church community.

Introductory Story from Shubha

One day we held a harvest festival celebration at our church. We had a great fellowship lunch after worship and everyone enjoyed the celebration. Then, as the congregation started returning to their homes, a non-Christian neighbour came to the church elders to complain that after every celebration we hold there are too many plastic cups thrown into the drain in front of the church. Often this blocks the drainage and she must beg the sanitary workers to clear the blockage by removing all the plastic covers and cups.

This incident questioned our Christian faith and witness in an ecological context and made us think about how we might need to change our behaviour. Plastics are not degradable and are often eaten by wildlife. When they end up in drains they can stop rain water from being able to enter the soil, and their production contributes to climate change.

In many churches in city and urban areas the church yard is cemented and there is no space for greenery. This makes the church lifeless, dry and exclusive to human beings. Through our anthropocentric activities, selfish motives and obsession with luxury, we contribute to the pollution and destruction of the environments around us. We keep our houses clean by throwing our wastes outside, with a notion "Not In My Backyard". These self-righteous attitudes thwart justice for creation.

The Earth suffers from mining, the rapid conversion of agricultural fields into human settlements and industries, the darkening of our air with smog, the way we are driving tigers, rhinos and many plant species towards extinction, the fish who eat our plastic and die, the birds that have no where to live on our barren, deforested land and our depletion of non-renewable resources. Mother Earth is being left naked, dirty and sick. These wounds are signs of our times. We must realise the sins we have committed towards our fellow creatures and listen to the groaning of God's creation. We are called to repentance. To undergo a complete transformation of our lifestyles, and to raise our voices for the quietly suffering earth. We must commit ourselves as both individuals and faith communities to lead the process of healing the wounded earth for Christ's sake.

Just as we all wet our fingers to eat the food, fruits, vegetables, milk, egg meat and grains from God's creation and breathe in the air that we obtain from nature, so also it is our inevitable and urgent duty to care for and to conserve the flora and fauna. As we seek the ways in which we as individuals and as church communities can be involved in practically engaging ourselves in caring for and protecting our creation, I hope this Section below may serve as guidance to express our faith in action by healing the earth, and being a good example to all our neighbours, both Christian and non-Christian.

"Shubha, how is the church taking leadership in integrating ecological concerns with church mission and ministry in India?"

The Church of South India (CSI) was the first in India to merge Environmental concerns with the mission agenda and ministry of the church. The Ecological Concerns Committee has been active since 1992, and CSI encourages her churches to incorporate ecological concerns in their order of worship and to include advocacy and direct action for social justice and the integrity of creation in missional activities.

The policies and programs of the Ecological Concerns Department of CSI are:

- Re-reading the Bible from an ecological perspective
- Planting trees
- Rain water harvesting
- Promoting the use of solar energy
- Green cooking and lighting
- Protecting threatened and endangered species and their habitats
- Waste management
- Educational campaigns
- Addressing climate change as a moral issue

- Environmental tithing by producing less waste
- Recycling and living more simply
- Encouraging rediscovery of old agricultural techniques
- Publicizing the ecological events happening through their newsletters and bulletin
- Promoting energy saving equipment
- Promoting smokeless and economical ovens/chulas
- Partnership programs
- Celebrating environmental festivals
- Green home /Church Eco Audits
- Campaigning against GM crops

This includes programs for:

- World Environmental Day celebrations and observation of days with ecumenical and ecological relevance.

- Eco missionary training programs and ecological workshops for pastors and heads of institutions

- Ecological and ecumenical conferences, consultations and camps at international, national and diocesan levels

- Inter- religious dialogue

- Press releases and statements on issues

- Inter-diocesan eco-fellowships

- Publications of bible-studies, liturgies, and other relevant sources to foster eco-sensitivity.

By drawing insights from local situations and relating them to the Bible, we have been able to re-read the bible from the perspective of the Earth. Based on this, three volumes of **Earth Bible Sermons** have been published as an effective tool to address various ecological issues like land degradation, waste management, pollution, climate change and mining in the light of Biblical reflection. **Eco-Bible studies** are also published through workshops or the Eco-Bible Study Program, which is conducted for clergy of various dioceses to discuss ecological issues. Work in this program on the Green Parables has resulted in around twelve eco-books being published by the CSI Synod Ecological Concerns Committee.

Other active groups include the: Green Teachers Fellowship, Green Clergy Fellowship, eco-clubs in schools, eco-missionary training camps, national and international conferences, people against nuclear energy, Eco friendly building construction, organic farming, promoting solar panels, groups introducing Green parish, Green School, Green Institution, and Green Home awards to promote Green Church Campaign, Environmental rallys, Rain water harvesting groups and Green School Project. These action-based groups and programs are enabling the Diocesan Ecological Committees to progress and grow engagement in ecological activities.

The CSI Synod Ecological Concerns Department also organized a **Visit to the War Affected Area** in Sri-Lanka, which was a meaningful visit for all the participants to become sensitive to the ecological damages of war. Seeing the collapsed water tanks and the devastated places was very powerful. The trip also enabled the Bishop and the Church of Sri-Lanka to view their own context from the perspective of wounded Earth.

The United Nations Development programme (UNDP) and Alliance for Religions and Conservation (ARC) have honoured the ecological contributions and long-term commitment of CSI in protecting the life on this planet by presenting CSI an award on the 3rd of December 2009. This was a historic moment for the church.

Making the environment part of your church's life

"Shubha, what are some of the ways the church can actively engage all ages in healing Earth?"

Worship and liturgy

Using eco-friendly symbols in worship like soil, water and fire as a sign of dedication,forming new orders of worship for environment-themed Sunday worship, **outdoor worship** in open air chapels or somewhere that is full of trees and plants. Celebrating the communion with **folk-lore worship** services, and Christian **folk songs** and **dances.** Focusing on the eco-theological dimension of our sacraments – for example in Eucharist and Baptism where we make use of the elements of the earth. We must widen our understanding, so that the bread which is broken, is not only for the broken humanity alone but also for the broken earth. God sustains the earth by God's broken body, the love that binds and nurtures. While we participate in the communion we celebrate this reality, entering ourselves into the reality in and through the suffering people and the suffering earth and we know that God is in solidarity with them and is present with us.

Children's ministry

As Sunday school is a place for providing Christian education to children, their curriculum should also involve ecological topics. Discussions and practices should include the problems of the use of disposable plastics, saving water and growing plants.

In Vacation Bible School one day can be observed as a '**green day**' where the school takes the children on a **procession** with charts and placards, with slogans on saving trees, cleanliness, and the need to protect environment.

Children can be taught simple tips to avoid wasting water like turning off the tap while brushing the teeth and saving electricity by switching off the power when it is not in use. Encourage them to make **reminder cards** which say "Unplug me" or "turn off" for their schools, Sunday classes and their homes. Encourage them to take simple actions to conserve energy and conscientize the children with ecological concerns according to their capacities through drawings, skits, paintings etc. Teach them simple and cheap ways to save rain water such as by using inverted useless umbrellas with a hole on the tip. Any simple initiative will make a difference.

Youth

Youth Fellowship can be actively involved in ecological activities by taking them out for an **Eco Tour** to a National Park or Bird Sanctuary, by **trekking** to nearby hill stations, or even to the slum areas to observe the life of the people living in those places and the crisis with which they are challenged. Organise a visit to the places where the life of the people are affected by the ecological crisis. Then organise a fun **Eco bible study** to reflect the on the biblical passages related to their exposure trip, raise their awareness of the ecological issues involved and discuss the ways they can be involved in addressing those issues and care for and protect the Oikos.

This might include the group cleaning the church campus once in a while, and **Eco- competitions** like **poster designing, pencil sketching, painting and essays** with specific themes that portray ecological damage. **Art from waste** can also be made to raise their awareness.

When there was flood in Chennai in 2015 the youth of the church were enthusiastically involved in the relief work both directly and indirectly. They contributed provisions and also visited the flood affected places to help the people. This was a fantastic learning opportunity for them, and a chance to see how human beings can suffer due to damaged environments. It was also a reminder that overexploitation and destructive attitudes towards environment are sins that we need to be aware of. Youth need opportunities to become made sensitive to, and heed, the cry of the nature. Being involved in disaster relief, and training through ecological retreats and workshops to become Eco- missionaries, can help them to actively engage in healing the environment.

Womens' and Men's Fellowship

When it is the season to get plenty of mangoes and guavas, bitter guards, drumstick seeds and other fruits and vegetables, the seeds should not be thrown away but rather collected. When it's a time for Neem trees to shed its fruit, **Seed Saving** can be done by collecting seeds and sowing them. You can then nurture the saplings to make your church and your home look green and to improve the indoor air quality.

If there are good cultivable spaces and water sources available on the church campus, then the Women and Men's Fellowship in the church can form a **kitchen garden, terrace garden or a herbal garden**. They can offer some vegetable seeds, plant saplings, and cuttings to church members to plant at home.

Shubha, what are some examples of Earth Healing activities?

Eco-friendly Church

If your church campus is already blessed with food trees, the booklet of St. Andrew's Church from Bangalore called **"Flora of our Church"** could be very helpful to guide you in caring for nature. Under the leadership of Presbyter Rev. Prem Mitra, a sub-committee called the Environment Committee was organized in this church to carry out ecological activities. Through this committee the trees in the church compound were identified, named and botanically classified. They determined the ways they could use those trees and expressed their respect and appreciation for the nature by caring for them and reflecting on how trees are an important source of spirituality in many cultures. This little **booklet** also helps its congregation to know their own church from earth perspective. They have also made their church a *plastic free zone.*

Eco-stationeries and Gifts

Gifts like cloth bags, jute bags, cardboard files, note pads with recycled papers, recycled paper gift wraps, greeting cards and reminder cards can be given as a sign of condemning the use of plastics. Solar cookers, solar torch lights, solar fans can also be promoted in this way.

Reduce Your Ecological Footprint

As individuals and as churches or as institutions we are called to commit ourselves to minimizing our ecological footprints. This means checking our lifestyles, our consumption, the smoke emissions from our vehicles, our carbon emissions, the CFCs from our refrigerators and air conditioners, how many trees we cut down and the pollution and plastics we create. We can then look at how we can balance these impacts by contributing positively to nature.

Carbon Fast

The CSI Synod Ecological Concern Department sent a Circular to all the dioceses to enable all its congregations to observe a Carbon Fast during the Lenten Season of 2017. This included simple ways that people could help to reduce their carbon footprints during Lent, such as:

To ride a bicycle, to buy a local produce, to reuse bags, to fix water leaks, to plant trees, to share rides, to compost, to choose to walk, to let nature do the work (by minimising the use of machines), to turn off lights when not in use and to use public transport.

Shubha, what are some important farming practices?

Promoting Organic farming

Panchagavya

Making natural fertilizers for the plants called panchagavya (in tamil) Pancha =five, gavya= products of cow. The five ingredients of this organic fertilizer are cow urine, fresh cow dung, milk, curd and ghee.

Mulching

Mulch fields and gardens by covering the surface of the fields with leafy wastes, field hay and left-over wastes from harvesting. This conserves the soil, retains the soil moisture and enriches the health of the soil by increasing the soil fertility. This improves soil productivity.

Organic Compost/ Vermi Composting

With the help of kitchen wastes like fruit peel, vegetable peel, wasted food, biodegradable wastes like dry leaves, saw dust, cow dung and soil, earthworms can prepare a compost that is great for and use in fields and farms for agriculture. As we often have multipurpose halls where weddings and other events are celebrated, or hostels and boarding homes, there are easy sources of continuous supplies of these food and other kitchen wastes. So, we should use these wastes as a source for composting or worm farms.

Crop Rotation

Productivity and biodiversity can be improved by avoiding monocultures and crops of only one plant (as is often used in commercial operations). Instead, used mixed cropping by planting nitrogen fixing plants, like marigold, agathi (in tamil) the scientific name of which is Sesbania pongamia perinata etc. This will enrich soil fertility and prevent the evaporation of water.

Green fencing

Strengthen the borders of your field or farm with green fencing by planting trees/shrubs.

Promoting Localised Market

In Tamil it is called *Ulloor sandhai*. Churches should take the initiative to mobilize the people to introduce localised markets. By doing so, they will help to increase the village economy of that place. Localised markets help to circulate the money from the food grains and vegetables grown by the village within their own area. It means better, more local produce, and the surplus can still be sold outside the village. It is also a way of respecting the hard work of the farmers in your area.

Jessica, what do you think is the most important action Australian churches have taken so far?

The Community Garden movement in Australia is where churches set up vegetable gardens on their land to allow local people who don't have space for a garden to grow their own food (because they are living in flats or high-rise buildings etc.). It has been growing massively and is very popular. It has been incredibly important because of the way it has helped to connect churches with their local communities (which can be a real challenge in the Australian context).

For example, when Port Melbourne Uniting Church were building their community garden and filling their wooden garden beds with soil (a time consuming and exhausting task), a neighbour they had never spoken to before popped his head over the fence and asked what they were doing. When they explained, he thought it was awesome, so he offered to fill the last bed with soil himself, so that they could go home early. This person, who they might otherwise have never connected with, became part of their community through the community garden.

The community formed around these gardens can also have powerful health benefits for people, particularly those with mental health issues, those who are lonely, and those who feel disconnected from their community for a variety of reasons (for example, if they have had to move to a new place for work). One rector I spoke to told me she believes their community garden has saved at least five lives through these connections. Many others involved in gardens nod when I tell this story, saying that this rings true to their own experiences of working with the communities in their gardens.

Community gardens are not going to work in every place and context, but the concept they represent, of gathering around a common environmental interest and working together as a community towards common goals, can be applied in many different ways. It is a key concept because it shows us how both people and the environment can both benefit greatly from joint projects, and that churches can facilitate these projects for their local communities, providing the leadership to make positive change and community possible.

Shubha, how can we heal ourselves to heal Earth?

Retrieval of Traditional Wisdom and Practices
We are part-and-parcel with nature. We depend upon nature completely for our survival, to breathe, for food, clothing, shelter and other essentials. By ignoring our dependency on nature, we are digging our own grave.

We have been carried away with industrial, scientific, technological and consumerist culture, and by ideologies of development and greed. These have dominated our lifestyles and practices and in our pursuit of their fake promises of better lives, we have lost the originality and the richness of our traditional wisdom, and traditional crop varieties, indigenous animal breeds, natural farming practices and organic seed conservation.

By begging multinational companies for seeds and dancing according to their demands, our fertile land has become barren, and our land owners ended up in huge debt, leading to farmers committing suicide. Our multiple cropping has been replaced by commercial and mono cropping, which exploits the land and poisons creation with pesticides and chemical fertilizers.

We must look at these signs of the time and repent. It is high time for us to retrieve our traditional agricultural practices for healthier living.

Promoting Natural Medicines

- It is good to know the usefulness of the plant and animals around us, to know their names and learn about their usefulness. Our ancestors had priceless traditional practices which were the secret of their healthy and prolonged lives and environment.

- Re-introducing traditional herbal medicines like Ayurveda and naturopathy and promoting them as they have no side effects for the body.

Health Care Activities

For example, free medical camps and awareness programs in tribal areas, villages and slums can be organized to discuss the prevention activities for dengue, malaria, HIV, cancer and other diseases.

Review Natural Lifestyle and Culture

All of us have been greatly influenced and carried away by globalization and consumerist way of living, including being profit oriented, focusing on accumulation, and a growing fast food and 'use and throw away' culture. These have deceived us by promising health, comfort and long life, but have delivered none of these. In the process, we have forgotten our own life affirming, and life-giving practices. There is an urgent need for us to unlearn these destructive cultures which alienate us from the earth- friendly living.

Jessica, what have been the biggest barriers to action?

The greatest barriers to church actions for the environment in Australia have been the interplays between resources and priorities. Most church leaders, and congregation members, think that it would be good to care for the environment, but they are busy and overworked, with limited finances and many demands on their time, energy and money, so the environment ends up low enough on the list of priorities that little, if any, action is taken.

One thing that is missing is a wide awareness of how good eco-theology and praxis can feed into all areas of the church, making congregations stronger. Instead of just being an extra thing on the list to do, approaching eco-theology and praxis as something to integrate into every part of church life, can revitalise congregations.

For example, talking about eco-theology can be a new and interesting way to raise a host of important theological questions with people of all ages. It can strengthen lay education programs and help people to make links between their theology and what that means for their everyday lives and actions. This makes our faith feel more relevant and alive.

Shubha, how can regional areas and dioceses get involved in healing the earth?

Regional Activities

In pastorates or in Area Women's Fellowship (once per month where women from all the churches in that specific area are gathered), **health awareness programs** about breast cancer, uterine cancer and other cancers, and HIV awareness programs can be organized to enable women to care for their health. We can also raise awareness about environmental health hazards, use of plastics, industrial waste, annihilation of life forms in rivers and lakes, and the need for the responsible water consumption. A resource person can be arranged to provide guidance for kitchen gardening, terrace gardening, and conducting **gardening skill training programs.**

In July 2016 a **retreat** was conducted for the women in Kolar Gold Fields area. During the games a bible quiz was conducted on biblical flora and fauna to orient the members to ecological perspective of the bible, and the bible study was focused on the book of Jonah. The winners were given a variety of vegetable seeds as an **Eco-gift.**

At diocesan level and at church level

Seminars and workshops can be conducted and experts can be invited to handle the specific topics. Some of the topics could be: 'Rain water harvesting and its importance'. 'Herbs and their medicinal uses'. 'Pollution in the name of Development'. 'Trees are the lungs of nature' and Workshop on water literacy, kitchen gardening and herbal gardening skills, and **installing recycling plants.**

Churches must join hands with the Non-Governmental Organizations and other people's movements that work on ecological concerns to make polices and initiate political actions.

Sextons Eco–Training Program

A Sextons Eco-Training Program can be organized when there is a church sextons annual get-together, or by organizing a regional sextons meeting to discuss making the church eco-friendly and plastic free, waste management and education about gardening skills and organic farming.

In church campuses, hostels, boarding homes, diocesan schools, other institutions and homes **Rain water harvesting,** mud pits or percolation tanks can be made to recharge the ground water. **Roof top harvesting** can be done in urban areas to save rain water for domestic purposes.

Interdenominational Programs

The Reformed churches with Roman Catholic and other church ecological concerns committees belonging to particular areas can get together can organize an **Eco-rally** and seminars and awareness programmes.

Interfaith Activities

Offering special prayers and readings from the Bible and from other scriptures will be helpful to see the face of God from the perspective of the earth. Interfaith views regarding ecology, eco-spirituality, the value and sacredness of nature, ecologically based ritual practices and their scientific significance can be shared in seminars by the religious leaders.

Shubha, what are some programs we can get involved with?

Women DARE(Dalit and Adivasi Rural Entrepreneurs):

DARE is a project introduced by Church of South India SEVA to bring to the fore the micro enterprise initiatives of different womens' groups in South India, particularly those Self Help Groups promoted and trained by the ministries of CSI diocese. This in turn encourages them to develop more self -employment models by promoting rural produce and local products. This sustains a life affirming local market economy and empowers women and marginalized indigenous communities.

'Give a cow' Programme

Rayalseema Diocese of Andhra Pradesh, in association with Mission Partnership India, launched a project in Madhanapalli and Aroghyavaram called 'Give a cow' programme with the intention that poor farmers' families are benefited with milk and dung for the agricultural fields. By doing this the church can support the farmers and also be benefited by agriculture.

Jessica, what would you most like to see churches do next?

As in India, celebrating the environment in worship is important in Australian churches. We hold worship outdoors, celebrate Harvest Festivals, host eco-retreats in the bush, conduct mindful or praise focused bushwalks, and hold all-age activities in National Parks and natural environments.

Many Australian churches also celebrate the Season of Creation – a series of services in September celebrating God's creation based on resources originally written by leading Australian eco-theologian Dr. Norman Habel (who is also involved in the Earth Bible Project). These resources are available to access at https://seasonofcreation.com/

Some churches also hold Blessing of the Animals services, usually on St Francis of Assisi Day (the first Sunday in October), where pets are invited to join the service. These events are joyous occasions, where people can bring the animals that are central to their lives to be blessed, and to help them celebrate all of God's creatures. They are also surprisingly powerful, as they challenge us to think about our place in God's creation as humans and affirm the spirit of God in our love for our animals, and their love for us.

These services are also another very powerful community outreach tool. People who want little to do with the church are often still keen to have their pets blessed, and when these services are held outside, I have seen people walking their dogs past come to join the service and ask for a blessing. They are also wonderfully intergenerational, as children love to bring their pets, and to have the opportunity to talk about why they are important in their lives.

Services are also sometimes held for World Environment Day, National Threatened Species Day and World Water Week. Some churches participate in Clean Up Australia Day each year during their service. Earth Hour is another exciting opportunity for services. I have never forgotten a service I attended at St. Paul's Cathedral in Manuka to celebrate Earth Hour. Outside the front door, we were handed candles, to light our way into the completely dark cathedral. We gathered in the pews in silence, with the feeling of the huge sacred space all around us. Then, a cantor voice rose from somewhere above us – high and pure, stunning. We joined in singing, and the liturgy continued with prayers and intercessions for the earth. The power of the atmosphere, of the darkness, of that space, and the singing in that moment is etched in my mind.

I would like to see all churches participating in at least one of these forms of environment themed worship. This is why holding an environmental service is one of the criteria for the first award in the Five Leaf Eco-Awards program I conduct (see https://fiveleafecoawards.org). Worship is the centre of our tradition, and where we learn and absorb most of our theology. Thus, eco worship is essential to helping our congregations see how central care of God's creation is to our faith. Through the mediums of prayer, singing, and hearing the word of God, we show our congregations what we believe about the environment, and how it should be treated. If we include the earth in our prayers each week, it reminds our churches that the environment is of ongoing concern and interest to God. If we thank God for the wonders and beauty of creation, we remind them that we can find and learn from God through God's presence in creation – both immanent and transcendent. If we bless people's pets, we tell them that we love and care for the things they love, and care about, and so does God.

Shubha, what are some important Indian Eco-Festivals and celebrations?

Festivals and celebrations are part-and-parcel of Indian culture and there are many festivals based on creation and its elements. Some of the festivals which reflect eco spirituality are:

Harvest festival

During the month of September or October (month may vary) every year, almost all the churches of the Church of South India celebrate an Annual thanksgiving festival called Harvest festival. During this festival, a portion of the yield from the land: fruits and vegetables, grains and pulses goats and sheep, livestock, hens, pigeons and love birds, food products and homemade sweets, and in urban areas household utensils, gifts, sarees and other articles are brought as a sign of thanksgiving to the church and these are auctioned. This will be celebrated with a communion service and accompanied by games, fun and fellowship.

On a less positive note, in recent years, this festival has been commercialised by introducing blessing plates ... alienating the 'have nots' by preventing them from participating happily and reducing them to mere observers. There is a struggle going on to restore and revive the earlier harvest festival which affirms life and happiness for all.

Thoppu thiruvizha

This is also called a 'festival of groves'. It is similar to a harvest festival where the worship is conducted outdoors in an open area with trees and celebrated in Kolar Gold Fields (KGF). In earlier days, all the CSI churches in KGF came together for a two or three-day festival with drama, and group singing, food stalls and games and bible quiz for women fellowship. However, as the years passed by church fellowships were lost and it is now celebrated as a harvest festival celebration by only one church, with singing and dancing by Sunday School children and youth and there is a spiritual convention meeting for three days. The ecological essence of this festival and its fellowship need to be strengthened.

Vana bhojanam: vanam = forest, bhojanam = meal. This is a festival of celebrating fellowship meal in the forest. The festival is celebrated by the churches in Vellore diocese, where people come together in a field area to thank God and all of God's creation.

Thoppu thiruvizha and *Vana bhojanam* are some of the ancient festivals celebrated by our ancestors to value the earth and all its creatures and to thank God for the life that was given to us as a blessing, and for all the goodness that we enjoy each and every moment from creation. There are many such festivals which we have forgotten or lost, and which need to be rediscovered and renewed to respect our creator God and to care for God's creation.

Vanamahotsava

This is an Annual Tree Planting Festival which was started as a movement in 1950. It is also called 'festival of forest'. It aims to conserve and plant tree saplings to increase the forest canopy and the density of the forest. In Karnataka it is celebrated on 1ˢᵗ of November every year. The significance of this festival needs to be revived.

Bhoomi Habba

Bhoomi=Earth and Habba= festival. This is 'The Earth Festival' which is celebrated at the Green Eco Sanctuary at Visthar campus, a place near Kothanoor in Bangalore. It is a day-long celebration to create public awareness of the environmental crises we face, and showcase inclusive and sustainable alternatives. The celebration includes painting, cartoon drawing, pot making, art, recycling workshops, environmental campaigns, folk music, theatre plays, storytelling for children and activities enable them to discover the beauty of nature. It also exhibits models or dolls that reveal eco-friendly living. Eco-friendly and organic crafts, seeds, food materials, and clay jewellery made by the tribal women are also exhibited and sold. Signatures are also collected for environmental petitions and eco-justice. The 2017 bhoomi habba was celebrated on 10ᵗʰ June with the slogan- 'Protect Earth Celebrate Life'. It had a focus on justice, peace and sustainable communities.

Thai Pongal Festival

On 14th and 15ᵗʰ of January every year, especially in India, this festival is celebrated. It is also a farmers' festival or Tamil harvest festival where they come together as relatives and friends with all their cattle- cows and buffaloes, herd of sheep and goats, hens and cocks decorated with painted horns, balloons and garlands tied around their necks. They are taken to the nearby temple to be blessed and to thank God for their agricultural abundance. Though this is a common festival for all, sometimes it is claimed to be a Hindu festival. However, it is always good that we thank God for the land and all the living creatures, which we benefit so greatly from.

Jessica, what have you found to be useful incentives for action?

One of the reasons I believe educating people about eco-theology is important is that theology helps as an incentive for action. It reminds us that the earth is the Lord's, and that we should love what God loves. A holistic eco-theology also points us to how this is a whole of life, whole of lifestyle approach as well. I often preach on how a Christian lifestyle should be recognisably environmentally friendly, and that people should be able to tell that we are Christians from how we love God's creation as well as each other.

Yet behaviour change does not always neatly follow theological awareness and insight. In fact, sometimes our behaviour changes before our theology does. One of the advantages of being in community is that the example of others can help us to live a more sustainable lifestyle even before we fully understand why this is a good idea theologically. So we can use our churches to normalise environmental behaviours and help people to automatically 'do the right thing'.

I think it is also worth remembering that you don't always have to take action in your church purely for environmental reasons. It is ideal if we can achieve multiple goals together. So an event might be a way of connecting with non-believers as well as a way of spreading environmental awareness. Or it might be a great all-age activity. We can share our faith while planting trees or develop leaders by asking them to lead our actions in these areas. Many Australian churches start becoming more environmentally friendly because they can save money with energy efficiency measures. This is great, because it still reduces carbon emissions, even if that was not the primary goal. In the act, they might get hooked, and find they want to do more for the environment.

People also like to do things that give them purpose, that are social, and that are fun. Even though caring for creation is serious business, not everything we do has to be serious! So let's act together, let's make it matter, and let's do it in creative and fun ways.

Jessica, what are 5 main keys to success in Ecological Ministry?

These are essential:

1. Resources

2. Communication

3. Education

4. Involving all ages

5. Establishing an environment group or committee

Jessica, how do you recommend we start to achieve change?

1. Start by establishing a Green Team/Environment Group or Committee. You can achieve change on your own, or in a small group, but it will be much faster and easier in a strong team.

2. Learn about your local environment and its issues.

3. Explore possibilities for your church.

4. Determine which are the most appropriate for your context (not too expensive, that build on the strengths of your congregation).

5. Widen your action steps – make sure you include behaviour change as well as technical changes. Consider incentives like awards programs or action frameworks to help with this.

6. Build a culture in your congregation of ongoing concern for God's Creation and review of what you are doing, and can begin to do, for the environment.

7. Create sustained change over time.

Conclusion

Many of the practices and guidelines in this chapter are not new, but things we need to re-discover or re-embrace. As Christians we need to avoid focusing only on individual salvation of the soul and ideas of escaping to heaven while ignoring the struggles of people and the earth here and now. We are called to heal and care for God's creation, which is suffering because of us. It is by returning to a natural way of living as an individual, as Christians and as churches, and by committing ourselves to be in solidarity with the suffering earth, that we can mend our ways and our lifestyles, and get involved in actively contributing to the process of healing God's Earth.

Questions for Discussion

1. How can your church help to heal God's Earth?

2. How can you inspire your congregation to reflect on eco-theology and God's love for creation?

3. What festivals and celebrations can you use to raise awareness of this theme? And how can you make them sustainable?

For Further Reading

Church of South India: A Seven Year Plan to Protect the Living Planethttp://www.arcworld.org/downloads/Christian-CSI-7YP.pdf.

Ecotheology Book series by the Church of South India David G. Hallman (Ed.)

Ecotheology: Voices from South and North https://www.amazon.com/Ecotheology-Voices-David-G-Hallman/dp/1606089099

Five Leaf Eco-Awards (Australian Environmental Award program for Churches)

https://fiveleafecoawards.org/Eco-Church https://ecochurch.arocha.org.uk/resources/

CeliaDeane-Drummond. *A Primer in Ecotheology: Theology for a Fragile Earth* https://www.amazon.com/Primer-Ecotheology-Theology-Fragile-Companions/dp/1498236995/ref=sr_1_1?s=books&ie=UTF8&qid=1526516097&sr=1-1&keywords=ecotheology

Reflection

Rev. Shuba Keerthana has explained all the ecological activities which we are doing in CSI very elaborately. The CSI Church Constituted an Ecological Committee in 1992 and we have completed 25 years in our journey. The CSI is the only Church in India which has mentioned Ecology as a mission in the Constitution and in the Mission statement. For CSI, Ecological work is not a social service, but it is a part of our faith. Only Church in India, recognised by UNDP with an eco Award, in 2009. The Green School Programme of CSI is getting good momentum. The CSI is promoting the values of sustainability in all our development projects. Living sustainably is about doing more and better with less. It is about knowing that rising rates of natural resource use and the environmental impacts that occur are not a necessary by-product of economic growth. The well-being of humanity, the environment, and the functioning of the economy, ultimately depend upon the responsible management of the planet's natural resources. Evidence is building that people are consuming far more natural resources than what the planet can sustainably provide. Many of the Earth's ecosystems are nearing critical tipping points of depletion or irreversible change. Christian ethics also goes a long way in helping Christians to cultivate sustainable lifestyles. We do not have to wait until there is a law to compel us to act responsibly; our ethical values and principles should help us to make the right choices. The right place to teach the values of sustainability is at school. Hence the CSI Synod Department of

Ecological Concerns promotes Green School Programme. In the life and ministry of the Church, the CSI would like to promote sustainable development practices and to build power for change. Hence, the CSI Synod published the '# GPGD 12 Points: Green Protocol for Green Discipleship - A Guideline of 12 Points for the CSI Dioceses to develop Green Congregations'. We hope and pray that all the parishes in the CSI would abide by this Green Protocol and would thus effectively participate in the 'Green-Discipleship' of our Church. As the CSI is committed to protect the integrity of the creation, we do believe that the Green protocol should be reflected in the life and ministry of the Church. We do believe that the Church should respond prophetically or lament like Jeremiah when people exploit the natural resources and consequently crucify God's creation, the flora and the fauna.

Mathew Koshy Punnackad

Section Three

Eco-theology and Eschatology

CHAPTER - 7

Endings ... and Beginnings:
A Conversation

Gracy Christina & David Reichardt in Conversation

The Christian faith is one of hope; it looks towards the reconciliation of all things in Christ. However, our ecological practice has to be realistic. The seriousness of the situation in which humanity finds itself is such that it is too late for some things to be reversed.

Editor's Note

This chapter, written by Rev Gracy Christina Mercy R. and Rev Dr David Reichardt, has also been edited into the form of a conversation.

Introduction

David

This book has been written in response to the increasingly serious threat posed by human activity to earth's global and local environments. Our planet is suffering

SCIENCE AND RELIGION FINALLY AGREE!

increasingly from ecological trauma, and its inhabitants are being forced, increasingly, to respond.

Christians share a particular perspective in this great, worldwide discussion. Typically, Christians believe that a good and powerful God created this good and bounteous earth, and has a good purpose for it. That purpose and future is not just for humans; it is for the whole "cosmos", all of God's creation. Therefore, the Christian faith is hope-full; it looks towards the reconciliation of all things in Christ. An Indian friend once put it like this: "The good thing about Christianity is that it has a happy ending!"

Gracy

Every beginning has an end point and every ending paves a way for the new beginning. But the happy beginning may end with sadness, and the sad beginning may end with happiness. The end depends upon how responsible we are throughout the journey. In particular, we should be serious about the beginning and end of the ecological crisis which has emerged in our times.

David

However, many scientists and some religionists disagree. For many scientists the world's ecological situation seems to contradict this hope. Ecological degradation is now so serious that many ecologists believe that it is too late for some of it to be reversed. Where is hope in the realisation that our descendants will very likely live in a significantly degraded earth?

Gracy

As Christians we need to take our stands. It is not too late but we must do it 'here and now'.

David on apocalyptic Christianity

Additionally, some Christians, at least of the western tradition, find their hope in the belief, influenced by the Greek philosopher Plato and supported by passages such as 2 Peter 3.10,[1] that this world will be destroyed by fire. This text seems to find good support in Scripture.[2] Some of these passages speak of judgement, and others of destruction. There is also the statement in I Thessalonians 4:13-17 that Christ will come for believers, both living and dead, in the "rapture" to meet Christ in the air. And Revelation 2:1 then says: "...I saw a new heaven and a new earth; for the first heaven and the first earth had passed away, and the sea was no more."

Hence the view of some within the Western tradition that believers will be saved, but that this world, along with non-believers, will be destroyed and replaced by a completely new one. Such is the hope of some, expressed in the statement, "What is the point of eco-theology? This world is going to burn anyway."

Gracy on biblical interpretation

There are various ways of reading, interpreting and quoting the Bible according to the context and the experience of the individual. Interpretation may bring out the various theological concerns. As we know we need to be careful about ideologically rigid interpretations of Scripture, both at the conservative and at the liberal ends of the theological spectrum. A particular Biblical interpretation should not lead us to stand far away from reality and responsibility. Appropriate interpretation of the scripture should help us to know the concerns of ecology.

Anthropocentric interpretation hinders us from being eco-friendly. For example, although 75% of the earth is covered by water humans call the planet "Earth" rather than "Water" because we live on the earth. We emphasize our belongings and we highlight what is ours! Since we are unaware of the full extent of the present crisis in the ecosystem, we give less importance to what Scripture says about ecological concerns. More often we overlook the scripture, not prioritizing the concern it raises or considering it as not contemporary. Blindfolds that hinder our reading of Scripture should be removed by identifying ecologically concerned verses in the Bible. We often skip some verses without noticing, thinking that we understand them because of the presupposition we apply to them. Frequent use of the scripture means it is all the more necessary to read the scripture with new eyes each and every time we encounter it.

[At this and several other points in our conversation Gracy demonstrated the link of apocalyptic eschatology with the very beginnings of the Bible. David returned to the cartoon, then resumed speaking about Hope, his main focus.]

David on "New Creation" and Hope

As the cartoon shows, science and "apocalyptic" Christianity seem to have converged, prompting a loss of hope for this world. Yet in recent times many theologians have been revising our understanding of the nature of God's plan of salvation for all of creation. This renewed understanding of salvation is called "New Creation" by its supporters. It involves re-reading and re-interpreting the Bible, and it results in a hope that is neither simply wishful thinking that humans will ourselves solve the awful problems we have created, nor that the souls of believers will be saved while our bodies and the whole physical creation will be destroyed.

But what it is about the Christian gospel that gives hope in the midst of ecological despair? Ironically, the Christian linear view of time and the Christian belief that God will set all things to rights at the last time have been distorted into myths of this worldly progress, unending economic growth, and even, in its most general sense, of evolution. Many argue today that the myths of progress and unending economic growth are major causes of the behaviour that is causing ecological degradation. But it is the Christian view of hope in a time of growing ecological despair that may point us back to a proper view of time. So let us look at hope.

Hope is defined as "a feeling of expectation and desire for a particular thing to happen".[3] The difference between hope and despair is a good night's sleep," Al Gore[4] told his climate change slide show trainees. For many years Mr Gore has been at the forefront of efforts to present the science of climate change so that it is easily understandable to the general public. For over a decade he has trained thousands of "climate change presenters" to communicate both his deep ecological concern and his hope that humankind will do what is needed to limit the ecological damage we have caused and build a better future for the planet. He insists that despite the seriousness of the situation there is hope, and he retains a belief that despite the denial and obstruction of those with vested interests in the current economic system, humanity will "do the needful" and make the transition to a clean energy future and a civilization that loves nature.

This is hope "in the natural", hope that humans, without (obvious) divine intervention, have the ability and the will to solve the gigantic problem we ourselves have caused. As evidence for this belief Gore points to remarkable things that human beings have achieved when we have cooperated: the moon landings, peacefully ending apartheid in South Africa and communism in Europe. India's rise from the devastation caused by British occupation and their hasty departure to the state of India today[5] can also be numbered among these achievements.

Gracy on biblical interpretation & Hope
But why are you telling about non-biblical hope when there is so much of significance in the bible that speaks of both ecology and a hopeful ending...and beginning?

David
Tell me what you are thinking.

Gracy continues
We believe in Creator God also basic attribute of God is creation. Thus we accept the supreme power of God is revealed in creation. We are God's Image and likeness out of the dust of the ground also the other animals were created out of ground (Genesis 2.19) Very attribute of God and his will is revealed in the nature as Theologians say that creation is a natural revelation of God.[6] We should be conscious that if we are threat to the nature; we are destroying the very signs of God's revelation. It is time for us to pay keen attention to the ignored values of the scripture and understand and interpret in the eco-concerned views for not to be too late.

Hidden treasures of ecological truth in the scripture should be evaluated in order to know the purpose of God in the creation as a whole. The Garden of Eden was the place of God's presence where God met Human and the place where God saw good in everything and it was very good; creating Man as male and female is a portrait of God's image and likeness.

Blessings to Abraham, Isaac, Jacob, Joseph and the 12 tribes were in terms of ecological ideologies. Hundredfold yield of Isaac was the expression of God's abidance, through the dream with stars and sun, cows and ears are as the fore telling agents of God's plan, land of Canaan represented God's blessing in terms of honey and milk. In the wilderness God revealed himself to Israelites by providing Manna, water, pillar of cloud and pillar of fire, meat which were the elements of God's provision. Wine and fig represent restoration and healing respectively. The rainbow in the sky was the sign of God's covenantal compassion that he kept as a reminder.[7] Former Rain, later rain, seed time, harvest, summer winter, day and night and the seasons all represent God's providence.[8]

God's supreme power is revealed in the creation. Heaven and earth is full of his glory and the whole eco-system narrates how powerful God is. God is a good shepherd for he leads on the sides of the calm water. Israel was called as seeds of the generation of the Fathers. The relationship between God and people is expressed in terms of wine and the farmer. The coming messiah was also called The Root of David.

The Kingdom of God is revealed through Jesus. And the cosmos is the expression of it. Jesus was an ecologist; he used eco-friendly metaphors to reveal the most hidden truth of God. The Kingdom of God is compared to a sower, God's providence was understood by seeing the birds of the air and flowers of the forest; the judgment of the lord is explained in terms of wheat harvest.

The Word become flesh ('bashar') Jesus interpreted himself metaphorically as Light, Lamb, Life, and Bread. Wine and branch are the ultimate metaphor to be connected with Christ to be fruitful. Jesus' triumph over the death was revealed upon the tree (Col. 2:15) Jesus was hanged on the tree[9] through which the victory has been celebrated. The ultimate revelation of God's love in the death and resurrection of Christ was in wood – on a cross. The trees were in the middle of the Garden of Eden; also 12 trees in heaven[10] which refers to prosperity and healing. Water was the sign of God's deliverance; crossing the Red Sea, salvation at the time of Noah through rain, baptism in New Testament, living water in and through Christ. In the book of Revelation the Kingdom of God is as pure as water. In other words it was like a sea of glass. Salt of the sea and figs were the instruments of healing in God's creation.

Jesus wanted his disciples to be the fishers of humans, not entrepreneurs. After the resurrection of Jesus he renewed the call of John to be a Shepherd. Paul talks about the field of God compared to children of God. Jews and Gentiles for God are like grafting of the tree.

God is personified as spirit or air. God created man out of mud and he breathed into man's nostrils the breath of life. Jesus breathed on them and offered The Holy Spirit. The Holy Spirit is 'pneuma' or 'ruach' which is 'air' in its literal understanding. And the spirit of the Lord dwells in us and we are expected to yield the fruits which are called as Fruit of the Spirit. The restoration will be taken place through the spirit/breath.[11] Breaking the phenomenon of anthropocentric ideology through the psalmist and prophet[12] God reveals that he will pour his spirit on all flesh[13] also the spirit of the Lord in all the creatures. And the permanent agent of the Spirit is tree.

Thus the culture of Israel in eco-friendly and the community has experienced God and his sovereignty. Creation is the treasure of God which God loves and wants to preserve and restore.

David continues on Hope

I agree that God is sovereign and loves Creation. Christians affirm that the fate of the earth rests neither in human hands nor in chance, but with God. Intrinsic to Christian faith is the belief that not only is this good earth God's creation and property, but God is intimately engaged in and with it.

The Bible's perhaps best-known verse[14] says in more literal translation that "God loved the world *like this*: He sent His only Son..." That is, Jesus was sent for the sake of *the World*! Humans are, of course vitally important to the world and to God's plan of salvation for it. Jeremiah has God reassuring the exiled people of Judah that "I know the plans I have for you...plans for your welfare and not for harm, to give you a future with hope."[15] And yet, ecological degradation and especially climate change loom as huge threats. Can Christians and Christian theology offer hope as a resource in meeting the gigantic challenge that climate change and human obstructionism are causing?

Hope is an important characteristic of Christian faith. One way of gauging how important this theme is in the Bible is to count the number of times the word "hope" occurs, and to compare its frequency with that of other important words. Given some variation caused by different translations the word "love" occurs about 730 times in the Bible. 'Faith" recurs about 530 times. We meet the word "Peace" 340 times, "Joy" nearly 270 times. The words "money" and "possessions" occur a combined 230 times. "Grace", a central concept, occurs 125 times. "Hope" occurs just over 200 times. It is an important biblical concept, though not as important by this measure as several concepts it is often found together with.

However, frequency of use is only a crude indicator of importance. One must also analyse the importance of this concept in its various contexts. There is not enough space to do this in this present book, but a few examples may demonstrate that hope is important.

Jeremiah 29.11 has already been mentioned.

There is an "in spite of everything" quality to biblical hope that Lamentations 3.19-24 expresses well:

"The thought of my affliction and my homelessness
    is wormwood and gall!
My soul continually thinks of it
    and is bowed down within me.
But this I call to mind,
    and therefore I have hope:[16]
The steadfast love of the Lord never ceases,
    his mercies never come to an end;
they are new every morning;
    great is your faithfulness.
'The Lord is my portion,' says my soul,
    therefore I will hope in him.'"

Indeed, in contrast to secular hope, biblical hope can be defined as "confident expectation". The apostle Paul explains why in Romans 5.1-5, a passage in which most of the Bible's much-used words mentioned above feature:

> "Therefore, since we are justified by *faith*, we have *peace* with God through our Lord Jesus Christ, through whom we have obtained access to this *grace* in which we stand; and we boast in our *hope* of sharing the glory of God. And not only that, but we also boast in our sufferings, knowing that suffering produces endurance, and endurance produces character, and character produces *hope*, and *hope* does not disappoint us, because God's *love* has been poured into our hearts through the Holy Spirit that has been given to us."

God's love is the source of and the reason for human hope, even in the ecological sphere. As Paul put it, "And now faith, hope, and love abide, these three; and the greatest of these is love."[17]

Gracy on the theology of New Creation

We Christians are called to bring hope in midst of hopelessness. Christian eschatology can provide a happy ending and it can provide a sad one. Whether it is happy or sad depends upon how responsible and truthful to our calling we are. A wrong understanding of the eschatology leads us to end up in tragedy. Most of us wonder what the use of eco-theology is when God is in control of everything. Many think of God as the Creator and Sustainer, the Supreme Power and Lord. We think that it also is his will to destroy the creation on the Day of Judgment.

But we need to understand that God has no plans of destroying the world but the day of the Lord is the day of the division. A wrong understanding of Christian faith leads us to give up our responsibility of custodianship and stewardship. We believe in eschatology where it is said that the whole cosmos becomes new. When the new comes the old perishes. We should be aware of it that the plan of God is replacement of old earth with new earth and old heavens with new heavens.

David

Yes, I'll talk about that sort of thing in a little while when I talk about theologies of Hope. But you were saying?

Gracy on eco-justice and God's love for God's Creation

There is a kind of reverse image here as India steps towards industrialization and modernization. In India the influence of these two '-izations' are certifying the fields as Barren lands. With the certification entrepreneurs are forced to or inspired to turn the fields into factories and Malls for the best price that they could offer. The bible provides us with a precedent in the story of Naboth's Vineyard. (1 Kings 21):

> King Ahab wanted Naboth's vineyard which was next to his palace. He made a good offer to Naboth in terms of land or money (1 Kings21:2,6). But Naboth did not want to sell it or make business out of the Land which was his ancestors' property. Naboth was the steward of the Land and Ahab represented (and had) power. When Ahab wanted to buy the vineyard using the power and position of his royalty Naboth refused to sell. In other words he resisted playing with the "global business of real estate". He wanted to retain the land; it was his ancestors' property, for which he had sentiment of his forebears and retain ecological concern also took stand for it. But the dominant political power wanted it. Even then Naboth refused to make a deal. For being the Voice of resistance he had to give up his life, yet he proved that his was the voice for justice of the Land.

There is a similarity in this incident with the restoration and renewal of the cosmos. Today because of the Global market and modernization we are replacing fruitful land with buildings, multistoried buildings and factories. Although the New Jerusalem will descend to earth[18] the new heavens and new earth will not be replaced with buildings as development; rather, old earth will be replaced by new earth and heaven with new heaven. Our eschatological understanding is that in Christ we are new creation and reconciled through him.[19] God so loved the world that he gave his only begotten son to save it.[20] If God would want the world to perish then why he should love the world? Or if God had a purpose to destroy it why did He give his only begotten son to save it? Thus God's ultimate plan is not to destroy the world but to save it and restore, reconcile and renew the cosmos. Jesus is called as Last Adam,[21] yet he is not the last man of creation but he is the first man of the new creation. Through the death and resurrection of Christ the mystery was revealed that God could change even death into resurrection. The physical body of Jesus rose in glory on the third day. There is a suffering between beginning and ending but the hope of glorious ending will never fade. Even our bodies will be sown as perishable, in dishonour, weakness and as natural. But they will be raised as imperishable, glorious, powerful and spiritual bodies.[22] Thus in Christ we have a hope of new beginning but not the despair of a miserable ending:

> "For the earnest expectation of the creature waits for the manifestation of the Children of God for the creature was made subject to vanity, not willingly, but by reason of him who has subjected the same in hope, because the creature itself also shall be delivered from the bondage of corruption into the glorious liberty of the children of God. For we know that the whole creation groaning and travail in pain together until now." Rom. 8:19-22.

God Loves the World which he created out of nothing,[23] and he wants to save it. So He gave his only begotten Son so that through Him everyone shall believe in Him. Also we are called as sons and daughters of God to channelize the mission of God. Through Jesus, we as cosmos are waiting for the salvation. Our mission is to be salt of the earth which preserves but is not used to destroy it. May that hope in Christ be alive in us, and may it be constructive, not destructive.

David on Theologies of Hope

I'd like to go back to theologies of hope for the last part of our conversation. If we quoted each of the Bible's 200 or more references to hope in isolation we would not find much of a contribution to a Christian response to ecological degradation. It is the task of ecotheology to think theologically about what these hope-full texts say in relation to ecology.

The German theologian Jürgen Moltmann has written extensively on both hope and ecology.[24] Although his *Theology of Hope* is a ground-breaking study on the nature of Christian hope and eschatology[25] it contains little about ecology. When Moltmann wrote *Theology of Hope* people were only starting to become aware of this subject. Twenty years later Moltmann made up for this with "God in Creation: An Ecological Doctrine of Creation"[26] A great achievement of "God in Creation" was to locate ecotheology within the doctrine of creation. Ecotheologian Celia Deane-Drummond has concluded "Ecology in Jürgen Moltmann's Theology"[27] with these words: "If ecotheology is to have a message for this ecologically damaged fragile earth, it has to include Moltmann's concept of hope in God, who through Christ makes all things new."

Others have also strengthened the connections between ecology, theology and hope. For example, Mark I. Wallace has suggested that:

"…we refer to the Spirit in our time as the 'wounded Spirit' or 'cruciform[28] Spirit' who, like Christ, takes into herself the burden of human sin and the deep ecological damage this sin has wrought in the biosphere. But, as Christ's wounds become the eucharistic blood that nourishes the believer, so also does the Spirit's agony over damage to the earth become a source of hope for communities facing seemingly hopeless environmental destitution. The message of the cross is that senseless death is not foreign to God because it is through the cross that God lives in solidarity with all who suffer. Now the promise of new life that flows from the suffering God hanging from a tree is recapitulated in the ministry of the wounded Spirit whose solidarity with a broken world is a token of divine forbearance and love…Hope, then, for a restored earth in our time is theologically rooted in the belief in the Spirit's benevolent cohabitation with all the damaged and forgotten members of the biosphere - human and non-human alike."[29]

Note how Wallace has drawn upon resources of traditional disciplines within theology: pneumatology[30] and the doctrine of the Trinity.

In "Surprised by Hope" N.T. Wright has, similarly, described the fundamental structures of Christian hope.[31] Noting that the clearest statements of Christian hope are found in the writings of Paul and the Book of Revelation Wright named three great theological themes: the goodness of creation, the nature of evil and God's plan of redemption, as he began his treatment of theological hope. Before this, however, Wright critiqued currently popular beliefs about the cosmic future which, although very different from each other, are both sometimes confused with Christian belief. The first is "the Myth of Progress". This is the belief, strengthened by Darwin's theory of evolution, that everything is, in the words of the Beatles' song, "getting so much better all the time."[32]   One particularly destructive aspect of the Myth of Progress is what the Australian author Clive Hamilton has called the economic "growth fetish" and, to invent a word, "affluenza."[33] That the myth of progress demands continual economic growth in a world of finite resources is dangerous enough, but N.T. Wright argued that the Myth of Progress's fundamental fault is that it cannot cope with evil. It has no adequate explanation of evil, and cannot hinder it. Nevertheless, although the past century has seen two devastating world wars, the threat of nuclear holocaust and now the additional threat of ecological catastrophe the Myth of Progress is still commonly believed.

The second option, though very different from the first, is also commonly thought to be Christian. It is the belief that the most appropriate human task is to get in touch with true reality, which is beyond space, time and matter. As was discussed in Chapter 1 this thinking originated with Plato, but most Christians think that Christianity is committed to at least a "soft" version of Plato's position. The created world is thought by many to be "at best an irrelevance, at worst a dark, evil, gloomy place. Many Christians believe that the purpose of being Christian is simply, or at least mainly, to 'go to heaven when you die'..."[34]

The result is, as many opponents of Christianity have pointed out, that Christians have contributed to ecological disaster because they do not think that, ultimately, this world matters. When many Christians speak of the hope that is ours in Christ they mean the eventual destruction of the created order and a destiny that is purely 'spiritual' in the sense that it is completely non-material.

N.T. Wright argues, over against both these popular but mistaken views, that the central Christian affirmation is that what God has done in Christ, and supremely in Christ's resurrection, is what He intends to do for the whole world, the entire cosmos:

"Only in the Christian story itself - certainly not in the secular stories of modernity - do we find any sense that the problems of the world are solved, not by a straightforward upward movement into the light, but by the creator God going down into the dark, to reduce humankind and the world from its plight."[35]

Noting that for the past two hundred years western thought has overemphasised the individual at the expense of the larger picture of God's creation Wright began his exposition of biblical hope with the bible's vision of the future world - a vision of the present cosmos renewed from top to bottom by the God who is both Creator and Redeemer. It is in that context that one can speak of the significance of Jesus' bodily resurrection, and of the 'second coming' of Jesus. Wright grouped the key New Testament texts that speak of the cosmic dimension of Christian hope into six main themes.

In 1 Corinthians 15 Paul uses the images of '*first fruits*'.[36] The offering of first fruits signifies the great harvest still to come. Paul then continues with a quite different image, that of a king establishing his kingdom by subduing all enemies. In describing a theology of *new creation* Paul says that every force and authority in the cosmos including, finally, death, will be subjected to the Messiah. That means that the massive, destructive forces of the universe - entropy, chaos, dissolution - will be transformed by the Messiah, who is the agent of the creator God.

A third theme employed the image of *the Roman colony*, found in Philippians 3.20-21. It says that, as the inhabitants of Roman colonies such as Philippi and Corinth were Roman citizens, so God's people are citizens of heaven who are colonising the earth. That is, followers of Christ are not escaping earth to go to heaven, they are seeking to make earth more heaven-like in anticipation of God's eventual and victorious transformation of the whole cosmos.

Returning to 1 Corinthians 15 for the fourth theme we find Paul declaring that as the goal of history God will be "*all in all*" (15.28). Romans 8 contains the fifth theme, that of *new birth*. Paul utilises this commonly-used Jewish metaphor for the emergence of God's new age: birth pangs. This he uses to denote the church, the Spirit, but also, in v. 22 the creation itself. Like the baby emerging from the womb there will be trauma, conclusions, contractions and radical discontinuity as the new creation emerges from the present creation and separates from it.

The sixth theme, *the marriage of heaven and earth*, is perhaps the Bible's greatest image of new creation. It is found in Revelation 21-22. In chapter 21, as in Philippians 3, the heavenly Jerusalem, which stands for the people of God, comes to earth rather than the faithful going to heaven. There is no temple; God dwells with God's people and Jesus, the Lamb, is as a husband to the Church. The first five verses of Chapter 22 describe the River of the Water of Life flowing from the throne of God and the Lamb out into the City. As Wright sums it up:

> "It is the final answer to the Lord's Prayer, that God's kingdom would come and God's will be done on earth as in heaven....It is the final fulfilment, in richly symbolic imagery, of the promise of Genesis one, that the creation of male and female would together reflect God's image into the world....And it is the final accomplishment of God's grand design, to defeat and abolish death for ever - which can only mean the rescue of creation from its present state of decay."[37]

That is the basis of Christian eco-theological hope.

David - Science and Christian Hope

Science, however, does not seem to share this hope. As the cartoon at the beginning of this chapter shows, science and fundamentalist Christianity seem at last to have something in common to be unhopeful about! This is reflected in at least four aspects of current scientific thinking: the destruction of the environment; mass extinctions of species; the end of the Sun; and the end of the Universe whose rate of expansion is increasing. All of these topics warrant theological attention. So, too, does the likelihood of massive, civilisation- and life-ending catastrophes - collisions with asteroids, nuclear war and the like. Behind all of this destruction lies the concept of entropy. Contrary to the theory of evolution, entropy describes the tendency of the universe to move towards greater disorder or randomness. That, of course, points to the eventual death of all life, which in turn asks sharp questions of the theological concepts of "old creation" and "new creation".

These important matters, and the vast size and age of the universe, all need much closer theological attention than this book can give.[38] However, the question of how Christian theology can speak of hope and new creation when the evidence that climate scientists produce points increasingly to the earth's environment being badly degraded is a good example of this tension between faith and science. Writing Australia's largest catchment area, the Murray-Darling Basin, Paul Sinclair has written:

> "On a 100-year time scale…the ecological changes caused by agricultural and urban development and regulation of the river have been severe. On a 1000-year time scale these changes remain profound. On a 100,000-year time scale human activities begin to fade, although they will remain significant. On a million-year scale most human impacts are relatively minor compared to changes caused by geological disruptions. On a billion-year scale even a human-caused mass extinction of plants and animals, which many scientists currently believe to be occurring, would cause only an interesting ripple on the fossil record."[39]

Even within the conservative/evangelical traditions of the Christian church there is sharp disagreement about the age of the universe. Some are convinced by biblical study that the earth is not more than some thousands of years old. Others, who do not think that their commitment to scientific truth clashes with biblical truth are comfortable believing that the earth is billions of years old. In any case, two things can be said briefly in defence of Christian hope against this seemingly crushing weight of science's belief in a vast, old universe. One is called "the Anthropic Principle". This term generally refers to the remarkable degree of "fine-tuning" observed in nature. Physicist Freeman Dyson put it this way:

> "As we look out into the Universe and identify the many accidents of physics and astronomy that have worked together to our benefit, it almost seems as if the Universe must have known in some sense that we were coming."[40]

There is, of course, much debate about the Anthropic principle. (Isn't it, too, very anthropocentric?) However, the argument that the Universe is formed in such a way that life, and in particular life that is conscious of itself, can be sustained and even develop in it points for many to there being a Creator.

This also supports the other point in defence of hope, which is that death has been defeated.

> "Listen," wrote St Paul, "I will tell you a mystery! We will not all die, but we will all be changed, [52] in a moment, in the twinkling of an eye, at the last trumpet. For the trumpet will sound, and the dead will be raised imperishable, and we will be changed. [53] For this perishable body must put on imperishability, and this mortal body must put on immortality. [54] When this perishable body puts on imperishability, and this mortal body puts on immortality, then the saying that is written will be fulfilled:
>
> 'Death has been swallowed up in victory.'
> **55** 'Where, O death, is your victory?
> Where, O death, is your sting?'"[41]

Indeed this is a mystery, but it is a hope-full mystery. Paul described Death as 'the last enemy'. It is for life what entropy is for creation in general. And ecological degradation is a particular form of death, dealt by the living, on the living. The existence of life helps us to comprehend that there may be a Life-giver. And the resurrection of Jesus Christ from the dead points to the general resurrection, the New Creation that God intends for Creation. This is the nature of Christian hope. Given recent scientific discoveries about the sheer size and age of the universe it is tentative. But Christ's resurrection, as scandalous and seemingly impossible as it is, gives us confidence.

Gracy responds

These days the ecological views of scientists with all that they are saying about species extinctions are stunning. And when they say that the world will face its end soon, that is an expression of hopelessness. Nevertheless we need to pay our attention to these scenarios of sad endings of the cosmos.

For we are also nearing the end. But we believe everything will be renewed and reconciled in Christ when he comes again. Until then we need to be trustworthy, patient but active and not passive Christians, which means to be hopeful Christians. Everything will be made new in Christ II Peter 3:5-7,13 says:

"...for they deliberately overlook this fact that the heavens existed long ago and the earth was formed out of water and through water by the word of God, and that by means of this the world that then existed was deluged with water and perish. But by the same word the heavens and the earth that now exist are stored up for fire, being kept until the Day of Judgment and destruction of the ungodly. But according to his promise we are waiting for heavens and a new earth in which righteousness dwells."

With the above knowledge of the scripture one could get a wrong understanding: that God destroyed this world with water and that God is planning to destroy it with fire. If that is so, what is the point of eco theology? We need to understand the disaster at the time of Noah. The disaster took place because of the corruption of the people (Genesis 6:6-7). But when God planned to destroy he had given a grace period for all to turn to God (I Peter 3:20). Noah was not only asked to build an ark but also he preached the good news to turn their hearts to God from their evil doings. (Genesis 6:19, 20) They formerly did not obey when God patiently waited in the days of Noah, while the ark was being prepared.

In other words Noah was an 'eco-missionary', an "anti-corruption campaigner" who escaped from the disaster. He took part in the mission of God's saving act. But people never understood what he revealed. The unique responsibility of stewardship was given to a human (Noah) to nurture nature but not to abuse it. And through his work eight persons and all the species of creatures were saved.

God made His promise not to again destroy the earth by disaster. But the scriptures also predict a disaster caused by fire or global warming. Peter predicts that: fire will be the weapon of the great disaster. It is the time to emphasize that global warming may lead us to a pathetic and miserable ending. Even the scientists say that the world is going to be destroyed as the planet can be destroyed in a fire ball.

The Lord is our God of covenant who promised to Noah that he would retain the seasons and not destroy anymore. Destroying the earth is not God's will; rather, nurturing it is. Now it is the right time for us to have a right understanding of the creation of God, to restructure our theological concerns and to take up the responsibility towards ecology. Today our stands and responsibility should be realistic. Here and now and should not be too late.

Conclusion

At a time when the very title given to the epoch in which we live – the "Holocene" – has been changed to the "Anthropocene", what does the future hold? How shall we then live at a time in which, regardless of religious and scientific beliefs, we humans are having a greater effect on the planet in which we live than ever before. What does this have to do with Christian faith and Christian theology. To the great, world-wide ecological discussion Christians can contribute a renewed theologies of Creation, and of Hope, stimulated by the conviction that a good God never intended to allow this good creation to be expunged. Rather, it will be transformed into God's New Creation.

Questions for Discussion

1. Do you have hope? Why? Why not?

2. What do you believe that the future holds?

3. What does this have to do with your Christian faith?

For Further Reading

Dean Drayton. *Pilgrim in the Cosmos: A Spirit Journey*. Adelaide: OpenBook Publishers, 1996.

John Eldredge. *All Things New: Heaven, Earth and the Restoration of Everything you Love*. Nashville: Nelson Books, 2017.

Clive Hamilton & Richard Denniss *Affluenza. When Too much is never Enough* Allen & Unwin, 2005.

Jürgen Moltmann. *Theology of Hope: On the Ground and the Implications of a Christian Eschatology*. Minneapolis: Augsburg Fortress, 1993.

N.T. Wright. *Surprised by Hope*. London: SPCK, 2007.

Endnotes

[1] "But the day of the Lord will come like a thief, and then the heavens will pass away with a loud noise, and the elements will be dissolved with fire, and the earth and everything that is done on it will be disclosed."

[2] Eg. Psalm 102:26; Isaiah 24:19; Isaiah 34:4; Isaiah 51:6; Micah 1:4; Matthew 24:35; Matthew 24:43; Luke 12:39; 1 Corinthians 1:8; 1 Thessalonians 5:2.

[3] Oxford Dictionary of English.

[4] Former Vice President of the USA and now one of the planet's great "climate warriors". That phrase he uttered at a training session for climate change slide sho presenters, September 2007, Melbourne at which the author was present.

[5] As argued by Shashi Tharoor in *Inglorious Empire: What the British Did to India* London, C Hurst & Co., 2017.

[6] For example, St. Thomas of Aquinas in *Summa Teologica*, published 1485.

[7] Genesis 9:1-17.

[8] Joel 2:21-27.

[9] The tree is called as *zilon* which means stick or wood.

[10] Revelation 22:1-5.

[11] Ezekiel 37:5.

[12] Ps.104:29,30; Joel 2:28.

[13] Bashar which gives the understanding of flesh irrespective of particular image.

[14] John 3.16.

[15] Jeremiah 29.11.

[16] Italics the author's.

[17] 1 Corinthians13:13.

[18] Revelation 21:2.

[19] 2 Corinthians 5:17, 20.

[20] John 3:16.

[21] 1Corinthians 15:45.

[22] 1 Corinthians 15:42-44.

[23] 'Creatio ex nihilo'.

[24] His "Theology of Hope: On the Ground and the Implications of a Christian Eschatology" was published in German as early as 1965, before Lynn White's famous article "The Historical Roots of our Ecological Crisis".

[25] The study of the last things.

[26] Jürgen Moltmann *Gott in der Schöpfung: Ökologische Schöpfungslehre* Munich, Christian Kaiser Verlag, 1985.

[27] Celia E. Deane-Drummond *Ecology in Jürgen Moltmann's Theology* Eugene, Oregon, Wipf & Stock, 2016, p.257.

[28] Cross-shaped.

[29] Mark I. Wallace, "*The Wounded Spirit as the Basis of Hope in an Age of Radical Ecology*", pp.51-72 in Dieter T. Hessel and Rosemary Radford Ruether, Eds. *Christianity and Ecology: Seeking the Well-Being of Earth and Humans*, Cambridge MA, Harvard, Harvard University Center for the Study of World Religious Publications, 2000

[30] The study of the Holy Spirit.

[31] "N.T. Wright, Surprised by Hope, London, SPCK, 2007, pp. 104-109.

[32] Getting Better, Writers Paul McCartney, John Lennon.

[33] Clive Hamilton & Richard Denniss *Affluenza: When Too much is never Enough* Allen & Unwin, 2005.

[34] Wright, pp. 102-103.

[35] Ibid., p.99.

[36] 1 Corinthians 15:20, 23.

[37] N.T. Wright *Surprised by Hope,* London, SPCK, 2007, p.119.

[38] Dean Drayton has faced these issues squarely in his theological autobiography *Pilgrim in the Cosmos: A Spirit Journey*, Adelaide, OpenBook Publishers, 1996

[39] Paul Sinclair, *The Murray: A River and Its People* (Carlton South, Vic.: Melbourne University Press, 2001)., 31.

[40] Freeman Dyson, *Disturbing the Universe,* New York, Harper & Row, 1979, p.250.

[41] 1 Corinthians 15:51-55.

ॐ

Reflection

The chapter addresses the fundamental question of End and Hope in the context of ecological crisis faced by humanity.

Eschatology, or the doctrine of the last things, is reflection on the Christian hope for the completion of human life in perfect fellowship with God and others and for the consummation of God's purpose for all creation.[1] A doctrine of creation would be incomplete if it failed to emphasize that the creation still groans for its liberation and completion (Romans 8:22).

Our eschatological vision is distorted due to the emphasis we have given on desperation (gave rise to extreme apocalypticism) than on hope. It differs fundamentally from the hope of the New Testament. Such an eschatology is a serious departure from the hope based in the gospel of Jesus Christ.

In contrast to such a distorted eschatology, the New Testament hope is centred not on a blessed rapture but on the coming of the crucified and resurrected Jesus and the accompanying call to faithful discipleship in the here and now. It is a hope focused on the redemptive power of God, whose judgement is real and severe but whose mercy endures forever.[2]

Christian hope must include, hope for the *fulfilment of personal, communal/corporate* and *cosmic life*. The final victory belongs to God, not to death (1 Corinthians 15). It encompasses the entire creation.

The fulfilment for which we yearn cannot be found apart from the renewal and transformation of the heaven and the earth to which we are bound in life and death.[3]

What should we do?

- Should we continue a linear understanding of eschatology? God's vision for the creation is restoration not destruction. It is New Creation.
- The language of Christian hope is mired in images; therefore, it needs to be properly interpreted and not taken literally.
- The eschatological symbols must be interpreted non-dualistically and must be shown to encompass the quest for fulfilment and wholeness in all dimensions of life.[4]
- Biblical eschatology is intrinsically connected to Ethics. Christian hope should evocate, motivate and give birth to creative human activity. It is a commission for a task – to 'till' and 'keep' the creation.
- Reading the Bible greenly, i.e., to re-read the Bible from ecological eyes.
- Search for new hermeneutical tools. Reinterpretation of scripture not in terms of destruction in the end but by preservation and keeping it safe.
- Dramas/skits in the church services on ecological crisis and biblical reflections thereafter. Highlight what belongs to all the creation not just the earth dwellers.

Endnotes

[1] Daniel L. Migliore, *Faith Seeking Understanding: An Introduction to Christian Theology*, 2nd ed. (Grand Rapids, Michigan/ Cambridge, UK: William B. Eerdmans Publishing Company, 2004), 330.

[2] Ibid., 337.

[3] Ibid., 340-41.

[4] Ibid., 341.

Samuel George

CHAPTER - 8

Living in the Here and Now

Seforosa Carroll & Chilkuri Vasantha Rao

Editor's note

In this final chapter Rev. Dr. Seforosa Carroll and Rev. Dr. Professor Chilkuri Vasantha Rao employ a handful of case studies to examine how a Christian environmental ethic might be applied in particular situations. Issues of climate justice naturally come to the fore

Seforosa Carroll

Part A

The life of our individuals and communities is intertwined within the inter-relatedness of life in human beings, in trees, in plants, in insects, in birds, in fish, in reptiles ... our life can never be separated from land, sea, river, air etc. If we try to separate ourselves from land and look at it objectively as just the source of resources for economical development we may not respect its spiritual existence, thus we destroy life in its inter-relatedness and inter-dependence. Our existence and our survival can never be separated from our land and sea. Our life in God is in creation. God is our bread of life and our water of life in our land and sea ... Our tropical forest is the home and garden of many species as well as our human communities ... Our land and sea are us and we are them. Do not separate us. If you do so, you are murdering us.[1]

Introduction

Global warming and rising sea levels are part of a much larger shift that is a movement away from the Holocene to the Anthropocene. In terms of climate justice (a fraught term) it is widely recognised that those most at risk in this emerging environmental crisis are not those who belong to land and cultures which are economically privileged. It is usually the poor, those without a powerful voice and the most vulnerable. They are often the least responsible for the effects of climate change and are dependent on those responsible for climate change to own and fulfill their moral and ethical responsibility to the environment.[2]

The impact of climate change is anticipated to displace up to 250 million people worldwide by 2050. (Sunjic, 2008). The office of the United Nations High Commissioner for Refugees (UNHCR) estimates that 'an annual average of 21.5 million people have been forcibly displaced by weather-related sudden onset hazards – such as floods, storms, wildfires, extreme temperature – each year since 2008' (Internal Displacement Monitoring Centre, 2016). The Internal Displacement Monitoring Center's (IDMC) 2016 global displacement report recorded 19.2 million NEW displacements across 113 countries as a result of disasters in 2015 (Internal Displacement Monitoring Centre, 2016).

In this chapter, I present an overview of the impact of climate change in the Pacific, in particular, the role of theology in bringing about transformative change as well as how the received legacy of a particular way of thinking about creation has been a barrier to effective change. Although the Pacific and India are very different contexts, it is hoped that there might be common experiences and theological wisdom that can be shared across both contexts that may help to guide, shape and provide hope for communities living in the here and now; in the face of ecological destruction and the impending loss of home.

Firstly, why the Pacific? I am a Pacific Island migrant woman. I have been living in Australia (Sydney) for the past thirty years. I grew up in Lautoka, the Western side of the island Viti Levu. Lautoka is known for its significant Indian population, a legacy of the indentured labourers scheme that brought many Indian labourers to Fiji in the late 1800s. I am a Minister of the Uniting Church in Sydney Australia. I am currently serving in a placement with the Uniting Church Assembly as the Church Partnerships manager for the Pacific region. My role entails frequent visits to the Pacific, supporting our church partners in their mission and ministry, and wrestling together to create life affirming faith responses to issues such as climate change and domestic violence. What I have found working with Pacific island communities is that faith and church are critical to bringing about transforming change in the Pacific.

The Pacific is among a number of countries in the world on the forefront of climate change. For those in Tuvalu, Kiribati, Marshall Islands time is already running out for them. Their future is uncertain and they are destined to lose their home, it is a matter of when. Within the last two years Tonga, Vanuatu, Fiji and Samoa have experienced destructive category 4 and 5 cyclones. The effects of El Nino are currently being experienced in the highlands of Papua New Guinea, parts of Vanuatu and Fiji. Many continue to die of hunger due to famine. It is expected that 4.37 million people in the Pacific are likely to be affected and at risk from drought. These cited examples are only a handful of destructive climate disasters with many more to come. Climate change impact now characterises life in the Pacific.

It is perhaps too easy for us to say to a Tuvaluan or I-Kiribati or a person from a severely climate impacted country to consider relocation. In response to this a Tuvaluan young man has said "People are saying relocate to another country, if you have been affected by climate change, move elsewhere. But wherever we go climate change will always catch up with us".[3] This insightful quote highlights how climate change will eventually affect us all. Climate change is everyone's problem and everyone's responsibility – some more than others. Climate change requires an ongoing concerted international response to address this very real threat to our earth and its human and non-human inhabitants.

Climate Change exacerbates poverty and gender inequality. The poor are particularly vulnerable to climate change. In this instance women are doubly marginal, as they make up 70% of the worlds poor. Generally, the poor are affected and further disadvantaged by climate changes such as disruption to rainfall and seasonal weather patterns which affect traditional agricultural and fishing cycles as it incapacitates the poor's ability to grow and harvest food, fish and collect reliable drinking water. Large-scale climate disruption due to disasters further disturbs agricultural and other seasonal cycles that the poor depend upon.

Women naturally bear the full brunt of climate change more than their male counterparts as they are the caregivers and nurturers of these communities. They are predominantly responsible for the household or community management of food production, water supply and energy for heating and cooking. Rev Maleta Tenten, Secretary for Mission of the Kiribati Uniting Church states, "Climate change increases the workload of women at home – care-work for children, the sick, the elderly, the disabled ... Women bare the brunt of climate change".

As climate change impact increases, these tasks become more difficult to do. Women face difficulties in terms of the general accessibility of financial resources, capacity-building activities and technologies. It has been recognised, however, that women have knowledge and coping strategies that give them a practical understanding of innovation and skills to adapt to changing environmental realities as well as to contribute to the solution. Unfortunately, these strategies to deal with climate variability are still a largely untapped resource. In addition Rev Tenten expressed concern for the correlation between the increase of violence (against women) and climate change impact.[4]

There are additional challenges that come to bear on the Pacific. The excessive use and dependence on fossil fuels by countries in the West has had an ongoing detrimental effect on the Pacific. In addition excessive mining and logging has left many Pacific countries economically vulnerable. The need to balance a healthy and viable economy with the management and sale of natural resources has left many Pacific countries vulnerable to climate change. For low lying atoll countries like Tuvalu, Kiribati, Tokelau, Marshall Islands and the Maldives (often referred to as "disappearing islands") the effects of rising sea levels is leading to the increased loss of inhabitable land, drinking water, health problems and increasing solastalgia.[5] An equally grave challenge islanders are facing in the midst of devastating ecological destruction is faith.

Wolfgang Kempf observes that "what we rarely find in debates within the humanities and social sciences on the consequences of climate change and sea level rise for the Pacific Island states is systematic attention being given to how Christianity has influenced local perceptions of this thematic complex.[6] The reason for this omission Kempf argues lies in the contradiction between science and religion and the struggle experienced by Islanders (and many other Christians) "to reconcile scientific findings and projections about climate change and sea level rise with their own Christian convictions".[7] There are a number of reasons behind the resistance to and the inability to engage with the challenges of climate change and its impact on Pacific communities by church leaders.

The legacy of Christian theology received in the Pacific has encouraged and endorsed a dualistic thinking in terms of thinking about the relationship between land and people. Pacific islanders have been influenced by a particular interpretation of the Genesis creation story. This understanding of the Genesis creation story privileges the human being as having full authority or dominion over creation and lead to the eventual misunderstanding and separation in the relationship between humans ad creation. The ancient Pacific worldview was to understand people, land, sea and creation as interdependent. Leslie Bosetto's quote at the beginning of this chapter attests to the intimate relationship between Pacific Islanders and land as well as the imperative need to reclaim indigenous worldviews that affirms interdependent relationship.

Secondly, the personalised/individualised understanding of salvation and redemption has been very influential in the Pacific. In the context of climate change this understanding has led to a two-pronged response. The first is manifested in a passive faith which believes that "God will save us" and that all that is required is "to faithfully wait". Secondly, the effects of climate change is seen as a form of punishment by God for sin(s)[8] and a visible sign of an imminent *parousia* which cultivates an attitude of resignation at best and a deep sense of hopelessness at worst. Finally, the understanding of home as the "heavenly home", whereby heaven is spiritualised as a paradisical afterlife has led to a strong understanding that "we are passive recipients in the here and now".

In the context of Tuvalu and Kiribati there are two interrelated themes at play. The first is the impending loss of home; the second is the necessary migration that the loss of home will compel. This impending sense of deep loss has precipitated an understanding of salvation that will come in the form of another Noah's Ark. In this context the Noah story has been interpreted to be about claiming the promise, the covenant made by God with Noah never to flood the earth again. The current rising sea levels presents a stark contrast and often raises two sets of responses. The first is to stand rigidly by the promise that God will save or that the flood will never come to Tuvalu or Kiribati. The second response is to ask "where is and how is God present in our suffering"? The later response requires a courageous shift in thinking and imagination. It entails an openness to undertake a journey that encourages a new interpretation of the Noah narrative. Alternatively, it presents an opportune time, a *kairos* moment to find new biblical stories and texts that resonate with our experience in the here and now with and in the hope of what has been promised to come.

Kempf suggests that a reinterpretation of the Noah story can act as a positive counter narrative to hegemonic climate change discourses or empire citing the 2004 WCC Otin Taai declaration as an example.

> We would like to say a word about God's promise to Noah not to flood the earth again. Some Christians view this covenant as a guarantee that they are not at risk of flooding from climate change. But the sea level is rising and threatening Pacific Islands with flooding from high tides and storm surges. This is not an act of God. It is a result of human economic and consumer activities that pollute the atmosphere that lead to climate change. Our response to God's covenant with Noah should be to act in love toward God's creation and to reduce pollution that is contributing to climate change. By placing us on earth, God has given us both the right to use it and the responsibility to do so with care.[9]

The *Otin Tai* declaration does not shy away from engaging with the Noah narrative but rather makes the case that contrary to the biblical narrative where the flood was sent as an act of punishment by God; the current ecological crisis is not an act of God or divine displeasure but is a result of human activity. In this way the Noah narrative functions as a prophetic call by calling into account our responsibility as custodians of creation. On the other hand the narrative can be interpreted as a wake up call to us Christians. The I-Kiribati composer Nenem Kourabi composed the song *AI Kamira Kanoan Te Bong*[10] based on his interpretation of the Noah narrative. He argued that Noah had been warned by God that a flood would come and God's instruction to Noah was to "be prepared". In his interpretation of the story within the Kiribati context Kourabi understands the narrative as a call to "read the signs of the times". In this sense Kourabi reads "the scientific forecasts as a warning and equally as an opportunity to shoulder responsibility by taking whatever steps were necessary".[11] Kourabi emphasises that

> what I had in mind, what I was getting at, were the words "be prepared"… Noah was given adequate warning… And now, in our own day, scientific prediction is a sign or a warning given to us… Be prepared before it happens! (cited in Kempf 78-79)

The work needing to be done in the Pacific with regard to climate change impact is manifold. These can be divided into two parts. There is a need for internal and external work. The internal work relates to theology and the recovery of and relationship with Pacific indigenous epistemologies. What is required is a life affirming theological response that reframes understanding of salvation as the flourishing of God's household.[12] It is also to understand redemption as that which is about reconciling, healing and the proper custodianship of our resources. It is to understand our relationship with creation as interrelated and interdependent. The practical outworking of this understanding is to cultivate an ethic of care that values relationship, interconnectedness and interrelatedness of our relationship and place with the earth. It will require a shift in thinking, practice and developing new habits or homemaking practices. Homemaking practices are intentional habits that make the ideal of home (the way God had initially intended) possible. Home then is eschatological. We know what home can or should be but we live in the reality of what home is not.

Home and homecoming is in the journeying that is home. Ernst Conradie describes this journeying as oikeiosis, which can be translated as the making of a home.[13] It is Conradie's conviction that we humans are not yet at home on the earth. He coined the word oikeiosis to describe the journey towards reconciliation with ourselves and our place in the larger scheme of things. That larger scheme of things is God's oikonomia. Here home is not so much about a goal or arrival at a destination; home is in the actual journeying or movement itself in and through which we ourselves are changed. In a very broad sense home is about how we choose to faithfully live out our Christian discipleship and also how we respectfully manage our relationships with others and place in the here and now. What we do here and now matters!

Rev. Dr. Cliff Bird suggests five basic rules or principles for homemaking practices and earth care. He argues that when the metaphor of home is applied to how we understand the earth as home, this can "transform how we live, walk and work for both our family homes and the Earth".[14] These rules are expressed in the following way:

- Take only your share;

- Share what you have;

- Clean up after yourself;

- Give the respect that is rightfully due to others; Keep the house in good condition and repair for others.

The first rule sets the limit on what one should take and use. It works on the ethic of self-restraint and self-control. It seeks to ensure that one consumes and utilises resources responsibly and with care. The second rule works on the premise that the benefits and resources exist for the whole human and non-human household. As such they should be regulated on the principle of sharing and reciprocity so all may have enough. The third rule emphasises the need for members of the household to keep the home clean and tidy. It is a caution against polluting and littering the home in which we all share and live. The fourth rule ensures that each human and non-human members of the household are respected for they are. It is to respect the dignity and integrity of the whole of creation on the grounds that all bear the image of God in some intrinsic way. The fifth rule seeks to safeguard the well being of the earth for the future. It stresses the need to keep the home in a healthy and viable state for future generations to continue to live in. In this respect present dwellers are called on to exercise proper care and custodianship for the earth for the sake of its future.

Finally, the external work that is required beyond the Pacific to do with advocacy and climate justice. This is work that is required by countries and churches outside of and in partnership with the Pacific. Pacific Islanders feel a deep sense of injustice and powerlessness. They have had very little to do to cause the predicament they find themselves in. Their foremost concern is calling polluting countries to account for their actions and to reduce their emissions and/or contribute to finding ways (and paying for costs) for adapting to the effects of climate change. Underlying this overwhelming concern is the hope that if emission levels are kept to a safe minimum, than there is the possibility that Pacific Island countries may have a longer time and opportunity to save their homes. This, however, does not address the likelihood of future inevitable migration. But this does not mean that migration is not an option that has not been considered. A point of contention for the Pacific concerns when climate change migration will become a prominent policy issue to be discussed between countries of likely origin and possible destination, as well as between Pacific Island countries and greenhouse emitting countries. Although it is recognised that dialogues such as this should happen this has not always been the case. New Zealand has by far been the exception resolving in November 2017 to consider creating a climate change refugee status for people displaced by rising seas. How and whether this policy is developed remains to be seen.

This in turn raises another challenge, that of climate justice. It is not clear, though, what climate justice might mean in actual practice. Addressing carbon emissions and rising temperatures may not necessarily address historic injustices brought about by the colonial systems of the past several centuries. Climate change does not take place in a vacuum. It is a result of development policies, inequalities within and between countries, global justice and the lack of solidarity between states. As Henry Shue contends there is a two-fold process embedded into narratives of climate justice, but it is not clear which one of the two – seeking to regulate climate or redeeming injustice – should be given priority.[15]

Chilkuri Vasantha Rao
Part A

From the Indian side I would like to begin with my own observations about the situation in the Pacific region and specifically in Tuvalu. While at a consultation of the Council for World Mission in Manila, Philippines, on 23th April, 2015, in my devotion I remarked:

> Maina Thalia from Tuvalu, Pacific region, explains that none of the Christian partner churches responded to a crisis situation, whereas the other people of other faiths not only came to rescue but also asked about the absence of the Christian church. The Christian church in the region of Tuvalu missed being in the *Missio-Dei*, it also missed being in the interfaith co-operation, it missed showing love to the brothers and sisters in crisis, it earned the mistrust of the fellow humans and the creation in distress. The other religions people were engaged in the *Missio-Dei* and not the Christian church. (See Youtube: CWM Consultation in Manila, Philippines, devotion by Rev. Dr. Chilkuri Vasantha Rao, CSI, 23.4.2015, accessed on 12th May 2018 at 10 PM.)

While I make a remark about the floods in Tuvalu and the danger of the island being inundated in waters, the Indian situation is predominantly the scarcity of water, of course not ignoring the flooding events.

Although I am all set to explain the response of the Church in India to the climate change and global warming this has been taken care of in chapter six. Hence, I would then concentrate on the responses and engagements in India.

The global climate has changed and it has affected the ecology, environment and resources. It also has its impact on the bio-diversity on the planet. Global warming, climate change, pollution and ecological balance these are some of the major ecological concerns. It is also a day to day concern and calls us to mend our behavior and nature of relationship with the creation that God has given us freely to keep and care. This task of caring and keeping requires a vision and mission so that God's purpose of creating the creation is continued and sustained for the betterment of whole of God's creation.

Here I would like to place before you a few intervention measures carried on to combat ecological crisis to bring change and positive impact. The eco-measures that are taken by the Government of Telangana are commendable, such as:

Mission Kakatiya - Renewal of village water Tanks

Tanks are the life line of Telengana State. The State's agriculture is highly dependent on the tanks which are spread across. The topography and rainfall pattern in the context have made tank irrigation an ideal type of irrigation by storing and regulating water flow for agricultural use. Due to lack of maintenance, dumping wastes, siltation, breaches, and encroachments led to the disappearance of village water tanks leading to acute drought.

Realizing the importance of reclamation of water tanks, the Government of Telangana State has taken up the programme of restoring the minor irrigation sources with the title "Mission Kakatiya (*Mana Ooru Mana Cheruvu* – Our Village our Water Tank)". The mission aims at retrieving the lost glory of minor irrigation in the state with community participation for ensuring sustainable water security. As per the enumeration, the total number of tanks is found to be around 46,531 and storing 265 TMC Water across the state. The irrigation department determined to restore all the 46,531 minor irrigation sources in the state in next five years, taking up 20% of the tanks each year. The objectives of the mission are to enhance the development of agriculture-based income for small and marginal farmers, by accelerating the development of minor irrigation infrastructure. It is a people's program to safeguard life on the earth.

As a result, it helped to increase the irrigated area. It also increased the bio-diversity, reduced usage of power (electricity), which was used to pump water to the fields. It also helped to increase the water storage capacity and ground water levels. In Telengana Rural Villages this mission has been very successful.

Rain Water Harvest

A recharge pit allows the rainwater to replenish groundwater by recharging the ground aquifers, which can be built to recharge a bore-well or just to help water infiltration in an area. It is a pit totally invisible when finished, filled with stones and does not present any danger. The percolation rate of a recharge pit is much less than of an open well. The water percolates slowly because there is no hydrostatic pressure in the pit. The rainwater harvesting –Recharge Pits are very successful in Rural villages such as, Thonda and Phanigiri villages of Telangana State among others. The government is financially supporting this project under the village development schemes.

Haritha Haram (Increasing Forest Cover)

"Plant a Tree and Plant a Life." Haritha Haram is a large-scale tree planting program implemented by the Government of Telengana to increase the amount of tree coverage in the state from 24% to 35%, which is being achieved in several phases. Its objective is planting trees in the areas outside the existing forest in order to rejuvenate degraded forests. This program also is protecting the forests from threats such as smuggling, encroachment, fire, and grazing. It is adopted to increase intensive soil and moisture conservation measures based on a watershed approach to maintain environmental stability and ecological balance which is vital for the sustenance of all life-forms, be it human, animal or plant.

The program uses multiple planting models: Avenues Plantation: Planting trees at road-side avenues-National Highways & State Highways, river and canal banks, barren hills, tank bunds and foreshore areas, institutional premises, religious places, housing colonies, community lands, municipalities and industrial parks. Block Plantation: Planting trees in waste lands and common lands. These plantations are raised in the vicinity of the villages. Institutional Plantation: Planting is done at Schools, Colleges, Government Institutions, Hospitals, Graveyards, *Smrithi Vanam*

(Memorial Parks) & *Mukti Vanam* (Liberation Grove), Private Institutions and Industries. Tank Fore Shore Plantation - Planting is done at Tank Fore Shores. Homestead Plantation - Planting will be around the Houses and colonies to meet Household needs. Agro Forestry Plantation - Planting is done on farmlands. Barren hill - Planting is done on Barren Hillocks. In the 1st phase - 15.86 crore seedlings were planted and in the 2nd phase 186 km land was planted with 31.67 crore seedlings. These plants were watered and fenced so that they grow and yield fruits.

People's initiative for replenishing depleted forests

The residents of Narapally, Uppal, Hyderabad district, have a commitment for replenishing the forest area in their geographical limits. The depleted forest is replenished with people's initiative. Before the onset of monsoons, the residents of Narapally, with the help of a Non-Governmental Organization, voluntarily dig pits in all the open spaces in the forest. These pits are well placed all along the slopes, ensuring that the pits will gather rain water during the rains. While digging the pits the soil is placed right on the edges of the pits. It is on this loose soil, at the edges of the pits, selected saplings are planted which could take root easily by absorbing rain water from the pits. This practice year after year has made the forest dense and the selected species of plants grow fruits and gives other important yields for the usage of the residents around the forest.

This forest, due to its increased density, has attracted the vultures to settle down and make it as their choice habitat. Today this forest serves as a natural vulture breeding centre. The residents take much care by time to time getting information from the government by way of Right to Information Act (RTA) to know if any projects are being planned which could jeopardize the forest by human presence in it. They ensure that the forest is not damaged. Forest is their good neighbour. The Narapally people's commitment looms as a model to all communities to rise up to the occasion and fight air pollution and check forest depletion and support life, increase flora and fauna and their own healthy sustenance.

Government's initiative to curb air pollution

The Capital city of India, which is Delhi, has suffered severe air pollution. Delhi air pollution has crossed all levels of reasonability and beyond the capacity of the meters that read the air pollution levels in the city. The thick smog has reduced the visibility on the roads becoming a big obstacle for the commuting traffic causing accidents, it also resulted in delay and even cancellation of public transportation of some buses, trains and flights.

Pollution related diseases and health hazards have increased. The Delhi government has declared a health emergency. The Indian Medical Association has advised the inhabitants of Delhi to stay indoors to avoid the ill effects of high levels of pollution on their health. International officials of high ranks representing their counties in India having their Consulates in Delhi were discouraged from staying in Delhi.

Delhi government has taken measures to control air pollution in the Capital by various methods, such as; the Delhi Transport Corporation has converted its buses to run on eco-friendly alternative fuel i.e., Compressed Natural Gas (CNG) thereby arresting exhaust. The Supreme Court made it mandatory for all taxis to convert to CNG and not to allow commercial vehicles registered before 2005 into Delhi. The Apex Court has banned the registration of luxury SUV's and diesel cars above 2000cc in the Delhi limits. Commercial vehicles that enter Delhi limits are to pay a high green cess. Both the central and state governments are directed not to buy diesel vehicles anymore. The diesel vehicles that are in use at the moment are to be phased out.

In order to further reduce vehicular emissions, the administration has come out with Odd/even rule, thus the cars with plates having odd numbered registration are to ply on odd dates and even numbered registration plates are to ply on the even dates.

Directions banning 'burning of waste', 'burning of crop residue' and fine on the 'emission of construction dust' have been issued by the National Green Tribunal and the concerned authorities have become strict in taking action on the offenders. This is one example as to how a government is serious and active in controlling air pollution in India, which stands as an initiative for all cities to be emulated.

In my recent visit to Aizwal, Mizoram, we took note that the Aizwal City Administration, in order to control air pollution and traffic congestion, has made a rule that the vehicles number ending corresponding to the date of the day would not be driven on the roads on that particular day. This would mean, suppose a vehicle ending with the numeral "XXXX5" would not be on the roads three times in a month, i.e., on 5th, 15th and 25th, and so is the case with every numeral. This is being implemented and the results are encouraging.

Domestic Solar Panels

In order to decrease pollution solar panels over the roof of houses and Churches are being used as the main source of energy instead of regular electricity. By using solar energy, fans, lights, water heaters and other appliances are put to use.

As one example from among the many churches we take note that the CSI St. Peter's Church, Suryapet, Karimnagar Diocese (Telangana, India) is completely run by using energy which comes through solar panels. The Andhra Christian Theological College, Hyderabad, apart from its solar lights, solar water heating, it has also erected solar panels that generate huge solar power, which is being sold to the State Electricity Board. In Kacheguda and Secunderabad Railway Stations this alternate energy is used to run fans, lights and other railway appliances. In many of the villages in Telangana and Andhra Pradesh, solar panels are used for street lights. Many secular educational institutions as well Christian educational institutions are switching to solar energy.

Government is also providing subsidy and loans for those who come forward to use this as their main source of power/energy.

Solar Farms or Solar Fields

While home owners use solar panels on their roofs, aim to generate power to cover their individual energy needs, large utility-scale solar farms are designed to generate enough electricity to power thousands of homes and businesses. A solar farm is a collection of solar arrays on unused land for the purpose of generating power from the sun's energy. Large commercial photovoltaic (PV) solar farms typically use hundreds or thousands of photovoltaic panels covered to convert the sun's rays into electricity.

Indian Government is concentrating and encouraging agencies and individual land owners to convert their unused land for generating power through solar fields or farms which produce no pollution of any kind, for e.g. Kurnool Ultra Mega Solar Park is a solar park spread over a total area of 6000 acres in Panyam mandal, Kurnool district, Andhra Pradesh. Kadapa Ultra Mega Solar Park is a solar park spread over a total area of 6000 acres in the Galiveedu mandal, Kadapa district, Andhra Pradesh. The Nambulapulakunta Ultra Mega Solar Park, also known as Ananthapur Ultra Mega Solar Park, is a solar park spread over a total area of 8000 acres in Nambulapulakunta mandal, Ananthapur district, Andhra Pradesh, which is supposed to be one of the world's largest solar parks. By using power from the above solar farms/parks/fields, Andhra Pradesh government is supplying power to the nearby villages.

In Kerela, the Cochin International Airport, is the first of its kind in the world to become fully solar powered airport. The airport has erected scores of acres of land with solar panels generating solar power for their own consumption. This initiative has been recognized by the United Nations and is a model to all airports world over.

The unused lands in our Churches, premises, institutions, compounds and missionary fields could be used for the above purpose thereby becoming partners in generating power without pollution.

Wind Energy Plants (Wind Mills)

As one passes through the villages of Kalyandurg, Uravakonda, Kadiri and Ramagiri, Atmakur, Beluguppa, Honnuru, Kudair, Pottipadu, Singanamala, Talaricheruvu, Tallimadugula and Vajrakaruru of Ananthapur District, Andhra Pradesh, one can find giant wind mills pointing the landscape making it into a 'City of Energy'.

Wind energy plants are nothing but producing power by using the unidirectional flow of the wind on the hilly and mountain areas. This wind will rotate the huge fans where the mechanical energy produced by the rotation of the hugs fans is converted into electrical energy which is again non-pollution.

Switching onto Electric Vehicles

According to the Economic Survey conducted in India over the last year, an increase in available disposable income among citizens has led to an increase in the purchase of vehicles and a reduction in the use of public transport. Roads are the dominant medium of travel in the country, and as of 2016 there were 229 million vehicles on the road. With over 3 million vehicles sold in 2016-17 in the four-wheeler segment alone, the total number of vehicles burning petrol and diesel, and spewing dangerous fumes into the air is over 230 million. Despite the increasing pollution in India's cities, vehicles that run on conventional fossil fuels continue to be sold in massive numbers.

India has begun to take the alternative path of arresting pollution; for example, in many metropolitan cities, for easy parking and easy driving, many youngsters, especially software engineers have already begun to use electrical cars and electric two wheelers, for which their companies are providing charging points at parking junctures. It is very gratifying to note that upon my visit to the Believers Church Theological Seminary in Thiruvalla, Kerala, electrical two wheelers are used.

Use of Biogas

In the present-day context, worldwide interest in renewable energy sources is gathering momentum. Biogas production is growing steadily, as more people are setting up biogas plants to produce biogas as alternate energy. The waste food and vegetables are put into the biogas plant and the plant produces gases like methane, hydrogen, and carbon monoxide (CO) and these gases can be combusted or oxidized with oxygen. The energy released out of this chemical reaction is nothing but biogas which in turn is being used as a non-polluting fuel for heating and cooking purpose.

In the rural agricultural setup farmers are more and more reverting to Biogas, which is eco-friendly, simple and low cost with circular benefits.

Institutions like the United Theological College, Bengaluru is using this biogas as alternative energy in the hostel and guest house kitchen.

Vermi-compost or Vermi-culture

Vermi-compost or Vermi-culture means artificial rearing or cultivation of worms specially earthworms to create a mixture of decomposing vegetable or food waste and other decomposable materials. Vermi composting has gained popularity in both industrial and domestic settings because, as compared with conventional composting, it provides a way to treat organic wastes more quickly. VISTHAR an organization in Bengaluru, India, promotes this in the educational institutionals and churches in India.

Conclusions

Chilkuri Vasantha Rao

The Indian response to ecological crisis of climate change and global warming is very encouraging. There are number of initiatives pressed into action by the Governments, Non-Governmental organizations, Churches and the Christian institutions. Moving forward in this direction would only mean that the Indian nation is all set to mitigate the repercussions of the climate change.

Sef Carroll

In this here and now the Pacific church is faced with a challenge. It is called upon to make a journey. This journey is not just simply a physical moving from one place to another. This journey is both spiritual and theological and requires leaders that will rise to the challenge of seeking an eschatological vision of a new heaven and new earth by drawing from both their deepest Christian convictions and Pacific wisdom to lead, sustain and nourish them in this journey. This journey will require different kinds of movements and shifts in thinking about biblical texts, God, theology, Church and HOME. It will mean rethinking that God will save in the form of another Noah's Ark to a God who journeys with us to new places and new dreams. In this sense migration and identity do not necessarily take the form of physically leaving Tuvalu or Kiribati but rather in the form of reinterpreting what migration and identity mean in the face of preserving home amidst the reality of the possible future loss of home.

Questions for Discussion

1. What are some of the similarities and differences between the Pacific context and your context in terms of your understanding of the role of faith in caring for the earth?

2. How do you understand the story of Noah's Ark? How would you interpret that story in a time of climate change impact?

3. How do you understand the relationship between human beings and creation? Following from that understanding, how is God asking us to care for the earth?

4. What are some homemaking practices you could start now to make positive changes for the future?

For Further Study

Books

Ayre, Clive. *Earth, faith and mission: the theology and practice of earthcare*. Eugene, Oregon: Wipf & Stock, 2015.

Delgado, Sharon. *Love in a Time of Climate Change: Honoring Creation, Establishing Justice*. Minneapolis: Fortress Press, 2017.

Doran, Chris. *Hope in the age of climate change: creation care this side of creation*. Eugene, Oregon: Cascade Books, 2017.

Gardiner, Stephen M, Simon Caney, Dale Jamieson, and Henry Shue, eds. *Climate Ethics: Essential Readings*. New York: Oxford University Press, 2010.

Videos

Tuvalu: Faith in a changing climate, https://vimeo.com/239577029

Anote Tong: "My country will be underwater soon – unless we work together" https://www.ted.com/talks/anote_tong_my_country_will_be_underwater_soon_unless_we_work_together.

Tuvalu: Islands on the frontline of climate change, https://vimeo.com/4997847

UN Climate Summit Poem "Dear Matafele Peinem by Kathy Jetnil-Kijiner https://www.youtube.com/watch?v=DJuRjy9k7GA

Endnotes

1 Leslie Boseto, "Do not separate us from our land and sea", *Pacific Journal of Theology*, 13 (1995), p.71

2 See Donald A Brown, *Climate change ethics: navigating the moral storm.* London, New York, Routledge, 2013 and Stephen M Gardiner, *A perfect moral storm: the ethical tragedy of climate change,* New York, Oxford University Press, 2011. Stephen Gardiner argues that climate change must be seen as a moral problem. He uses the metaphor of a storm to demonstrate how three particular problems (storms) converge or intersect to hamper responsibilities and obligations to act ethically. Building on Gardiner's work Dan Brown proposes and maps strategic ways forward on what should be done to address the barriers that Gardiner raises to ethically based policy.

3 From a video interview with a young Tuvaluan man speaking about the impact of climate change on Tuvalu and its future.

4 Author's conversation in 2015 with the Secretary for Mission, Rev Maleta Tenten of the Kiribati Uniting Church.

5 The term solastalgia was coined by Australian environmental professor Peter Albrecht. According to Albrecht solastalgia as "the pain experienced when there is recognition that the place where one resides and that one loves is under immediate assault (physical desolation). It is manifest in an attack on one's sense of place, in the erosion of the sense of belonging (identity) to a particular place and a feeling of distress (psychological) about its transformation. It is an intense desire for the place where one is resident to be maintained in a state that continues to give comfort or solace. In short, solastalgia is a form of homesickness one gets when one is still at home." For further reading see his article "Solastalgia" in http://www.psychoterratica.com/solastalgia.html.

6 Wolfgang Kempf, "The rainbow's power: climate change and sea level rise and reconfigurations of the Noah story in Oceania" in *Pacific Voices: Local government and climate change*, edited by Ropate Qalo. Suva, Fiji: University of the South Pacific 2014, p. 78.

7 Kempf, "The rainbow's power...", pg. 68.

8 Ministers have sometimes commented that churches are often full after a natural disaster believing that this is due to people feeling that natural disasters is God's way of dispensing punishment for sin.

9 The *Otin Tai* declaration, World Council of Churches, 2004. https://www.oikoumene.org/en/resources/documents/wcc-programmes/justice-diakonia-and-responsibility-for-creation/climate-change-water/otin-tai-declaration

[10] How amazing are the events day by day
The global changes
The rising of the sea level,
Is affecting Kiribati

If this is really going
To happen,
Why don't
We get prepared?
The flood in Noah's time
Acted as a warning
The rainbow appearing in the sky
Was the sign of salvation

Listening to scientific advice too
Is a way to salvation
What are our responsibilities?
We have to be prepared.

[11] Kempf, "The rainbow's power…" 78-79.

[12] See Sallie McFague. *A New Climate Change for Theology: God, the World and Global Warming* (Minneapolis: Fortress Press, 2008).

[13] Ernst M Conradie. *An Ecological Christian Anthropology : At Home on Earth?* (Aldershot, U.K.: Ashgate, 2005), 6.

[14] Cliff Bird, "Oceanising" John Wesley? Toward an ecological-ethical reading of John Wesley for contemporary Oceanic Methodists". Unpublished paper presented at the meeting of The Methodist Consultative Council, Pacific in Tonga May 1 -6 2018,12.

[15] Henry Shue, *Climate Justice: Vulnerability and Protection*, (Oxford: Oxford University Press, 2014).

Reflection

Eco-ethics was the focus of the chapter. How Christian faith should propel us to care for creation? It comes under the purview of ethics – environmental ethics. Environmental ethics is the discipline in philosophy that studies the moral relationship of human beings to, and also the value and moral status of, the environment and its non-human contents.[1]

The job of environmental ethics is to outline our moral obligations in the face of such concerns. In a nutshell, the two fundamental questions that environmental ethics must address are: what duties do humans have with respect to the environment, and why? The latter question usually needs to be considered prior to the former.[2]

What about Christian ethics? Does it address adequately the environmental issues? What about our moral obligation towards the creation? Earlier in this book, we have seen how the 'inherited' theologies have side-lined or even neglected the aspect of care for creation. This has affected our ethics too. One of the major flaws of our theologizing is the dualistic approach to creation. This chapter rightly points out that Christian theology as it was 'offered' to the Pacific communities were based on this dualistic approach. Individualized and personalized notion of salvation was offered as the gospel to the communities. This has adversely affected the Christian communities' approach to nature.

Whereas, the traditional Pacific spirituality talks of interdependence between people, land, sea and creation. Shouldn't we go back to these wisdoms that are available in the Pacific spirituality?

The ecological crisis provides us with a *kairos* moment to find new biblical stories and texts that resonate with our experience in the here and now with and in the hope of what has been promised to come. This should propel us to action plans for caring for the creation. The chapter has enough practical suggestions, to, which we add few more that will provide us ways to move forward in the impending crisis that we face.

What should we do?

- A wholistic approach to crisis. This journey will require different kinds of movements and shifts in thinking about biblical texts, God, theology, Church and HOME. Everybody has to chip in to face the challenge of ecological degradation.

- Preservation of bio-diversity should be focused as an ethical goal.

- Need for a creation-centred ethics (not anthropocentric).

- Get the churches and homes to conduct an energy audit and implement improvements.

- Plant deciduous trees along the south side of the house to save on cooling costs.

- Focus on three **R**'s: reduce, reuse, and recycle. Suggestions can be found at www.earth911.org

- Reduce fossil-fuel dependency.

- Practice sufficiency and contentment in all your purchasing decision.

- Practice carpool.

- Take a day of rest – no shopping, no work, no driving – once a week. This will reduce carbon footprints.

Endnotes

[1] Andrew Brennan and Lo, Yeuk-Sze, "Environmental Ethics", *The Stanford Encyclopedia of Philosophy* (Winter 2016 Edition), Edward N. Zalta (ed.), URL = https://plato.stanford.edu/archives/win2016/entries/ethics-environmental/ (accessed August 23, 2018).

[2] Alasdair Cochrane, "Environmental Ethics," https://www.iep.utm.edu/envi-eth/ (accessed August 23, 2018).

Samuel George

Epilogue

I was taken aback to be asked to write the epilogue for this book. What does one say to you, dear reader, when you have just finished reading eight chapters warning you of the impending disaster for planet Earth and seeking your help in facing this future.

This is far worse than an Himalayan avalanche rumbling down from distant peaks, surging along precipitous ravines with rock smashing roar, thundering toward the plains, growing evermore destructive, annihilating all in its path. Or a break in the continental crust near the Andaman Islands, fracturing the sea floor, up and down, pouring almost limitless energy into a giant tsunami that races towards the Eastern coast and surges in for tens of kilometres destroying all before it.

Of course one would act as soon as possible to help put in place early warning systems to alert those in danger and give some the chance to escape these natural disasters. How much more so is the reality when a disaster of human making, global warming, threatens the whole world with higher and higher temperatures, with rising sea levels flooding the coasts of every continent, unleashing extreme weather, threatening apocalyptic social scenarios and irrevocably changing the environment in itself. Some monitoring the rise in carbon dioxide levels warn that already critical systems for weather and the rise in sea level are at "tipping points". This is bigger than we can envisage. But so far the response has mostly been a fatalistic shrugging of the shoulders, a leave it to others to deal with, a turning back from doing anything, continuing on in the private world of our own dreams.

WHAT ARE YOU GOING TO DO!!!
There are a limited number of options.

NOW you could say "I am busy and have a full diary of meetings and commitments. I will think about it later." Ah, we have an infinite capacity to return to normal. Our own urgent overwhelms the world's important, or in this case, the ordinary cannot cope with the coming disaster.

OR MAYBE "That was an interesting book about an issue that already affects us all." There are a number of practical things I can do at home, and I will look up one or two of those organisations mentioned and start to see what I can do.

OR HOPEFULLY "This disaster requires me to come to terms with why it is the world procrastinates in the face of this difficult issue, and find the resources in our faith and theology to sound a clarion call to those in our communities with whom I worship.

As this book makes clear, It is vital we are clear about the Jesus is to whom we draw attention.

For too long we have majored almost exclusively on the humanity of Jesus. It is important to realize he was incarnate as one of us, God with us, entering into the web of human, social and environmental networks as we do. What is remarkable is that he did not allow these relationships to squeeze him into limited views. He brought love and life to human relationships, justice and truth to social relationships and made the environment transparently the basis for teaching and demonstrating the Kingdom of God.

The scope of this crisis that threatens us, however, requires us to rediscover that he is also the cosmic Christ, the Son of God bringing salvation to these same relationships refashioning and restoring them in the shape of the Creator. The Greek world for salvation is worth considering from this perspective. It can be translated in at least three ways depending on the context, with the chosen translation including the other two associations. The Greek word 'swzw' can mean salvation, healing, or restoration. Jesus Christ the great healer of creation, the restorer of creation, the saviour of the creation. Jesus Christ confronted the many facets of sin with the reality of the kingdom of God in himself in the decisive act of his life, cross, resurrection and ascension. He is the way the kingdom comes in our midst. In global warming we have another consequence of the human abuse of God's world brought to our attention. As his people can we sit idly by when from the perspective of the Scriptures this is a sin against a restored creation, and future generations including our own grandchildren?

For too long we have read Scripture from the point of the individual, rather than God's care for the whole planet and more. The issue of global warming is part of the Holy Spirit's wake up call to the church to see how the word of God speaks into our societal setting as well as our personal and family setting.

This is shown in the book by the way Jesus parables speak into this issue. They remind us that Jesus was a rural and urban preacher who embeds the flowers of the field, the birds, and the fig tree in the parables as a way of pointing to the reign of God in our midst. This is an invitation for us to see how parables enable ecology to give vital insights for placing the individual in the world at large. The writers use of the parable of the prodigal son was illuminating. The prodigal is seen as western consumption selling the past for the sake of a western future that has ended up with us trashing the world, leaving it as a pigsty. It took awhile before the prodigal came to his senses and headed back to the wisdom of his father. How will the world come to its senses.

Over the last few years I worked with Chris Dalton, while he was wrestling with the environmental damage that flowed from the rational economic consequences of increasing progress as the only way forward for society. The breakthrough came for him when the parable of the Good Samaritan led him to see the land of Australia as a person left beaten on the side of the road. The bleeding land, lying there helpless, needs to be recognized as a neighbour, not just as someone to be used, abused, and left without a voice. It was the break through that enabled him to see the world in a new way. It was not a call to do more so much as a call to live in a different world, treating the planet as a neighbour. It led him to re-imagine Australia as the beloved companion.[1]

As is documented in the book each year brings further encroachment of the sea on their low lying islands of Tuvalu and other places in the Pacific. Some there wondered how God could let their Islands be flooded again after the promise of the Noarchic covenant that God would never do this again. Scripture was carefully considered and they came to see that it was not God doing this. It was the result of the lifestyle of their fellow humans on the planet.

As the authors have shown Scripture can provide us with new lenses to see our world differently. A promised land of plenty was given to the Israelites. In the New Testament the land of promise is a new creation given by God in and through Jesus Christ. It is now obvious that we are living in an age when this world which bought in to a promised land of fossil fuel energy has belatedly found that it brings with it the curse of a blighted planet. As the good law becomes a curse when we fail to see the one who gives us the law, so there is an urgent task for us all to receive the world as a gift from God. Scripture provides resources for us to help rediscover a gracious caring view of planet Earth and its future.

We are entering a new era - the Anthropocene - in which the human race impacts directly on the future of the planet. Whether plastic contamination or the destruction of the ozone layer, higher levels of carbon dioxide in the atmosphere or radioactive waste, the killing of other species and the destruction of habitats or the acidification of the seas, the human footprint leaves a toxic residue for the future. What then reader will you do? The authors invite you to be the agents of grace for the planet in the role that you have, not adding extra jobs but changing direction in all that you do in ministry and life for the sake of God's good creation. It is time for us to act in ways that treasure the earth, our island home in space, a beloved companion on our journey to God's future.

Endnote
[1] Dalton, Chris,*From Terra Nullius to Beloved Companion: Re-imagining land in Australia,* (Inhouse Publications, 2017).

The Pigsty

God

said "this

is your inheritance.

The Earth is a good creation

so go forth and multiply,

have dominion over

the whole

Earth".

The younger son

enjoyed his freedom

and what great fun he had.

What a wonderful lifestyle he led!

What profits there were to be made.

A virgin earth, waiting to be exploited

by mining, technology, transport, farming.

He had a ball, but even so the angels wept

as cities got polluted, crops failed,

people starved, wars started,

living standards plummeted,

earthquakes destroyed,

tornados raged and

Earth became a

Pigsty.

"Inevitable,"

the angels mourned,

"humanity got its just deserts.

Such prodigal, selfish living that

wasted God's inheritance".

And God wept.

Then

a flicker of light,

barely discernible, almost going out:

humanity, in despair, seeking God's comfort.

God rejoiced, all the bells in heaven rang for a feast of celebration,

and the angels protested: "Humanity had squandered

its right to receive anything from you", they said.

God smiled, compassionately,

and created for all the

abundance of

Shekinah

R.D. Drayton

ॐॐ

Eco-theological Sermon - 1

Preached at Manali Masihi Mandali (CNI) Church, Manali, Himachal Pradesh,

11 January, 2015

Texts	Genesis 1:26-27; Psalm 127:1-2; Matthew 7:24-27
Theme	Dominion over the House
Idea	The whole world is the house of God.
Preacher	Rev. Dr. David Reichardt

Editor's note

In 2013–2015 Dr Reichardt lived in Manali while travelling around the CNI Diocese of Amritsar and beyond, working as a volunteer eco-theological consultant.

Introduction

I thank Pastor Ji for requesting me to preach today.

The task that the Lord has given me here in India is to start ecological projects in the churches, schools and hospitals of Church of North India in the states of Himachal Pradesh, Punjab and Jammu & Kashmir. The biggest challenge and opportunity I must meet to be successful is to convince the people in the churches - people such as you - that caring for God's creation is an important part of being a follower of Jesus. So today I shall preach for the first time one of the sermons I plan to use in churches around northwest India this year. Please give me your feedback after this service!

Let us pray. May the words of my mouth and the meditation of my heart be pleasing to you, O LORD, our rock and my redeemer. (Psalm 19.14)

The Sermon

Have you thought about what it means for humans - that means you and me - to have dominion over the whole earth? And have you ever thought about what it means to be made in God's image? We need to know something about being God's image-bearers before we can understand what it means to have dominion over the rest of creation. So then, what does it mean to be made in God's image?

I wrote this part of the sermon at Johnson's Café, Manali, which just now is being extended. My friend Pia, the owner of Johnson's, is doing in a very small way what God does in a very big way: she is building!

Like God, humans are builders. Much of our time and energy goes to building houses that become homes for ourselves. I have lived in many places. My wife and I have bought 3 houses, and sold 2 of them. Wherever we have lived, we have tried to make the house into our home. For that reason the biblical image of "The House" is one we can relate to.

Just as we build houses to live in, we also build our lives. The American Christian songwriter and singer Michael Omartian wrote a song called "See this House" that expresses this thought well:

"See this house I've built.
It stands so strong,
It took so long.
Placed so high on this hill.
No one sees in,
They never will.

Board by board I willed the walls into place,
And the roof went on with my dreams.
As nice as it is on the outside,
You know it's still not all what it seems.

Inside it's all run down.
Lonely and bare,
Dark everywhere.
Confusion all around.
Things to be sold.
Love to be found.

Down the hall, that room's been locked up for years.
And neglect has misplaced the key.
It's full of memories I bought for a price,
At a time when nothing came free.

But You.......
Opened the door.
And there was light like there's never been before.
Then You......
Gave me the key.
And there was love there to set me free and
Until You........
I was like sand,
Blown out of hand

See this house I've built.
It stands so strong,
It took so long.
Inside it's been made new.
It's all I have.
It's all for You."

In this song the house means the singer's own life, which he has built.
On the outside it looks great, but on the inside "...it's all run down./

Lonely and bare,/ Dark everywhere./ Confusion all around./ Things to be sold./ Love to be found."

But when Christ enters this house it's made new. Light and love enter with Him. Because the builder has given his life's house to Christ it now stands strong.

****

Jesus told a parable that means much the same thing. I learnt a song in Sunday School that expresses it:

"The wise man built his house upon the rock,
The wise man built his house upon the rock,
The wise man built his house upon the rock,
And the rain came tumbling down.

The rain came down and the floods came up,
The rain came down and the floods came up,
The rain came down and the floods came up,
And the house on the rock stood firm.

The foolish man built his house upon the sand,
The foolish man built his house upon the sand,
The foolish man built his house upon the sand,
And the rain came tumbling down.

The rain came down and the floods came up,
The rain came down and the floods came up,
The rain came down and the floods came up,
And the house on the sand went "SPLAT!"

So, build your life on the Lord Jesus Christ,
Build your life on the Lord Jesus Christ,
Build your life on the Lord Jesus Christ,
And the blessings will come down.

The blessings will come down as the prayers go up,
The blessings will come down as the prayers go up,

The blessings will come down as the prayers go up,

So, build your life on the Rock."

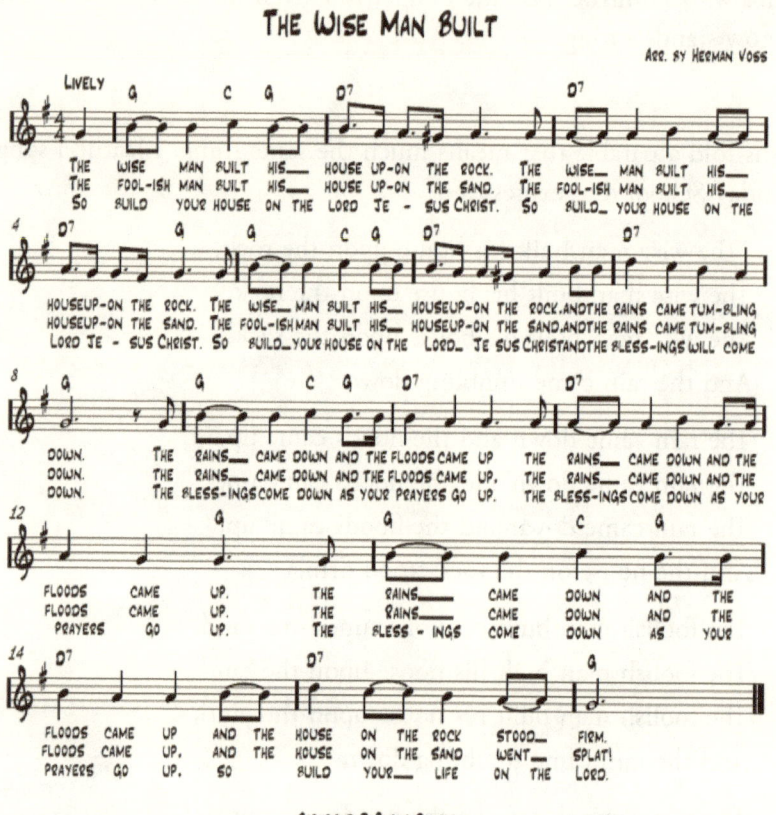

This biblical theme, "The House", stands for our lives. If we build the houses of our lives on the rock of Jesus' teaching we'll stay firm and safe through life's storms. Every other foundation is sand.

You get a still deeper understanding of how important this theme "The House" is from the very next verse, Matthew 7.28: "*And when Jesus finished these sayings*, the crowds were astonished at his teaching." Go looking in Matthew's gospel and you'll find the phrase "When Jesus Finished" repeating itself five times. Matthew 11.1 says: "*When Jesus had finished instructing his twelve disciples*, he went on from there to teach and preach in their cities." Matthew 13:53 says: "*And when Jesus had finished these parables*, he went away from there." Matthew 19:1: "*Now when Jesus had finished these sayings*, he went away from Galilee and entered the region of Judea beyond the Jordan." And lastly, Matthew 26:1: "*When Jesus had finished all these sayings*, he said to his disciples..."

The same phrase is used five times: "..."

Each time the phrase "When Jesus finished" signals the end of a block of teaching in Matthew's gospel:

Now THAT'S important because Matthew was comparing Jesus with Moses, and what Jesus was doing with the Exodus. Jesus' Sermon on the Mount reminds us of Moses receiving the Law on Mt Sinai. And Jesus' five blocks of teaching in Matthew's Gospel point us to the first five books of the Bible: Genesis, Exodus, Leviticus, Numbers and Deuteronomy. These are called the "Pentateuch" in English, because "Penta" comes from a Greek word meaning "five". In many languages they are called the "Five books of Moses".

Many bible scholars believe that making five blocks of teaching is Matthew's way of telling his mainly Jewish audience that Jesus is like Moses, but that He is greater than Moses. That is why Jesus could teach by His own authority. He is the one greater than Moses who has come to lead His people to freedom. And in His great warning at the end of the first block of teaching Jesus uses the Parable of The House: "If you do what I have told you", He said, "you'll be like the House built on the foundation of rock...If you don't you'll be like the house built on sand."

This little song I learnt at Sunday School more than 50 years ago is much deeper than my teacher knew! And the version of it we sang in Confirmation Camps for Swedish youth that I led in Sweden 20 years ago is much deeper than I understood! *Firstly,* of course make sure that you build the House of your life on the Rock of Jesus and His teaching! But *secondly*, "The House" is an important biblical theme.

We see that when we think of the greatest house in the Bible: the Temple in Jerusalem. The Temple was what Celtic people call "a thin place", that is, a place where heaven and earth come close together. It was God's House. After the Temple's dedication God came to King Solomon at night. God said, "I have heard your prayer, and have chosen this place for Myself as a house of sacrifice...If my people who are called by my name humble themselves, and pray and seek my face and turn from their wicked ways, then I will hear from heaven and will forgive their sin **and heal their land**." (2 Chronicles 7.12-14)

We learn at least 2 things from this important passage. As King Solomon had just that day said in his prayer of dedication, neither the earth nor the highest heavens can contain God, so a temple made by humans is completely unable to do so. *Yet because Solomon's attitude was right* God decided to accept this building as a house of sacrifice.

And **secondly**, God restated the Covenant agreement between Godself and Israel. Now the Covenant between God and Israel is stated a number of times in the Old Testament. Simply put, it goes like this: "If Israel obeys God's Laws and live in relationship with God, then you will prosper. But if you do not, then you will suffer."

This version of the Covenant is particularly interesting: "...I will hear from heaven and will forgive their sin **and heal their land**," says God. From the idea that if Israel humble themselves, pray, seek God's face and turn from their wicked ways God will heal Israel's land there are 2 more important consequences: **First**, God's plan is not just to save us from the land, this earth. It is to save the earth itself in, through and together with the salvation of humankind. That's why Paul wrote in Romans 8.19-23:

> "For the creation waits with eager longing for the revealing of the sons of God. 20 For the creation was subjected to futility, not willingly, but because of him who subjected it, in hope 21 that the creation itself will be set free from its bondage to corruption and obtain the freedom of the glory of the children of God. 22 For we know that the whole creation has been groaning together in the pains of childbirth until now. 23 And not only the creation, but we ourselves, who have the

first fruits of the Spirit, groan inwardly as we wait eagerly for adoption as sons, the redemption of our bodies."

Humans will not be saved FROM creation. The future of humans and of creation is all bound together! God intends to save creation through and together with the salvation of humans. I have read, and seen on video fantastic stories of land and nature regenerated and huge crops produced by communities who have come to faith in Christ. I believe these stories point to the wonderful, worldwide restoration of nature that will occur when Christ returns.

RESTORATION! And so, **secondly**, we return to God's original purpose for humankind. Genesis 1.26 says God gave humans "dominion" over the whole earth and all living creatures on it. And there's the problem! The word "dominion" has come to mean "rule, control, domination". If I have dominion over you it means that I rule over you. *I* get to do whatever *I* like, but *you* have to do whatever I *want.*

We have seen some of the terrible effects of that understanding of dominion in the behaviour of the Islamic State fighters and terrorists in Iraq and Syria: beheading people, enslaving women and children and so on. And we also see it in the cruel and selfish ways in which humans treat nature: clearing forests, enslaving animals, polluting rivers, oceans, the skies and the land and so on.

BUT THAT IS *NOT* THE WAY IN WHICH GOD EXERCISES DOMINION!

"The earth is the Lord's and the fullness thereof, the world and those who dwell therein," says Psalm 24.1. But the bible's most famous verse, John 3.16, says that "God so loved THE WORLD, that he gave his only Son, that whoever believes in him should not perish but have eternal life." God has dominion over creation, but in Christ God SERVED creation. And God's purpose for humankind is to be **servant leaders** in creation.

Or to say it another way, we humans are stewards of God's house. You know that Jesus told several parables about good and bad stewards, don't you? In these parables the owner of the house or the farm in which the stewards exercised dominion stands for God. So the house stands for or means the whole world.

There is a Greek word, "oikos", which means household, house, home. That Greek word oikos has given English 3 important words:

- "oikonomia" meaning economy, the law, or ordering of the household;

- "oikologia" meaning ecology, the study of the household;

- and "oikumene" meaning the whole inhabited world, giving us the word "ecumenism". The whole world is the house of God.

And that, my sisters and brothers, is why we must love it as God loves it. We are the stewards of God's good and much-loved earth. We are the gardeners of God's beautiful garden. We are the builders in God's great house. Though the life, death and resurrection of Jesus Christ and the efforts of His people God *is restoring* God's house, God's Kingdom.

I love building. In each of the houses we have owned I have done some building. And each of the gardens we have lived in we have tried to improve. Let us join God, not only in seeking the salvation of souls, but in restoring God's house, this good earth. For that is also an important part of following Jesus.

Amen.

Eco-theological Sermon - 2

Preached at Normanhurst Uniting Church, Sydney, Australia

11 September, 2016

Texts:	Psalm 24; 2 Chronicles 7:11-14
Theme:	Land Sunday in the Season of Creation
Idea:	The earth is the Lord's and the fullness thereof.
Preacher:	Rev Dr David Reichardt

Welcome to the second service in this month-long Season of Creation.

Last Sunday I introduced the Season of Creation, and explained the concept and how it is being adopted into the Church's year by more and more of the Church worldwide.

I played short video clips by Pope Francis and Bishop Emeritus Desmond Tutu to demonstrate that concern for Creation is not simply my hobby horse that I want you to ride too!

Impelled by the worldwide ecological crisis, which many people now regard as the most dangerous issue the planet faces, increasing numbers of Christians around the world are acting to restore local environments; reduce our impact upon them; and limit and counteract climate change.

I have now visited 160 people connected with this congregation and I've heard that many of us are engaged in this "ecopraxis". From the

vegetable garden to the bushwalking group; from the cyclists - we even
have a family that runs a cycle shop in Turramurra - to those who have
put solar panels on our roofsyou are a congregation that is both engaging
in practical measures to help God's creation, and enjoying living in
creation. And that is what we are called to do. We are stewards of God's
earth. We are God's gardeners. That, I believe, is what the Good Book,
the Bible tells us.

Last Sunday we looked at oceans by way of a worship song and a
video clip that shows the animals of the deep seas. Today, I have no video
clips to share with you, but I aim to show you what the Bible says about
the Land. My theme is "Land - the Earth is the Lord's and the fullness
thereof" Is land a gift for all or a commodity for a few? Can we even say
that the Land belongs to humans? Land is a theme which is interwoven
in the history of God's people.

There are several key themes which emerge from a study of the Bible's
texts that speak about the Land. I am much indebted to the great old
Testament scholar Walter Brueggemann for his insights here. Brueggemann
has written a great deal on the biblical theme of "The Land". He has
identified four sub-themes and seven biblical principles which I would
like to take us through now.

1.   Land as a Promise and Gift

The Old Testament is a tapestry of stories in which land features as
an alternating promise and gift. The Bible's first 5 books - called the
"Pentateuch" - describe the covenant relationship that unites God, the
people of Israel and the land. The Bible begins with the gift of land in
the Garden of Eden and then other gifts and promises of habitable land,
often to the landless:

 – Goshen, 'the best land', to Joseph and his clan in Egypt;
 – the land flowing with milk and honey to the Israelites;
 – and a chance for the exiles in Babylon to return.

But the gift of land does not come without conditions and responsibilities!
The landless people of Israel receive a promise of security and belonging in

a covenant with God, but they lose this conditional gift when they abuse the land, making it an object to be bought, sold and accumulated. The land belongs to God, and the people are called to rule with justice and mercy. The legal codes, particularly in Exodus and Leviticus, and in the Wisdom literature, appeal for the equitable distribution and redistribution of land and wealth.

The Prophets warned against mismanagement, injustice and oppression. For example, this from Jeremiah 2.7: "I brought you into a fertile land to enjoy its fruits and every good thing in it. But...you entered my land and you defiled it and made loathsome the home I gave you." But despite the efforts of the prophets the land was exploited, polluted and defiled, and the covenant with Yahweh was broken. As in the beginning in the Garden of Eden, the people were punished for sin and banished. Samaria fell to the Assyrians, Jerusalem to the Babylonians, and the people were cast out of their land.

2.   The Earth is the Lord's

While humans were given the often misinterpreted command to "subdue and have dominion over" the earth (Genesis 1:28), we were also instructed to "till and keep" it. (Genesis 2:15). The Earth is the Lord's. It has been given as a conditional gift to human beings. Land is held in covenant with God. This covenant is conditional on right relations between God and people. No one may be deprived of their possession and use of land – not even by a king.

As evidence of that, read the account of Naboth's vineyard in 1 Kings 21. King Ahab was NOT to take Naboth's vineyard from him. In Israelite society a king did NOT have that right, even though Ahab's pagan wife Jezebel assumed that her husband did. The Biblical story of the people of God makes plain that the promise of God was **also** a promise of land to the landless. Accordingly, the Bible expresses strong moral condemnation of greed and the abuses of the rich who force the poor and small farmers to give up their land: "Woe to those who join house to house, who add field to field" thundered Isaiah in ch 5, v. 8.

And "They covet fields and seize them; and houses and take them away; they oppress a man and his house, a man and his inheritance". (Micah 2:2)

There is thus no unconditional right to private property. Rights must be exercised for the benefit of others, to satisfy human needs and not human greed, and in ways that are not destructive of the land.

3.   Jubilee

In the biblical notion of Jubilee we see God's lordship in social, economic and ecological issues. It is specified that during a Jubilee year:

- Land and houses must be returned to their original owners.
- People can return freely to their families and properties.
- Land must be allowed to rest.

Already implied in the idea that 'the earth is the Lord's", Jubilee announces justice on the accumulation of property and land, since these deny a large part of humanity their just portion of the fruits of the earth. The basic underlying intention is clear: God destined the earth and all it contains for all people so that all created things would be shared fairly by all. Justice should go hand in hand with charity.

It is also significant that the Jubilee provisions include that the land too has 'rights' and must be left fallow in the Jubilee year. Not only does this contain an environmental component, but "during the period of recovery of the fruitfulness of cultivated land, its fruit is available to the poor and to the wild animals and birds."

4.   Jesus' Announcement of the Good news of the Kingdom - Jubilee and Shalom

Jesus is concerned with issues of land and rural justice. A Christian theology of land starts with an awareness of Christ's reconciling power, It must take into account the inter-relatedness of human beings and soil, water, plants and animals and rediscover a reverence for the earth as God's creation. In doing so, we do not only look back to creation or a past 'golden age'. Christians look forward in hope and faith to the coming reign of God where the dominant vision is that of Shalom– a comprehensive Shalom of well-being, peace, justice and right relations.

So, as Christians, we are required to re-examine the ways in which we relate to the land and each other. Without sustaining the life of earth, sustaining life on earth is made impossible. If reconciliation is about right relations, then in Christ we see people reconciled with people, with God and with creation. So…having examined 4 biblical themes that have to do with the relationship between God, humans and the land I'll conclude by naming Brueggemann's 7 biblical principles regarding the question of land:

1. Land is a **gift from God**, to be justly shared for the benefit of all humanity.

2. Land is the **place of life**, the place where life is lived and celebrated, the place that gives life and identity. Land has a social function.

3. 'Ownership' of land is never absolute; we are **stewards** of God's land.

4. We must recognise the present day tendency to turn land into a **commodity** for profit, leading to the exclusion of the poor and the denial of their rights to land. Our interventions must work to ensure there is fairness.

5. The Jubilee tradition affirms **God's commitment to the poor** in seeking to ensure just and equitable access to land and resources.

6. Human work on the land should express the **dignity of human labour and the joy of participation and cooperation** because it is a privilege to be co-creators with God in the unfolding story of creation.

7. It is **against God's will** to strip the earth of its fertility and to rob future generations of its benefits.

This biblical teaching about the land teaches us that social justice

- is a vital aspect of the Gospel

- is not just about humans, but is about the "commonwealth of all being".

But 2 Chronicles 7.14 promises us that the God of wonders wants to cooperate with us in healing creation. One of my favourite summaries of the Christian message comes from Hans Küng: "God kingdom is creation healed."

Here is how that will happen:

"If my people, who are called by my name, will humble themselves and pray and seek my face and turn from their wicked ways, then I will hear from heaven, and I will forgive their sin and will heal their land." (2 Chronicles 7.14)

Amen.

How to Prepare
an Eco-theological Sermon

This eco-theological textbook has been written largely so that Indian pastors and involved laypeople will be better able to help their congregations think about and act "christianly" for creation and in the world-wide ecological crisis. Among a pastor's many tasks, expounding the Bible - preaching and teaching - are primary! If you as a pastor have been convinced that caring for creation is an important aspect of following Christ then you will probably feel called to preach on it. That is your job! That is who you are! But how do you prepare and deliver an eco-theological sermon?

Background Preparation
Preparing and preaching an eco-theological sermon is not different from any other sermon. When you preach you expound God's Word, and you seek to connect God's Word with your listeners and their lives. You seek, thereby, to glorify God.

Theological Background
It will be helpful to study this book and other material to gain a general understanding of ecology and eco-theology.

Biblical Background

Know your Bible texts that have to do with creation and eco-theology. Once you start looking for them you will find them throughout the Bible.

Prayer

Maintain a consistent prayer life yourself, and have a group of intercessors who pray consistently for you. As well as that, pray before, during and even after the preparation and delivery of your sermon.

Practice ("Praxis")

Become involved in some practical aspect(s) of environmental care yourself. In India planting and nurturing of trees and programs to clean up the localities in which people live have become very popular. These are great ways of becoming involved in your local communities

Know your people

Know what your people are already doing to care for their environment, and what their attitudes to environmental care and theology are. Encourage and help them.

Sermon Illustrations

Build up a store of environmental stories and even jokes as sermon illustrations!

Sermon Preparation

Choice of Bible Text(s)

You need to decide which bible passage(s) you feel led to preach on. Many church traditions follow a lectionary pattern of bible readings. They study set bible texts for each Sunday of the Church's year, often following a 3 year cycle. Other traditions allow the preacher to choose her or his own themes and bible texts. In either case you must study the text(s) you plan to preach over. Read them as long before you actually preach over them as you can. Ask yourself "Where is the gospel in this bible passage? What does this passage have to do with creation, the "cosmos" that God has created? And what does this passage teach me about the relationship between gospel and creation?"

Other than that…

Other than that, preparing an eco-theological sermon is very similar to preparing any other kind of sermon. At first I found that it was not wise to preach often on the environment to congregation(s) who were not used to thinking that creation care is part of the Gospel. However, as time passed my congregations came to trust that I would not "ride my hobby horse", and I have found more and more ways of integrating eco-theology with "general" theology. The Church of South India has a good program, led by Professor Mathew Koshy Punnackad, that gives presbyters experience in writing and delivering eco-theological sermons.

David Reichardt